ALAN DEAN FOSTER
SLIPT

D0124415

B®

BERKLEY BOOKS, NEW YORK

SLIPT

A Berkley Book / published by arrangement with
the author

PRINTING HISTORY
Berkley edition / April 1984

ISBN: 0-425-07006-9

For Sissy and Randy Shimp,
*   friends always there when you need them.*
For Rube Cozart,
*   who in never saying much, says a lot.*
And particularly for Jane Cozart,
*   self-proclaimed wicked witch of the west,*
*   who in reality is Glinda, the good witch of the east.*

Over the years the nightmares had grown less intense, but this summer they'd returned with a vengeance. Though six years had passed since the accident, in her sleep she saw it as clearly as if it had taken place yesterday. Dreaming did nothing to blur the details.

In some ways they were worse now than they'd been immediately following the disaster. Time slowed remembrance, making each second pass in slow motion. Everyone bled in slow motion as they died repeatedly in her mind. Died slowly.

Squeal of brakes and shockingly uncharacteristic curse from Mrs. Robish as she fought vainly to make the old schoolbus do things it was never intended to do. Thunderous overwhelming shriek from the train whistle warning of imminent doom. A sensation not unlike being caught in a big wave at the beach, tumbling her over and over inside the bus. A wetness salty but not of the sea as blood spurted from dozens of tiny torn bodies as the locomotive ripped broadside into the stalled bus.

Above all she remembered the calm which had enveloped her. She hadn't screamed like the rest of the children. She remembered thinking how like snow the inside of the bus became. She'd never seen snow, but imagined from pictures that it must have been something like the million shards of glass that filled the bus's interior as the windows caved in explosively.

The wave striking her again, tossing her around the back of the vehicle. She'd been sitting in the last seat. She remembered putting bb's in a tin can and shaking them around, making a crude musical noise. Shaking and bouncing them, the way her friends were flying around the inside of the bus that afternoon. Little soft bodies suddenly no longer alive, making wet sounds as they struck the unyielding walls. And then the bodies coming apart and her outraged little-girl mind blanking the sight out as best it was able, not letting her acknowledge the pieces of arms and legs richocheting around her.

She remembered watching Jimmy Lee Cooper go floating past her, his face kind of sad (what was left of it). Then a wrenching, numbing pain in her back that startled her even more than it hurt as she flew (just like the superheroes on the Saturday morning cartoons) through the broken-out rear window.

It was warm that day, even for the South Texas coast country. She recalled the warmth around her as she floated through the air, recalled watching the mangled wreckage of the schoolbus recede down the tracks as the mountain that was the train pushed it along. She never saw Jimmy Lee Cooper again. Only his casket, at the mass funeral.

Then she'd hit the ground and stopped bouncing and rolling. She'd been thankful for that because she was starting to feel kind of sick. She was numb all over, as though the dentist, Doctor Franklin, had given her novocaine all over instead of just behind the one bad tooth he'd fixed earlier that year. Drowning out every other noise was a sorrowful sharp screeching as the train fought to bring itself to a halt.

Soon there were people coming, coming down the road the bus had been on. They were getting out of their cars and running up the tracks toward the nearly stopped train and what remained of the schoolbus. The screech of the train's brakes was replaced by multiple softer screams. She'd never heard adults scream like that before and it scared her badly.

She never knew whether she'd tried to get up or not. She only knew that she didn't get up. Besides, she didn't feel much like moving. There was nowhere to move to. They were all going to be late for school, she thought, and wondered if a train hitting the bus would be enough of an excuse for Mrs. Romero.

She looked down and saw that her dress was all torn up, and that she was dirty all over. There was a lot of blood, too, but it didn't seem to be hers. She wasn't sure how she knew that but as it turned out she'd been right.

Then there was someone bending over her, looking down at her. A man dressed in blue coveralls and a white workshirt and a broad western hat. He just stood there staring at her, talking to himself fast. She didn't know why he'd been mentioning Jesus's name over and over because they weren't in church.

He knelt close and she remembered thinking that he had a nice old face, burnt brown by years in the South Texas sun. He pushed back the brim of his hat and then used it to shade her face.

The screaming continued somewhere far away. Then there was a new sound; the rising complaint of hurrying sirens. She hadn't been sure at first that that's what they were because she'd never before heard more than one siren at a time. When they all wailed together like that it was hard to identify them.

The man touched her then, running his fingers along her left side from her shoulder down to her leg. He pulled the hand away suddenly as if he'd touched fire and looked real funny. Then he stood up and spoke. She recalled his words very clearly, even though it had been long ago and she'd been very tired.

"Now don't you worry, little girl. You're going to be alright. I'm going to get some help and I'll be right back. Just don't try to move. Understand?"

She nodded. She wanted to say, "I'm not going to move, mister. I'm very tired and I don't want to get up." But she said nothing.

He smiled at her, a funny kind of smile not at all as comforting as he'd intended it to be, and went running away back toward the road. Back toward the sirens, she thought.

Soon there were other people bending over her along with the nice man. They were all panting hard, like they'd been running a lot. The farmer who'd found her was talking to one of the younger men in the clean white coats.

"I told her not to move," he said. "I don't think she has."

Then the young men were inspecting her, running their hands over her, and one of them looked at his friend and said quietly, "We've got to get her on the gurney."

The other man nodded agreement. Then there were hands under her. Gentle, careful hands, lifting. She remembered herself telling them, "It's okay. You're not hurting me. It doesn't hurt."

One of the men in the white coats had smiled down at her. He seemed to be trying real hard not to cry, which was a funny thing to see in a grown-up. She'd only seen it once or twice before when her mommy hadn't known she'd been awake. But she'd never seen it in a grown-up man before.

Then they were putting her on something flat and white. She almost started to scream when they lifted her, because it reminded her of that moment of flying around inside the tumbling schoolbus with her coming-apart friends, reminded her of flying out through the back window. But she relaxed a little when she realized she wasn't flying anymore, only being carried.

They slid her into a big car with a red light on top. An ambulance, she thought. She'd always wanted to ride in an ambulance. She remembered asking one of the nice men, "Will I be able to hear the siren?" He smiled back at her through his anxiety and preoccupation and said, "Sure you will, honey, sure."

They waited for the longest time. Then another pallet was brought and slid in next to hers. It had another little girl on it. Amanda thought it looked like Lucey Huddle, but she couldn't be sure because the face was all messed up.

About halfway through their ride (they were going very fast, she knew) the nice man who'd told her she'd be able to hear the siren pulled a clean sheet over Lucey Huddle's head. When he saw Amanda watching he whispered to her.

"It's okay. She's just sleeping. She'll sleep better this way."

Amanda nodded slowly, her first movement in a long time. She didn't reply because she didn't want to make the nice man feel bad because she knew he was lying and she didn't want him to know that she knew. He didn't say anything else, just kind of stared off into the distance. Every now and then, though, he'd bring himself back long enough to check on her.

It was strange, she thought as the ambulance careened down the highway. For a moment back there, lying on the grass near the cottonwood, she'd thought she'd been able to see herself from up in the air. That was a funny way to see things, she thought. She giggled, startling the nice man. Lying on the ground, it was kind of neat to be able to see yourself. She remembered seeing herself covered with blood. Her blue dress was shredded and both her shoes were missing (now where did *they* get to, she thought).

She'd been all twisted up like a rag doll, a real Raggedy Anne. Then the farmer and the men in white coats looking down at her.

She remembered it all vividly, much too vividly, as she woke up breathing hard and in a cold sweat.

She knew what had happened, made herself sit up in bed until she regained control of her breathing. She used the edge of the sheet to wipe away the sweat. A bad one, she thought. At least this time she hadn't woken up screaming. It hurt her to see the expressions on her parents' faces when she did that and they came running into her room.

She listened for them, but there were no sounds from their bedroom up the hall. Only the summer concert provided by the crickets outside, interrupted occasionally by the alarming drone of a cicada. When the crickets relented she could hear the faint slap of water against the seawall that protected the yard. Sometimes her dad snored and she could hear that, too, but not tonight.

She used her left hand to lift and push her legs over the side of the bed. Her arms were slim but far more muscular than those of the average sixteen-year-old girl. She used them to drag herself into the wheelchair. Her nightgown clung momentarily to one of the brake handles. She tugged irritably at it and it pulled away cleanly.

Twist and turn and wheel over to the window to sit staring thoughtfully at the night. The moon was nearly full, its glow like the beam of a flashlight on Lavaca Bay.

She remembered the strangest thing about the "incident," as her parents carefully referred to it. It had been there in the nightmare too, the only thing not nightmarish about it. There had been someone else standing there looking down at her little twisted body, only that someone hadn't been there. She knew him. An old man. Her Uncle Jake.

She frowned to herself as she always did at the memory, brushing long black hair away from her forehead. The moonlight pouring through the window gave her face an angelic cast, setting alive the coppery skin and sharp features that reflected her mixed anglo-hispanic heritage.

He'd been sorry, so sorry that he couldn't have prevented the "incident," couldn't have helped her somehow. But he had helped her, simply by being with her. Uncle Jake had always been with her. It was their little secret. When the hospital people had turned her mom and dad away outside the operating room, Uncle Jake had been able to go in with her.

She was thinking of him now, and she was worried, and she didn't know why she was worried, and that worried her more. He hadn't been hurt, hadn't been in an accident. If he had she would have known about it immediately. It would have awakened her faster than any nightmare because it would have been real. Everything that happened to Uncle Jake was real to her.

She'd known when he'd gone into the social security office that time and let his temper get the better of him. He'd gotten himself all worked up, which he wasn't supposed to do, and his heart, which was the weakest, oldest part of him had started to hurt.

The indifferent expression of the bureaucrat behind the desk had turned to alarm, and other people had been summoned. He'd come out of that okay. Then there was the time he'd been watching the Superbowl and his television had gone on the fritz. He'd gotten real excited and angry at the same time. His heart didn't hurt as badly that time, but it had scared her anyway.

She hadn't seen her Uncle Jake in person in many years. Only twice, in fact. Once right after the "incident" when he'd come to visit her in the hospital, and once a couple of years ago when he'd stayed for most of the summer. But he always sent her something for Christmas and her birthday, and he was always there when she needed to talk to him. That was their own little secret, their special secret, her and Uncle Jake, the crippled teenager and the arteriosclerotic old man.

She thought about her unfounded concern and wondered if she shouldn't ought to try calling him now. No, not until she thought about her feelings some more. Besides, it was late and she didn't like to wake him. An old man needed his sleep.

She put her hands on the smooth, cool chrome wheels, turned herself and rolled toward one of the two bookcases that rose from floor to ceiling. Both were full, their shelves lined largely with used paperbacks. That had never mattered to Amanda. After all, a book was a book, whether it had a fancy leather binding or a torn paper one. All that mattered were the words.

It was quite a library. Tucked innocuously between the tomes on plants and people and school subjects were books with funny titles, books even her mom and dad didn't pretend to understand. But at a quarter a book they didn't care what she bought on their family trips up to Houston.

She studied the shelves and used the mechanical picker to reach up and pluck out one particular volume. It had given her some understanding of herself. Maybe it would help her understand why she was concerned for her Uncle Jake. She worried about him a lot, because she loved him, and because he was special in a way not even her parents suspected.

She wanted above all to protect him. That was ironic, because except for his bad heart Uncle Jake was a robust, energetic man. No matter that he was already into his seventies. At least he could walk, which was something Amanda hadn't been able to do since the incident. It's in her back, the doctors had told her parents. It's in her back, nothing we can do, nothing anybody can do, sorry and shrug and good-bye. . . .

She remembered what walking was. A fading memory now, a sweet innocent remembrance that was one with all her other childhood memories. Pre-incident memories. Her legs now and forever more would be round and chromed and cold.

She turned on the little reading light over her desk and angled it on its gooseneck. Then she leaned back in the wheelchair and began reading. There were a lot of big words in the little book, words that wouldn't mean much to her parents, but she'd become comfortable with them. She was a good student, at times an exceptional one. But then, when one doesn't go out on dates or go to parties or go dancing or spend the weekend cruising, one has lots of time for study.

The sonorous dirge of the insects rose over the familiar complaint of the air conditioner and dehumidifier. Something was about to happen, Amanda felt. It somehow involved her Uncle Jake. Perhaps it might reach out to involve her as well, because she was linked as tightly to her Uncle Jake as he was to her. It's something bad, she thought anxiously. Very bad.

But at least it didn't feel like it involved trains, though she wasn't sure about buses. That thought let her relax a little. After a while she fell into a calm, nightmareless sleep. The book slipped from her limp hand to close itself against the floor.

II

The same fat, silver moon that gleamed on Lavaca Bay off the South Texas coast also lit a tiny valley just outside the city limits of Riverside, California. As only the moon watched, sixty and not six hundred rode down into the little valley of death. They were mounted on steel and rubber instead of horseflesh. There were no cannons waiting to blaze away at them. These were not the Crimean heights and the assault on the valley was being carried out with the utmost stealth and silence of which the invaders were capable.

The general who directed the attack held Ph.D's in chemistry and business administration. His soldiers were armed with graders and backhoes, diesel trucks and tracked dozers. The enemy they fought was as deadly as it was unseen. It did not inhabit the valley so much as permeate it.

Nothing lived in that bowl-shaped depression in the hills east of the sprawling Los Angeles metropolis. A few twisted, gnarled forms thrust bleached fingers toward the moon: the skeletons of the mesquite and cottonwood and scrub oak that had once thrived in the valley bottom. For the past fifty years the water table from which their roots had once drawn nourishment had been poisoned by a bewildering variety of indus-

9

trial wastes. Now not even a weed could grow there.

A deceptively innocent-looking pond of amber liquid flecked with dirty foam had collected at the valley's lowest point. The small army of heavily clothed soldiers treated the pool with especial caution. It was a mixture of rainwater and acids, sludge and things with long, tongue-twisting names. Around the central pool rusted and broken metal drums stood guard like heavily ribbed ghosts.

Quietly, quickly, the men and machines went to work. No one spoke. For one thing, the respirators and masks they wore made conversation difficult. For another, continued silence was vital not only to the success of their operation but to the issuance of triple-overtime bonuses for each worker. Those who worked with shovels and suction hoses pulled instinctively and often at the thick gloves protecting their hands.

On the hillsides to east and south a few lights shone dim against the late summer night. Once a backhoe's gears ground loudly in protest against its operator's too hasty shifting. Attentive mechanics rushed to mute its complaints, packing extra insulation around the transmission.

The attack had been well-rehearsed in advance. It proceeded with admirable speed. It was already well after midnight. Before the first light of the sun rose over San Gorgonio every worker and machine had to be out of the valley and the work had to be completed.

While the assault continued, similarly masked workers leaned against their trucks up on the east ridge. They conversed in low tones, watching the intense activity taking place below while they waited their turn. The beds of their vehicles carried an odd assortment of vegetation, parodies of the landscaper's art. There was young mesquite, some prickly pear, jumping cactus, manzanita . . . a cross-section of the wild chaparral which encrusted the dry hills of Southern California. No rose bushes, no delicate geranium beds this time. The landscapers who'd been hired to replace the natural vegetation murdered by industrial poisons thought the whole business was absurd. But they had been made to comprehend the urgency, and they certainly understood the money.

As the men watched and waited they occasionally glanced across the valley at the sources of the unwinking lights. But no one emerged from any of the tiny, ramshackle houses lining the opposite ridges to stare curiously at the work going on below. It was the middle of the week. Tomorrow was a work day, crucial to the survival of those inhabitants of the shacks and stucco homes lucky enough to have jobs. They ignored the faint noises in favor of more necessary sleep.

The valley was nothing to them, a dirty but seemingly safe playground for their numerous children. The parents were too occupied with the business of survival to trouble themselves about the valley. Most of them could not even read the long English words which were printed on the sides of some of the broken drums and cannisters lying on the valley's slopes.

Despite the lack of activity in the homes, other men waited opposite the clean-up crew and the landscapers. These men carried money and solid wood, to be used to discourage attention as the situation dictated. The hours went their way toward morning, however, without interruption from the sleepy citizens snug in their beds above the valley.

In less than an hour the vicious little pond had been sucked dry. The men who had drained it carefully folded up their hoses, mounted their trucks, and drove their armored tankers up the single dirt and gravel road. Intact crates and drums had been loaded into the backs of unmarked trucks which followed the tankers upward.

The graders and dozers went to work. Dump trucks were quickly backed into position. With speed and precision the top fifteen feet of lethally contaminated soil was excavated and loaded into waiting trucks. Thick plastic was used to cover the dirt and seal the loads from sight. Dumpers followed tankers and semis out toward the desert.

Now a perverse parody of the process by which the little valley had been poisoned was played out. Trucks rumbled down into the vale and fresh chemicals in benign combination were worked into the exposed soil. When this was finished it was the landscapers' turn. They came in with their pickups and flatbeds and proceeded to replace the flora which had once thrived here. As they did so they were careful not to come in contact with the recently treated earth.

Water trucks and men with tanks strapped to their backs moved among the gardeners. Each bush and shrub and patch of carefully manicured weeds was given a healthy dousing of clean, fresh water mixed with concentrated nutrients. Circulating among them all were men and women of different mien. They moved more slowly, more thoughtfully. The jeans and flannel shirts they wore hung unnaturally on them.

They avoided the gardeners and waterers as they stuck things into the ground as seriously as any doctor taking a patient's temperature. They extracted fragments of soil and crumpled roots, put them in test tubes and added liquids from ready droppers. They whispered the results to one another through their protective masks.

Here and there a few mop-up squads of laborers attacked isolated pockets of still unhealthy soil. The excision had to be total or the cancer might spread enough to ruin the whole night's work. Nothing could be left for the inspectors, not the slightest hint that fifty years of industrial sewage had been poured into this valley untouched and untreated.

The earth here had been horribly, callously injured. The repair work was thorough and expensive. But the repair was more cosmetic than absolute. The valley could never be the same again. The backhoe operators and landscapers and engineers were morticians, not resurrectors. When they were done the valley would look natural enough. Good embalming always does. But underneath, the substance of the valley, the thing that had made it a healthy, normal piece of the Earth, would still be just as dead.

Benjamin Huddy checked the sky, then his watch. The watch was very expensive and very accurate. Close to four. They'd have to wrap this up soon. The Board of CCM's western operations would be awaiting his report, back in the tall clean tower the company owned in West L.A.

It would be a pleasure to give that report, he mused. Nothing serious had materialized to challenge the work. There had been no unexpectedly deep pockets of sludge to excavate, no indications of subsurface volatility to avoid, no sign of a shallow aquifer to divert. Judging from the speed with which the landscapers were doing their job, within ninety minutes the valley would once again resemble its undisturbed neighbors which marched off in chaparral-covered anonymity to the east and south.

Nearby the twin bulks of Mounts San Gorgonio and San Jacinto rose nearly twelve thousand feet into the still dark sky. Huddy wished he were atop the latter instead of standing above the valley rubbing sleep from his eyes. It would be nice to take the tram down to Palm Springs. Check into the Lakes or some other resort, take a shower, maybe get in a little tennis. He deserved the rest after this job. Palm Springs and rest would have to wait a while longer though, he knew. The report to the Board and post-operative processing would have to come first.

When the first notification had crossed the desk of some CCM supervisor that the Riverside County inspectors had routinely included the valley on their list of suspected unauthorized chemical dumps, there had been panic stretching all the way back to corporate headquarters in New York. Someone had slipped up. All company dumping was supposed to have been contracted out to subcontractors who couldn't be tied solely to CCM. But the dump had been in use by CCM local operations for half a century and in all that time, no one had thought to discontinue its use.

Then the report showed up and some employee noted the potential danger to the corporation. Frantic outcries within the hierarchy of CCM's chemical division had been met by calm responses from those few who'd kept their heads. It was only a problem, albeit a serious one. It required only a solution.

Having risen just high enough within the company to be privy to such dangerous information, Huddy had been the one to come up with an answer. Sensing one of those rare opportunities which occasionally present themselves on the corporate battlefield, he'd worked all night and had appeared at the hastily convened board meeting with charts and statistics detailing his plan. He didn't mention that Ruth Somerset had helped him put it together.

The board had been impressed. Even Webster, the nephew of CCM's Chairman's son-in-law, had found himself shut out. With some reluctance but more relief, the board had agreed to turn the project over to him and an associate. That's when he'd mentioned Somerset's name.

Actually, as far as Huddy was concerned, the actual clean-up work was anticlimatic. The hard part had been the intricate maneuvering necessary to set everything up and to delay the inspection team. Persuasion and threat, argument and bribery had done their work, however. Tomorrow, maybe the next day, the county inspectors would arrive to find a simple, uncluttered little valley much like its neighbors instead of an ancient and ill-used dumping site laced with enough toxic chemicals to kill several thousand elephants.

Perhaps it wouldn't appear quite as lush as the valley next to it, but it would still look healthier than the homesites which ringed it. Not even mesquite grew up there. Only old tires, broken-down fifties cars, beer bottles and cans in ripe and rusted profusion.

CCM would then be able to point out with considerable corporate pride and not a little righteous outrage that the valley in which they were accused of dumping illegal chemicals was a far healthier place than the inhabited dirt road which ran along the surrounding ridges.

Huddy watched contentedly as the landscapers concluded their assignments and the monitoring/test crew moved efficiently among the newly planted trees and bushes. In less than six hours his crews had sanitized both in content and appearance over fifty years of unregulated dumping from Consolidated Chemical and Mining's Riverside, Barstow and Perris operations. None of the employees involved elected to protest the secrecy. Most of them were full-time CCM personnel who'd do exactly as they were told. For those who were not, large bonuses bought both silence and loyalty.

Besides, even if the operation was somewhat irregular, the end result, the cleaning up of the dump, was beneficial. Wasn't that all that mattered? No need to penalize the company for the mistakes of the past. If somebody spoke out, workers from the thirties and forties weren't the ones who'd pay with their jobs. The logic employed varied, but the result was the same. Each employee managed to rationalize the operation to his or her own satisfaction.

Why bring trouble down on themselves? If the dump was all that dangerous it would have been noticed by now, wouldn't it? Better just to keep one's mouth shut and do the job. Especially when a negative comment could result not only in losing that job, but in being blackballed by every large company in America.

It's tough to be outraged when your colleagues don't feel the same, or when you've a family to feed. No, better just to do your work and try not to dream about it later. The work crews operated with a unity of purpose, fueled by fear and greed.

Huddy could have checked on such matters himself but preferred to leave that phase of the operation to subordinates. He disliked talking to manual laborers. Beer and football were limiting topics for an intelligent conversationalist like himself.

He looked younger than his forty years, though the greying at his temples (carefully maintained by his barber to give him that distinguished young-executive look) hinted at his real age. He was tall and limber, an elegant scarecrow brandishing a pleasantly boyish grin which had gained him admittance to as many feminine chambers as corporate ones.

Ten years he'd been with CCM now. If everything went as planned and the county inspectors didn't find enough left in the valley to raise a stink about (he smiled to himself at the pun) there should be at least a senior vice-presidency waiting for him. When word was sent to New York, he might even get the call to move to Headquarters.

His gaze shifted toward the road slightly below. A blue-jeaned figure was climbing toward him. In shape it differed considerably and deliciously from most of the workers cleaning up beyond. In addition to the success the operation promised him, there was also Ruth.

She was ten years younger than he was, wiser in some ways, much less so in others. She was not his assistant. But as assistant chief programmer for CCM's Western States computer operations in West Los Angeles she had access to information outside his own department. Information to which he would ordinarily be denied access. She was his mole, his eyes and ears on the rest of the corporation's activities. On more than one occasion he'd used her information to outmaneuver his colleagues and competitors at the meetings and board room warfare where corporate chiefs were made or broken.

It wasn't unnatural that she be out on such a field expedition. Her own department would be busily altering dates and records and bills of lading to confuse inspectors and bureaucratic watchdogs.

Huddy planned to be present when the county inspectors finally got around to checking out the valley. He wanted to enjoy the looks that would doubtless come over their faces. They couldn't completely obliterate the history of the dumpsite, of course, any more than they could do so to the chemicals which had leached into the ground. But it would be enough. When the sun finally rose here there wouldn't be enough poison left in the valley to threaten anything bigger than a butterfly.

"Almost finished, Benjy," she told him.

"Almost." No one was watching them, so he allowed himself the luxury of a long embrace, a lingering kiss, and a delightful grip with both hands on her derriere.

"That was nice," she murmured as she pulled away and smiled saucily up at him. "Have to do it again one of these days." They'd been lovers for as long as they'd been intercorporate conspirators. "How about right now?" She reached for him again.

He put up his hands in mock defense. "Too many eyes around. Too many of the supervisors know me."

"It's dark." Her hand traveled up and down his thigh. He backed off. Slowly, smiling to show her that he wasn't irritated.

"Not here, anyway."

"Listen, everyone knows we've been working together on this project." She could be downright coquettish when she wished to, he thought.

"Yes," he admitted, "but not how closely we've been working together."

"Or exactly how we've merged our positions." She turned serious for a moment as she glanced back down into the valley. "Be done inside an hour and out of here before sunrise."

Huddy nodded. "It's gone well. Look, in addition to the triple over, I want both of the foremen on the heavy machinery crews . . . what were their names?"

It didn't surprise him that she recalled them instantly. Ruth was a lot like her computers. "Larson and Kilcallen?"

"Yeah. I want extra bonuses for them, on top of the promised."

"I'll mention it to payroll." She frowned slightly. "I don't know that they'll buy it, on top of everything else. This is costing the company a hell of a lot."

"Anderson gave me a blank check to go with the go-ahead I received from the board. You know that."

"No need to be profligate," she argued.

He shrugged. "A few individual bonuses won't make a dent in the overall cost. I may want to make use of Larson and Kilcallen some day. It's always a good idea to bind men like that tight to you when you have the chance."

"If that's what you want, Benjy." She made a mental note to inform payroll. Mental notes were the only kind that were necessary for Ruth Somerset to make. It was one of the things Huddy valued most about her. He disliked committing decisions to paper. Other people might read them someday.

Such a pretty head, too, he thought, though her coiffure hardly went with the sweatshirt and blue jeans. She'd forgotten to change that. He wouldn't mention it. Ruth could be funny about having her mistakes pointed out to her.

Not for the first time he thought how fortunate he was. Already he was farther up the corporate ladder than most men half again his age and better connected than most. A beautiful, devious woman stood at his side to assist him. At a discreet distance from his side, of course. She was as intelligent and ambitious as he was. Yes, he was lucky.

He thought back one more time to the board meeting. Ridgeway had told them that New York had bounced the whole problem right back in their laps, and they'd damn well better come up with a solution *fast*. Hesitation among his colleagues, confusion as they filed out of the meeting room. His hasty call to Somerset to join him at his condo that night.

Then the working up of the plan. The myriad details to be attended to, the careful timing, the methods by which they would delay the county's inspection: everything intricately plotted and graphed and then computer-printed and copied out.

Ridgeway's expression the next morning when Huddy had

confidently handed up the bound summary of the project. Waiting for word from New York. The official go-ahead with Ridgeway's reluctant but nonetheless admiring blessing.

And now it was nearly finished. All the weeks of worrying and planning, the concern that a late summer rain would ruin everything, were behind them. Even the last-minute scramble to locate sufficient quantities of a certain chemical neutralizer when it was discovered that none was available in company warehouses hadn't thrown them off schedule.

He chuckled at that memory. They'd been forced to purchase the neutralizer through a third and fourth party from one of CCM's biggest competitors, who would have been delighted to withhold the stuff if they'd known it would have resulted in CCM's public embarrassment.

Everything had gone as planned. Barring any last-second hitches the operation would be completed half an hour ahead of schedule.

He turned his attention from the valley where activity was beginning to diminish to the few lights from the small homes lining the far ridge. Streetlamps, mostly, he knew. It was too late for television and too early for coffee.

Greasers and wetbacks and bums, he thought dispassionately. He knew the names of every family that owned property bordering the dump. They'd been thoroughly and intensively researched. None seemed likely to make trouble about the dump. If any were so inclined they would have likely gone to the media long ago. None had.

A few of the houses had been here as long as the dumpsite. They were largely stucco over wood, with roofs of cracked red tile patched in places with corrugated steel. To Huddy's early dismay he'd learned that a couple had small gardens facing the dump, which the poor owners cultivated assiduously. But he'd relaxed after seeing the photographs. The gardens were up high on the ridge line. Surely a few struggling heads of lettuce or celery stalks couldn't send roots down far enough to encounter toxic wastes. Surely not.

No one had bothered to convey that information to the already frantic board. Huddy wasn't about to enlighten them. Anyway, it was a false concern, as he'd already decided.

"I know for a fact there'll be promotions out of this."

Somerset's gaze was still on the magically changing landscape below. "If the bonus that comes with 'em is large enough I'd like for us to take off someplace." She had the features of a movie star, he mused as she turned her face up to him. And behind it, the mind and morals of a piranha. "Let's take a real vacation for a change. Tahiti. I've always wanted to see Tahiti."

"You wouldn't like it," Huddy informed her. "Much too frenchified."

"Well, someplace else, then." She threw both arms around his neck, heedless of who might be watching, heedless of corporate propriety there on the hillside at sunrise. "Just the two of us on an island all to ourselves. The Bahamas, if you want to stay close to home. Jamaica. Barbados. I don't care. As long as it's got a warm beach and some privacy."

He smiled down at her and put his arms around her back, pulling her close. "Alright, I surrender, sweetness. As soon as this is all wrapped up and put to bed and our promotions are finalized."

"You know something yourself, then."

"Enough," he assured her. "It's only logical. We've saved the corporate ass, and that's always worth a step or two up the ladder."

"Stennet's job," she murmured, her eyes glittering expectantly. "I've wanted that sucker's job for more than a year. And when I'm head of all programming for Western Regional Operations and you're Senior Vice-President—"

"Why stop there?" he interrupted her. "Ten years," he said confidently, while admiring her aggressiveness, "give me ten years, and I'll be Chairman. And not just of Western Operations."

"What about me?" Her expression was full of mock-anxiety.

"You? You'll be Assistant Chairman, of course."

"How droll." She tapped him lightly where she loved him. "What about Webster?"

"Forget about him. He's a turkey, and no relatives in high places can change that. Not that he's a dope, he's not. But no guts. Hesitates to commit himself. New York would never name him to an important post because they know he'd vacillate over any deal he came in contact with.''

"Five years," she decided, watching him. "You won't need ten.''

"If we're lucky. If CCM isn't interested, there are other companies. When word of our success with this leaks out . . . and I'll make sure it leaks all over the place . . . our competitors will fall all over themselves offering me switch bonuses and perks. But I'd rather stay with CCM. I know the operation. Of course, if Exxon gets really serious. . . .''

She looked surprised at that. "You didn't tell me you've been in touch with them."

"Don't get excited. Just a couple of friendly lunches is all. Shop talk. You know how I always like to cover my rear.''

"Not as much as you like to cover mine." The glittering eyes again, only different this time.

He looked one last time across at the small homes across the valley. She followed his gaze, turned abruptly serious.

"There's been no trouble with any of them?''

"What kind of trouble could they make, even if they knew enough and had the inclination? Niggers and trash. But no, not a peep out of any of 'em. When I came through here a week ago to make the final sweep I contacted those who aren't getting welfare checks. I told them we were going to do some landscape work around here and that I'd appreciate it and so would my company if they'd make sure to keep their kids out of the way. Gave them fifty bucks a head. You should have seen them take off in their junkers. Straight for the nearest liquor store." He made a gesture of disgust.

"Of course, there were one or two I couldn't buy off, but we didn't have any trouble shutting them up. I had some friends pay them visits. Been no trouble. No problems at your end?''

She shook her head. Blonde hair rippled in the fading moonlight. "Below board level no one even suspects what's going on. All costs and equipment procurations are filed under 'Baja Exploration and Development,' along with our phosphate operations down there. It'd take a better programmer than the County retains to separate truth from fiction, and he'd have to know Spanish anyway. *Es verdad, amore*. Even if somebody tripped over the actual figures, the substance of the operation's as well hidden as a real Gucci bag in a truck full of Hong Kong fakes.''

Huddy nodded and gently stepped away. A man was mounting toward them. He was a big, beefy individual a few years older than Huddy. It was hard to tell. Physical labor aged you faster than desk work and his beer belly made him look even older.

This was Larson, and he had four kids and a wife prone to illness, Huddy remembered. All four kids still lived at—and off—home. None of them had a dope problem. He smiled to himself. He liked to know all about his subordinates. It helped him to identify with their petty personal problems. It also provided him with the wherewithal to wield more than just corporate power over their lives.

As one of the supervisors of the clean-up, Larson was in a position to have a pretty good idea what was going on. And to testify in court about it, too. But that would never happen, Huddy knew. The foreman needed this job too badly.

"Pardon me, Mr. Huddy,'' the foreman said, properly deferential. Big football star in college, Huddy thought. Second-team all Big-Eight at offensive guard. Didn't look much like it now. The only sweeps Larson led these days were with a broom. Good man, though. That's why Huddy had brought him in on this one. He'd keep his trap shut.

"What is it, Larson?''

He jerked a thumb down toward the valley. "We're just about through here, sir. As you can see.''

"Any trouble on the way out?''

"Not that I've heard. Hang on. I'll check.'' The foreman extracted a radio unit from his belt, muttered at it, listened, then clipped it back in position.

"No sir. None of the outgoing trucks have been stopped. Every driver's under strict orders to stay within the speed limit on penalty of forfeiting every nickel of their bonuses. No complaints from any of the local yokels, the Highway Patrol hasn't noticed us, and I've made sure the trucks are well spaced on the Interstate. The last of the dumpers is already out at the 'Springs. By rush hour they'll be on Highway Twenty-five and beyond any traffic. By tonight they'll be near Mexicali.''

"You're sure our people at the border know what to do?"

"Everyone's been taken care of," Larson said delicately. "The right people have been paid. The trucks'll go over, then cut through to the coast and rendezvous at the dumpsite we picked on the Gulf. By tomorrow night everything we trucked out of here will be a problem for the fish to worry about. Not yours any longer."

"Not *ours* any longer," Huddy corrected him.

"Right. Not CCM's, I mean. Excuse me."

"No sweat. You've done a great job, Larson, you and the others. There'll be an extra surprise in your paycheck next month, on top of what's already been agreed upon. I've already authorized it and Ms. Somerset here will make sure of it." She nodded at the foreman. He didn't acknowledge her smile. Being around her made him nervous and tend to forget his wife and family.

But he couldn't conceal his pleasure. Replace the old Datsun six months early, he thought. A new stereo, maybe. Maybe even enough money to help Frank out at the J.C.

He wanted to express his thanks to Huddy but held himself back. He knew Huddy didn't much like talking to him. That suited Larson just fine. Privately he thought Huddy a stuck-up asshole. Knew his business, though. Had to admit that. Anyway, you didn't have to like the guy. Just follow his orders and it was Christmas in September.

"I'll see that things are cleaned up proper, sir."

"I know you will, Larson." He said nothing else, ending the meeting. The foreman nodded once, then turned and headed back down the path.

As soon as he was out of sight Huddy put his arm around Somerset's backside.

"My place or yours?" she asked, running her tongue over her lower lip.

"Ours," he told her.

"Oh no." She slumped against him, disappointed. "Not more work. I thought we were through."

"Not quite yet. You know that, sweetness. Come on, you're twice as thorough as I am anyway. Let's not blow this by overlooking something important at the last minute."

"Oh, alright. But I'm damned tired of it, Benjy. Two days almost without sleep."

"I promise we'll make up for it. Starting tomorrow night, after I've been through the site in the daytime. I'll make up for everything else, too."

She snuggled a little closer.

III

The path led to a graded parking lot just over the hilltop. Down below lay the lights of Riverside and off to the north, San Bernadino. Huddy stepped up into the motor home and flicked on the light. No family recreational vehicle this, but thirty feet of sybaritic corporate luxury. Even the Captain's chairs forward were padded leather.

He drew a couple of drinks from the bar and added a few tablets from the pillbox he always carried with him to his own glass. They'd helped keep him going for the past week. Somerset plopped herself down in the chair opposite the computer terminal. Her fingers ran lithely over the keyboard, calling up figures and names which should not have been in CCM's corporate files.

That was the beauty of computer work, she thought. It was so quick and clean. No need anymore for bulky paper shredders or furnaces. You could wipe out illegal information at the touch of a finger, vanquish it forever from the realm of possible prosecution.

She knew what Huddy wanted her to check now. The dump itself was clean. The county inspectors would find only healthy vegetation and fresh air in its depths. Only people could cause them trouble now. Huddy would want to make absolutely sure of potentially troublesome people. He'd want to double-check to make sure everyone had been bought off or threatened into submission.

Huddy handed her the drink. That was one area where their tastes differed. He couldn't understand what she saw in the taste of gin, which to him had the flavor and consistency of machine oil.

He leaned close to her as she operated the remote terminal. The list she had conjured up contained the names of everyone, adult or child, who lived within a hundred and fifty yards of the dump site's outermost boundaries or had lived there within the last thirty years. It was not the kind of list that ought to be in the hands of a private corporation.

In addition to the usual vital statistics: name, height, weight, physical description and so on, the list also gave the employer's names for those who had jobs, the amount of monthly welfare each family received, which individuals were especially vulnerable to economic pressures (which included nearly everyone on the list), which were not, even the dates and descriptions of serious illnesses suffered.

It was the last statistic that Somerset and Huddy were most determined to keep from any other eyes. A doctor perusing that list would immediately have noticed something unusual. There were less than three hundred names on the list. For such a small grouping, with such a diverse ethnic background, the incidence of serious respiratory disease was exceptionally high, as were the number of deaths due to various cancers.

The statistics were not surprising to Huddy. He'd half expected something of the sort when he'd taken on the project. Unfortunate for those who happened to live near the site, but hardly his responsibility. The number of possible and known carcinogens which had been dumped at the site filled another long list.

Fortunately, few people lived in the vicinity of the dump for very long. They were scattered all over the Southwest and Mexico. Of those who remained, several had recently moved away, thanks to the indirect intervention of CCM, which, through Huddy's underlings, had provided unexpected financial windfalls or job offers elsewhere to families with an especially high incidence of cancer. The county inspectors would find no cluster of heavily diseased citizens living next to the site.

It seemed wondrous, for example, that a job had miraculously materialized for Mr. Gomez, despite his constant coughing. The family had long been dogged by tragedy. Both of Gomez's parents had died of liver cancer several years ago. So when the job offer had been made, the family readily accepted, delighting in the knowledge that even their move to Calexico would be paid for by Mr. Gomez's new employers.

No records had to be falsified, no one had to be asked to lie. The potential warning signs were simply induced to move away from the dump. All were grateful for the unexpected largess. None saw any connection between their good fortune now and their terrible luck in the past.

Only one remained that Huddy would've liked to be rid of; an old, long-time resident of the area, name of Jake Pickett. He reached past Somerset and touched the keyboard. The abstracted Jake Pickett sprang into prominence on the glowing screen. Somerset knew the name and looked sympathetically at Huddy. This Pickett had refused the first job offer Huddy's people had made him. For one thing, he was older than the Gomezes or any of the others they'd had to resettle. He'd lived next to the dump longer than anyone else. Unlike the Gomezes, he had roots there.

So he'd simply smiled patiently at the company representatives while politely declining their offers.

"This is my home," he'd told them. "I've lived here fifty years. I'm not about to pick up and leave now. What for? A job? At my age?" He'd laughed easily. "You've got to be kidding. I've got my social security and my modest savings. So you find some younger fella who really needs the job." And he'd closed the door on the discouraged representatives.

They couldn't tamper with his social security, Huddy knew, and the man's savings were secure in an insured bank account. He was too old to threaten bodily and probably too dumb to know better. He continued to read the screen, murmuring aloud.

"One sister, moved to Texas, died there age forty-two." He found himself nodding knowingly, dispassionately. "Lung cancer." He wondered if the woman had been a smoker and hoped so. Not that anyone was likely to pursue personal histories that far.

The best thing about Pickett was that he had a bad heart. Chronic history of heart arrest, angina, complicated by liver problems. Slightly overweight. Pickett had been a drinker in his youth, though apparently no longer. If only he'd cooperate and die tonight, Huddy thought. He considered having a couple of strong-arm types break into the old man's home and rough him up a little. Take a few things, make it look like a robbery. Maybe they could induce a fatal attack.

Trouble was, there wasn't much to rob, and just one suspicious county detective could really begin to mess things up. A better idea, Somerset had suggested, was to employ a bunch of barrio toughs. Unfortunately, the dump site was so far out of town that no home boys claimed the area as part of their turf. Besides, teenagers were unreliable, as likely to turn on you as help you. Too dangerous.

What really concerned Huddy was not Pickett's intractability or his family's medical history. They could tolerate a few remaining examples of disease. According to the reports, the man was something of a neighborhood flake. Not crazy, just independent and ornery enough to make trouble just for the hell of it and hang any consequences. He was an old man, lived by himself, with no close relatives within a thousand miles. There seemed no way to get at him.

Gomez, now, had six kids. If he hadn't accepted the Calexico job there were other avenues open to Huddy's people to convince him he'd better do what he was told. But there seemed to be no way to gain control of Pickett. He spoke perfect English, had lived next to the dump most of his life, and seemed damnably straightforward. Huddy definitely did not want him talking to the county inspectors.

The staged robbery still seemed like the best alternative. If caught, the robbers could claim they'd gone to the wrong house. It was a thin story, but a plausible one. The police ought to buy it. They might even be able to get away with having the old man "accidentally" catch a stray bullet.

"You know something?" Huddy said. "I worry too much." Somerset leaned back and put her hands against him.

Her head was thrown back and she stared up at him through exquisite lapis eyes.

"I've told you that, Benjy."

"Yeah. You know, when this is over, we really *should* take that vacation. Find an island and just sit on the sand for a couple of weeks. I'm sure the company wouldn't begrudge us the time. Hell, if we pull this off they won't begrudge us anything."

"That's my boy." One nail made circles against his belly. "What's the point of knocking yourself out if you don't take advantage of life once in a while?"

"Sometimes I just forget about resting." Privately he thought, that's the trouble with you, Somerset. Those who aspire to wield real power don't have time to rest. Lotus-eaters never get anywhere.

His own sense of superiority thus fortified, he turned his attention back to the screen. "I mean, what can we do about this guy? Likes to dress up on Halloween, play Santa Claus at Christmas, play with the neighborhood kids. A real retard. How do you manipulate somebody like that?"

Unpredictable, too, he thought. Just the sort who, if he was confronted by a health inspector, was likely to say something real dangerous.

He read on. "Graduated high school, no college." That figured. Actually, Huddy was surprised to see evidence of the high school diploma. Rural school, though. Virtually worthless. So he's not the brightest guy around. Good. He might have trouble putting his feelings and suspicions into words. Hardly likely to mention his sister, who'd lived with him for fifteen years. Probably both of them played down in the dump. Well, the sister was no longer a concern. She was long gone. Pity Pickett hadn't picked up the same bug as his sibling.

Somerset's hand moved to his collar and stroked his neck. Her fingers toyed with his hair. He sighed, tried to force himself to relax. Less than a week, he reminded himself. Less than seven days and we can forget all about this and enjoy the money and promotions.

Only Pickett still stood in his mind, blocking his delight like a black valentine.

He'd try the job offer one more time, only this time he'd make the proposal himself. That way he could at least size up his last roadblock to success in person. He had to ascertain just how dangerous Pickett might be before deciding on something extreme like the fake robbery. Hopefully the old man would come around and extreme measures wouldn't be necessary.

First thing in the morning, he told himself. Now he was exhausted and Somerset was right about him needing to relax. She was good at that. Real good. Huddy was certain he gave back as good as he got, of course. Sex was only another form of wielded power. He had no qualms about letting her feel she was in command at such times. It was good for her ego and he was hardly hurting as a result.

Yes, Somerset was nice to have around and not only for her encyclopedic mind. She knew that and it didn't cause her any problems. She was too well-balanced.

The computer continued to wink glassily at them as they moved from console to couch. He'd finish with Jake Pickett in the morning. Probably worrying about the old man needlessly. Everything else had gone so smoothly. One stubborn old man surely wasn't going to screw things up.

Somerset pulled him down on the couch and he forgot about Jake Pickett, forgot about the project, forgot about everything except the wonderful warmth and movement she was.

As usual they both enjoyed the hell out of their lovemaking, and, as usual, there was no love in it. . . .

IV

Surely a beneficent spirit was watching out for Benjamin Huddy, for he learned the next morning that the company's lawyers had scored yet another triumph of legal obfuscation, for which they were famed. They'd succeeded in delaying the inspection of the dumpsite not for another day or two, but for a whole week.

Huddy could scarcely contain his pleasure. A full week would give the landscapers several opportunities to slip down into the site and check on the transplanted chaparral, to add water and fertilizer and replace any plants which hadn't taken to the sanitized soil. It also let him return to the Century City office to take care of accumulated busy work before driving back out to Riverside the next day to confront the obstinate Jake Pickett.

The section of Riverside he had to drive through to reach the site was even more depressing in the daytime. This barrio was worse than East L.A.'s. There was no community spirit here, none of the pride which had produced the blazing murals which turned old buildings in L.A. into towers of light and color. He guided the Cadillac cautiously through garbage-lined streets, past ancient corner markets shielded by black iron grates.

Finally he was maneuvering the Eldorado out of the barrio proper and up the dirt road leading to the ridge bordering the dump. He wondered if maybe he should have sent an aide. But he was curious to see the site after a couple of nights' work by the landscaping crews, and knew he'd handle Pickett better than any assistant. They'd had their opportunity and had failed. Anytime you want something done right you've got to do it yourself, he thought sourly. They just hadn't handled the old man properly.

Also, it was a nice day to be out of the office. He wouldn't miss anything. He had a good secretary and Somerset would warn him if anything unexpected developed in relation to the project.

The dirt road which climbed the ridge did not show many tire tracks. Not everyone who lived on the road owned a car, though you couldn't tell it from their front yards, where deceased Chevrolets and wheelless Fords slowly disintegrated in the California sun, rusting dinosaurs from the fifties.

The valley looked odd from this angle. He was the same height above the site's floor, but everything else was different, including the position of the sun. It was a beneficial revelation, he thought. Beneficial to view the valley from any place where the inspectors could see it. And what they would see was a little geologic depression no different from the dozens which surrounded it.

The tallest trees had been planted in the center of the valley, where water was likeliest to collect. Hastily transplanted grasses and wild grains bent to the summer breeze. There was no sign that man had intervened in this place or that the natural order had been disturbed.

Something caught his eye. He frowned, stopped the car. The window hummed as he lowered it. There, on the far hillside. There was a patch of brush that appeared to be turning brown much too rapidly, even for late Southern California summer. He made a mental note of the spot. Have to get the landscapers up there to work on it, he thought, and a field tech to make sure the soil is clean.

Not that the county could make much of one little plot of poisoned flora, but Huddy wanted everything to look so normal, so natural at first glance that they wouldn't even bother to run a soil analysis on their way to the next locale on their ecological hit list.

He continued upward, thankful for the front-wheel drive which took the barely graded track easily, wincing every time a kicked-up piece of gravel struck the car and echoed through the padded interior.

Then he reached the end of the road, near the highest part of the ridge. A couple of battered white crossbars blocked his way. The Dead End sign that hung limply from the center was a mess of bullet holes, spray paint graffiti unintelligible to anyone outside the barrio, BB dents and rock scratches. The lower of the two horizontal barriers lay forlornly on the ground. Kids had jumped up and down on it until it busted off.

Those same children, who ought to have been in school, now appeared as if by magic from the yards surrounding the dingy, grime-encrusted houses. They clustered around the car, marveling at the fresh paint and polished chrome, and making Huddy uneasy. He decided the best thing to do would be to do nothing. The last thing he wanted was to antagonize these gutter brats.

He stood there for a moment, ignoring their giggles and wide-eyed stares as he studied the papers and map on his clipboard. Jake Pickett's house was straight ahead, up a trail which began where the road ended. The ridge was too narrow for a road beyond this point, hence Pickett's comparative isolation. He put on his best smile while he thumbed the car door lock. There was a click as both doors snapped tight. He pushed the door closed.

The children promptly shifted their attention from the car to its driver. Huddy was careful not to touch any of them as they crowded around him.

"Hi, mister." The boy who spoke looked to be about ten. He glanced admiringly at the Eldorado. "Nice car. Too nice for you to be from the welfare."

"That's right," he replied with forced pleasantness, "I'm not from the county, or the city."

"Well, where you from, then?" asked another boy curiously. His tee shirt was cut off just below the sternum, revealing his bare brown belly to the sun. Whether this was the result of local fashion trends or just poverty Huddy couldn't have said and didn't much care.

Nearby a little black-haired girl stared solemnly at him. Occasionally her stare was interrupted as sharp, racking coughs bent her over. Huddy knew that cough, could surmise its likely cause. Now that the dump had been cleaned up, maybe her cough would go away. Maybe.

It would be impossible for the county inspectors to prove anything from the few chronically ill people who remained around the dump. Besides, these people were habitually ill, weren't they? No telling where the girl's family had acquired their coughs. Probably south of the border. Likely as not, the little girl's parents were illegals. Huddy grinned. They'd no more talk to a government official than they'd take a union job. His attention went back to the trail.

"Hey mon, if you not from welfare," the older boy persisted, "then what you doin' here?"

"I'm going to visit a friend." He pointed toward the surprisingly neat little house not far beyond the dead-end barrier. "Does Mr. Pickett live in that house?"

"Pickett?" The eldest boy frowned while his gang clustered close around him.

"He means *el magico hombre*," one of the other boys finally said, *"stupido."*

"Who you calling *stupido*, Victor?" He started to push the younger boy, then thought better of it. He still wasn't sure this stranger with the nice car was harmless.

"Yeah, that's his place, I guess. He not in any trouble, is he? You *sure* you not from welfare?"

"Positive," Huddy reassured him.

"That's good," said one of the other boys. *"El hombre magico*, he's a nice old guy. Not too good here, though." He tapped his chest. *"Enfermedad del corazon."*

"Right," said Huddy, hoping he was. "Has he had any attacks or bad spells with his heart lately?"

"Hey, I'm no paramed, mon," said the oldest boy, shrugging. "We don' see him all that much." His attention shifted away from Huddy abruptly. "Hey, mama's home. Come on, Carmela. Come on, everybody. Maybe she got some soda.

"Adios, mister. You say hi to *el hombre magico* for us.

And don' worry about your car." Laughing and trailing fragments of clothes, the children ran barefooted down the street toward the house where a battered old Oldsmobile had just pulled into the driveway.

Huddy was glad to see the kids go. Making sure his tie was straight, he flicked dust from the hem of his jacket and tucked the clipboard under his right arm as he started up the shrunken road. Despite the older boy's assurances he didn't want to leave his car exposed to this neighborhood any longer than absolutely necessary. He'd make the interview with Pickett as brief as possible.

The slope was gentle and the walk not long. Standing in front of the little stucco palace Huddy had to admire the view. The top of the ridge commanded a sweeping view of the city of Riverside, the mountains to the north and east, and Corona to the south.

The beige stucco was not as badly cracked as some Huddy had seen, considering the house's likely age and the forces it had been subjected to down through the years. Stucco did not react kindly to water and earthquakes. A few ancient rose bushes shared space with newer irises. The roses were probably as old as the house.

He stepped up on the porch and put out a finger toward the doorbell, wondering if it would work. His hand never touched it. The door opened.

"Howdy." Pickett nodded down the trail toward the barrier, correctly interpreting Huddy's look of discomfort. "Didn't mean to startle you. Heard your car drive up and the kids laughing. Not many folks come up this way. Those that do are usually lost. They turn right around and go back down. You didn't. I expect it's me you want to see, then."

"If you're Jake Pickett." Huddy made a show of checking his clipboard.

"Unless my mother lied to me." He grinned, stepped aside. "Come on in."

"Thank you." This would be easier, Huddy thought as he mounted the porch steps, if Pickett were a grouchy, irritable old man. Not that it mattered in the end. Huddy wanted cooperation, not courtesy.

The interior was a surprise. It was far from immaculate, but it was a lot cleaner than many bachelor pads Huddy had seen. The small living room was dominated by an ancient sofa. Worn but clean blankets hid the rubbed places in the floral upholstery. There was an old rocking chair, an easy chair with overstuffed arms neatly patched, a very plain coffee table that had to date from the thirties, and a small TV sitting on a wooden stand. Huddy's eyes flicked from one opening to the next, missing nothing. From what he could see through the short hallways the rest of the house matched the front room in cleanliness as well as scarcity of furniture.

Pickett looked his age. He didn't seem particularly unhealthy, but not every cardiac sufferer wore the troubles of his chest on his face. He was slightly over average height, which surprised Huddy. He'd always thought of sick old men as small and crumpled, walking with heads bent forward and backs crooked. Pickett was as tall as Huddy, and he stood straight. A belly bulge showed through the clean brown shirt and the blue jeans billowed around thighs and calves where muscle had shrunk away. Pickett's shoulders were rounded as those of a career typist. His face was pleasant and open, the chin sharp, nose slightly hooked, the eyes bright and alert and blue. Thick white hair that showed little hint of thinning was combed straight back on top and sides in the style of fifty years ago. Funny, Huddy mused, how reluctant men are to change their hair style.

He extended a hand. "Benjamin Huddy, Mr. Pickett." The grip that enveloped his was firm but still only the shadow of what once was.

"You know mine." The old man's voice was strong, with no quaver whatsoever. Out of the corner of one eye Huddy read the label on the small bottle standing on the coffee table. The letters were red: Nitrostat. For angina, Huddy thought. It was comforting to see some sign of illness in this house. Pickett in person did not conform to Huddy's preconceived notions.

"Have a seat, sonny." Pickett slipped into the easy chair and gestured at the couch. "What can I do for you?"

Huddy sat down . . . and nearly lost his balance as he continued to sink. New furniture did not make you welcome like the old couch did. He flipped through the papers on the clip-board and assumed a serious mien.

"My information indicates that you've lived in this house for a long time, Mr. Pickett."

The old man nodded. "Most of my life. Grew up in this place, really."

"Then I can understand your reluctance."

"My reluctance?"

"To accept the job you were offered by the company I represent, the Masters Security Systems out of San Diego. You remember that?"

"Oh sure." Pickett studied the ceiling. "I do recall another young fella, younger than you, showin' up one day and offering me some sort of guard job down thataway. I'd just about forgotten it."

"It was a guard job, Mr. Pickett. In one of the numerous highrises Masters is responsible for. Late night work. You watch half a dozen television monitors and radio for help if you see any trouble. It's a good job for a man your age, Mr. Pickett. Wouldn't it be nice to have some real cash coming in? I know what social security pays.

"I believe Masters' representative also offered you assistance in resettling in a nice, modern new apartment in an adult retirement complex." He smiled ingratiatingly at Pickett. "You refused the offer. I'd like to know why."

"You with this Masters company, then?"

"I'm associated, though I don't function directly under them. We take care to choose the people we want to hire, Mr. Pickett. We're disappointed when it looks like we've made a wrong choice, and we like to find out where we went wrong."

"Not much to it," Pickett told him. "It's just what I told him. I grew up in this place, spent my life here. I've been to San Diego. It's a nice town. I liked Sea World and the Space Theater a lot. But I ain't interested in moving there. Also, I don't much like guns."

Huddy forced himself to be patient as he explained. "You don't have to wear a gun for this job, Mr. Pickett. All you have to do is watch the monitors. If anything serious appears, it's up to you to call in the men with guns."

"Don't sound like I'd be much of a guard, then."

"It's up to you whether or not you want to wear a gun, Mr. Pickett. You have a choice. What we really need is someone with good eyes who doesn't mind just sitting in one place for long periods of time. Not everyone can do that, you know. It's especially hard on younger men."

"Sorry," Pickett said. "Still not interested. You want a beer?"

Huddy did indeed, but he wasn't quite willing to chance the unknown that might emerge from this old man's refrigerator. "No thanks. I just had lunch. Tell me something, Mr. Pickett. Doesn't living here worry you? I realize you've spent your life here, but surely the neighborhood's changed drastically from when you were a child."

"It sure has," said Pickett. "Sure has. Didn't hardly ever used to be anybody t'come up the road. Wasn't even much of a road when mom and pop put this place up."

"And that doesn't concern you at all, Mr. Pickett? The adult retirement building in which you'd be living has a full security system, medical personnel on call, all kinds of privacy and protection."

"You don't understand." Pickett grinned at him. "I *like* the way this neighborhood's changed, Huddy. It used to be awfully lonely until the families started moving in—the Sanchezes, the Rials, the Diazes and Diegos and Dan Phungs."

"That doesn't bother you?"

"Naw. Told you, I like the company. I get a kick out of having all the kids around. Say, you know what they call me?"

"*El hombre magico*," said Huddy absently. "They told me."

"Yeah. The magic man. Ain't that a kick? An old fart like me." Pickett was obviously pleased with his title. "I do little parlor tricks for them, keep 'em amused when they're out of school which for some of them is most of the time. In return, their mommas do me nice. You know, handle some of my shopping and complicated laundry and stuff. I'm kind of the neighborhood baby sitter. By default." His grin widened. "That suits me better than looking for burglars and snake thieves." He nodded toward the far end of the room. "If I want to stare at the tube I'd rather watch Laverne and Shirley or football than some empty corridor. So if you're here to try and talk me into taking that job, sonny, I'm afraid you've wasted your morning." He hesitated a moment. "Say, maybe you can tell me something."

"If I can." The disappointed Huddy was preparing to leave.

Pickett gestured to his right. "It's about that old dump down there." Huddy tensed immediately. "That goo's been stinking and festering down there for as long as I can remember. And all of a sudden I wake up a few days ago and it looks like King Kong's been workin' down there with a bucket and spade. The whole place's cleaned out. Somebody must've been in a godawful hurry to do that, Mr. Huddy. I was just wondering if you might know who did it and why? Not the clean-up; that was years overdue. But why so fast?"

"Beats me," said Huddy carefully. "All I can think of is that the dumpers just decided it was time to clean the place up and they might as well get it done with."

"It was time, alright. It was time thirty or forty years ago." He winced and his hand went to his chest. It was just for a second and he didn't reach for the bottle of tablets on the coffee table.

"Better late than never, I suppose. Doesn't matter to me anymore. But kids play down there all the time, you know? Just like my sister and I did when we were growing up. Their moms and dads try to keep 'em out, but kids will play wherever they feel like it. I try to warn 'em away, but I don't know much of their lingo and some of them don't know much English. It's good to see the trees and grass down there now. Better for 'em."

"I'm sure whatever companies were responsible feel better for finally having performed the clean-up," Huddy said guilelessly.

"Yeah. Too bad they didn't do it a long time ago, though. I had a sister, you know? Lived with me here for a long time. Catherine. She moved away not long after mom and dad died. Died too young, Caty did. Always wondered if maybe the

stuff that was dumped down there"—and he gestured in the
direction of the valley once again—"might've had something
to do with her dying so young."

"People die young all the time," Huddy pointed out.
"What did she die of?"

"Cancer. Of the lungs and liver. Real pretty girl, Catherine
was. My folks both went with cancer, too. Guess I was just the
lucky one."

"You see," said Huddy, "it runs in the family. You can't
blame it on a single source."

"Yeah, maybe," said Huddy softly, "but we didn't have no
cancer in the family before dad died. Leastwise, none that I
ever heard tell of."

"Well, you know what old medical records are like. In the
old days they weren't always sure what killed people. Even
when they were, they gave the diseases all kinds of different
names."

"That's so," Pickett admitted, "but it don't matter much
now, I guess. What's past is past. I'm just glad to see the garbage finally cleaned up."

"Me too," said Huddy. He rose. "Well then, if I can't convince you to take our offer, Mr. Pickett. . . ."

"I'm afraid you can't, sonny."

"You obviously feel strongly about that dumpsite. I guess if
anybody asked you how you felt about it you'd tell them how
happy you were to finally see it cleaned up?"

"Sure would. Tell 'em the same things I told you. What's
past is past."

Huddy relaxed inside. This man is safe, he decided. "I want
to thank you for your time, Mr. Pickett. I guess Masters Security will just have to look elsewhere."

"Guess they will." Pickett rose and started for the front
door. "Tell me something, though, Mr. Huddy. Why are they
so keen on me? I've been retired for years."

"Good references. The social security department refers us
to such people. We like to try and help out our senior citizens
whenever we can. This job is suitable for someone of advanced age. I'm sure we'll have no trouble filling it."

"That's good, because I'm just fine and happy right here."
Huddy put one hand against the door. "Don't think I don't

appreciate what you're tryin' to do for me. I'm just not your man."

Now that the interview was over, Huddy was anxious to be on his way back to the office. He still would have preferred that Pickett accept the job, but after talking with him he was pretty sure the old man wouldn't say anything too upsetting to any nosy county inspectors who might come knocking at his door. He'd likely just go on about how nice the site looked now and how good it would be for the kids.

There was a knock at the door and the faint sound of giggling. "That'd be Ortuno and his bunch," said Pickett. "I guess Carlos' *mamacita* got back from the Safeway."

"I'll be on my way, Mr. Pickett. Thanks for your time, and if you ever change your mind, you have Masters' phone number."

"Yeah, I guess I stuck it around here somewheres when that other fella gave it to me. You take it slow, sonny."

"Sure will."

Pickett moved aside as Huddy opened the door. They both exited, Pickett following in Huddy's wake. Dirty, dusty children clustered around the old man, laughing and giggling and shouting at him in a local patois of Spanish and English. Two of them shoved pop bottles toward him.

"Now just hold on there a minute." Pickett made placating gestures with both hands. "I can't take everybody at once. Who wants to be first? Will it be you?" He pointed sharply at a little girl, who put both hands to her mouth and shook her head. "How about you?" The little boy singled out took a step backward.

"Or maybe it should be. . . ." He reached out fast and grabbed the head of the oldest boy, the gang leader who'd put the questions to Huddy on his arrival.

Something made Huddy hesitate, turn. Words ran through his head. "*El hombre magico*. . . . I do parlor tricks for 'em, keep 'em amused. . . ." He always did waste too much time indulging his curiosity. But Pickett resembled a magician about as much as he looked like a power forward for the Lakers. Huddy was mildly interested to see what the old man could do.

"Okay now," Pickett directed the youngster, "hold it steady." The boy held out the bottle of sickeningly sweet quasi-orange drink and closed his eyes. All part of the show, Huddy mused. Why am I standing here watching this? I've got work to do, and Ruth'll be wondering what the hell's taking me so long.

Pickett passed his hands through the air over the pop bottle, closing his eyes and mumbling something unintelligible under his breath. When he'd concluded, he snapped his fingers.

For an instant it appeared nothing had happened. Then Huddy saw that the cap had tumbled off the bottle and its owner was already guzzling down the tooth-destroying liquid.

"Okay, now the rest of you." One by one, Pickett removed the caps from another half dozen bottles. Each time Huddy moved a little closer, trying to see how the trick was managed. He was frowning. It seemed like such a simple trick, and yet for the life of him he couldn't see how the old man pulled it off.

Clearly the caps were not pre-loosened, because soda immediately fizzed out under pressure whenever a cap was removed. No matter how intently he watched, he couldn't see how Pickett managed the trick. The old man's hands never went within a couple of inches of any of the bottles. He even removed the cap on the bottle of the reluctant little black-haired girl he'd first approached, and she was standing at least three yards off to one side.

The children melted away down the trail, laughing and drinking. Huddy hesitated. The sun was hot and getting hotter. He had a lot to do back at the office and he longed for the coolness of the air-conditioned Century City tower. Despite that, he followed Pickett back toward the house until they were standing on the porch.

"I can see why they call you the magic man. That's a neat trick. Do you work with cards and canes and stuff also?"

"Naw, I just fool around." Pickett looked a little embarrassed. "Like I told you, I'm the local baby sitter. I've always had a knack for little tricks like that. Keeps the kids in good humor." He hesitated briefly. "You want to see it again?" He gestured down the road. "The parents don't care nothing about it."

"Yes. Yes, I would like to see it again, Jake. How about if I take you up on that beer?"

"Good. You wait right here." Pickett melted into the house, reappearing a moment later with a couple of bottles of dark green glass. That gave Huddy another mild shock and raised the old man a notch higher in his estimation.

"Okay now." Pickett handed both of the Heinekens down to his visitor. "You hold one in each hand and I'll do 'em both at the same time."

"From up there on the porch?"

"Why not?" Pickett smiled ingenuously.

Huddy didn't understand. When he didn't understand something, he was displeased. It bothered the heck out of him that he couldn't figure out how the old man managed the seemingly simple trick.

"What's the secret? How do you do it?"

"Now if I told you, wouldn't be a secret no more, would it?" said Pickett with a grin.

Huddy checked both caps, tugging on one with all his strength. It was on tight, wouldn't budge. He inspected each bottle for hidden strings, found nothing. Pickett waited until he was finished. He was still smiling.

"Well?" said Huddy.

"Well what, sonny?"

"Get going. What about your 'magic words'?" He gestured as he spoke, waving one of the bottles through the air.

"Oh, them. Them's just for the kids. Of course, if you'd like the whole show. . . ."

"No. Skip it. You do it however you want to."

"Right," said Pickett, whereupon Huddy gave a shake like a man with ten-second flu as the caps to both bottles promptly fell away from their seats. Beer bubbled out of the bottle he'd been waving and foamed over his right hand.

"Oops." Pickett clambered down the steps and hurriedly grabbed away the bottle. He took a long slug of the contents, wiped his lips contentedly. "Sure beats hunting for an opener, doesn't it?" He let out a short, sharp laugh.

Huddy sipped gingerly at his own beer. It was good and cold and he was glad he'd asked for it. It helped steady him. He'd seen the trick up close now. Maybe too close, because if his life had depended on him explaining how Jake Pickett had dislodged those two bottle caps, Huddy would be a dead man.

If the furiously thinking executive had thought to inspect either of the caps under a magnifying glass he might have had a clue as to what had taken place. He would have seen that some of the cork lining the caps seemed to be missing. But the caps were forgotten in the dirt and dust as Pickett escorted him down the trail toward the road barrier.

"That's a simple trick," Huddy said carefully. "Real simple." He didn't even notice the mud that was climbing all over his two-hundred-dollar shoes. "But I'm damned if I can figure out how you did it."

"Want to see some more?" Pickett looked pleased, like a little boy who'd just shown his parents a straight-A report card.

"Yeah." Huddy feigned disinterest. Board meetings gave him plenty of practice at that. "Yeah, I'd like to see some more. You going to get some more bottles?"

"Naw. You've seen that trick." Pickett leaned on the barrier. It creaked, the vandalized "dead end" sign threatening to fall permanently from its moorings. He nodded toward the Eldorado. "Your car's awful dirty."

"It's a dirt road." He wondered what Pickett was leading up to. At the same time he was irritated that the old man had noticed. There was mud coating the front end of the big car and the wire wheels were plastered with light brown.

"C'mon," Huddy urged him, "what are you going to do?"

"Already done it." Pickett stood up against the barrier. "Looked at your car lately?"

Huddy glanced over his shoulder and the sight hit him like a brick between the eyes. The mud and dirt had disappeared; not just from the front of the car but from the underside and the wire wheels as well. Slowly he walked around the Eldorado. Even the underside of the back end was spotless.

The soda pop trick had intrigued him. The business with the beer bottles had really piqued his curiosity. Now he just stood there stunned, gaping at the car. Easy, he told himself. Don't rush things. Look for the logical explanations. Don't go off half-cocked.

"How did you do that?"

Pickett shrugged. "Like I said. It's a trick. It's nothing special."

"I don't see any water. There's no air hose. How did you *do* it?" His tone was running away with itself and he forced himself to relax, to calm down. "Mr. Pickett, would you mind taking a medical exam?"

"Now I told you, sonny," the old man reminded him, "I'm not interested in your guard job or any—"

"No, no." Huddy hastened to reassure him. "Nothing like that. Forget about Security Masters . . . Masters Security," he hurriedly corrected himself. "What I mean to say is, the exam date is already set up for you. The doctors involved are company. If you don't show for the exam the doctor in charge will just get a couple of hours off. Seems a shame to waste it. I meant to mention it to you before. You'd end up with a complete rundown on your general physical condition, at no charge."

"I don't like hospitals." Pickett frowned uncertainly.

"Neither do I. I use these same doctors," he lied feverishly. "You'd get executive care."

Pickett chuckled then. "Sounds like fun. I haven't been to the doc in quite a while. Medicare and Medicaid don't like to pay for general checkups. Don't guess it would hurt me none."

"Of course not, not at all. Like I say, it seems a shame to waste the opening. Don't worry about the money. It means nothing to the company."

"I still feel a little funny about it, Huddy. Me not accepting the job and all."

"Look on it as a repayment for the beer," Huddy said soothingly. "My company likes to do things for senior citizens. If we can't persuade you to take the job, at least we can leave you as healthy as when we found you. We do this sort of thing all the time."

"Can't you give some other guy my spot?"

Huddy shook his head. "Our appointments aren't set up that way. Either you use this one or it goes to waste. Come on, Jake. Our company doctors make enough as it is without having to work for it."

That hit a nerve. Pickett had seen plenty of what went on and didn't go on in the offices of physicians who accepted many Medicare recipients.

"Sonny, you've got yourself a deal."

"Thanks, Jake. You know, seeing you living here like this, above a chemical dump, there's no telling what might've gotten into your system. Our doctors are a cut above the kind the county works with. If there's anything that's gunked you up inside, they'll find it and fix it."

"Okay, okay, you've sold me. You sure there won't be no charge, now?"

"Not a dime," said Huddy briskly. "I promise you." He hefted the bottle and took another swallow as if to demonstrate his good intentions.

"Well, when's my appointment?"

"Couple of days. I don't remember exactly."

"Don't you have it down with those papers?" Pickett nodded toward the clipboard.

"Uh, no. No need to carry that information around with me. Why? You planning to be out of town?"

Pickett laughed. "I've got more time than anything else, Huddy. Where do I have to go?"

"I'll send you all the information as soon as I get back to my office." He looked around the dead end. "Do you have a car?"

Pickett turned and pointed to an ambiguous blue frame parked down the street. "That's mine. She's old so she's hell on gas, but she runs. Just because I ain't got no room for a garage doesn't mean I'm afoot. Remember, sonny, I'm a native Angelino."

"Silly of me. You think you can find the office I'll direct you to?"

"Just because I live out here in the boonies doesn't mean I don't get around, Huddy. I've driven this country all my life. You just have your people shoot me the instructions and I'll find my way."

"Fine. I'll be in touch, then. You're doing a right thing, Jake."

"I try to." He reached out to shake the younger man's hand, waited until Huddy switched the bottle to his left palm. "Hey, don't get the idea I'm not appreciative. I am. Just wanted to make sure you don't plan to have some young fool standing by to point out what great medical care I'd get if I accepted your job."

"Don't worry about that," said Huddy softly. "I promise you that your exam will be a completely relaxing experience."

ant lions. The security guard waved at him as he drove past.

He slipped into his spot, took the express elevator to the twenty-eighth floor, and headed for his office, barely acknowledging the waves and comments of his coworkers. Shawna, his secretary, was waiting for him.

"Hello, Mr. Huddy. You've been missed." She checked a pad. "There are six calls you have to return. The first was from Mister—"

"Hold everything." He waved a hand at her, the hand holding the clipboard.

"But one of the calls was from—"

"I said *everything*, Shawna. I'll get to them as soon as I can."

"Whatever you say, sir." She watched him curiously until he'd disappeared into his office.

Beyond the glass windows, endless waves of homes and concrete stretched off into the smog. On a clear day you could see the Pacific from Huddy's west-facing window. But today was not a clear day. Late summer days in Los Angeles rarely are. Like most of his fellow citizens, however, he'd acclimated himself to the brown-yellow haze which passed for air in the L.A. basin. The view was old-hat anyway.

He spent a moment behind his desk contemplating the grain in the walnut, then thumbed the intercom. "Shawna?"

"Yes, Mr. Huddy?"

"Ring Ruth Somerset for me, will you?"

"Yes sir." A pause, then, "No answer, sir."

"Damn. Forget it." He flipped off the com and turned to the computer terminal which occupied the left side of his desk. Carefully he activated the screen. Ruth could do this much faster, he knew, but since she wasn't available he'd try locating the information himself. He was too anxious to wait for her return. Nothing else mattered now. Not the calls he was supposed to return, not Ruth, not their planned vacation. All that mattered was finding an explanation for Jake Pickett's little parlor tricks.

The computer responded promptly to the secret key which protected the information concerning the site clean-up project. Discreet codes brought forth a list of several hundred names. A list very dangerous to CCM. It gave the names and backgrounds of everyone who had lived in close proximity to the dump whose illnesses the toxicologists believed were directly attributable to that proximity.

It took only seconds to find Pickett's name among them. Some would have taken longer. Those who now lived in Mexico, for example.

PICKETT, JAKE. Black letters on a white screen stared back at him. Huddy balanced his chin in his left hand, the index finger slowly stroking the slight cleft there as he studied the readout.

The information was not new but he reread it anyway. Pickett had grown up next to the dump. So had his parents. That was something of a surprise. The stucco house didn't look that old, but it wasn't hard to stucco over older materials. Stone, for example, or adobe.

This time he paid particular attention to the history of the sister Pickett had mentioned. She'd moved away subsequent to the death of both parents. Ended up in Houston, where she'd married. One daughter, apparently normal (so far, anyway, Huddy thought). Divorced. Died. The basics of one's life can be compressed into a very small space. Huddy read on.

The daughter's name was Wendy. She would be Pickett's niece. Moved out of Houston and eventually married the part owner-operator of a commercial fishing boat, an Arriaga Ramirez. Two children: a son Martin, currently a junior at Texas A & M, and a sixteen-year-old daughter named Amanda. Both children likewise apparently healthy and normal.

That is, they had been born that way. The daughter had been paralyzed in both legs since a bus accident at the age of ten. Tough, Huddy thought. It's a tough world.

Both of Pickett's parents had died young. Three deaths from cancer in the same family, the source of which might lie in the now sanitized dump. Huddy felt no remorse over the deaths of Pickett's mother and father and sister. That had all happened before he'd come to work for CCM. He bore no moral responsibility for what had happened to them. He was sorry for the grandniece, though. A lousy thing to happen to any kid.

What was important was that there was ample evidence for

the theory that living so close to the dump for so long had affected the bodies of the Pickett family. Why be afraid of it, he told himself? Where there's evidence of genetic damage there can also be genetic improvement. Since the cleansing of the Cadillac a single word had erupted in his mind. It was still pulsing strongly there, still waiting to be denied.

Telekinesis. The ability to move objects without touching them physically, through the use of some sort of mental energy. Scientists scoffed at it, magazines drew readers by mentioning it, tests regarding it were often maddeningly inconclusive. What sort of tests? Bottle caps slipping untouched from their bottles? Dirt tumbling from the underside of a mud-spattered car? Were those valid tests, on which industrial empires might be raised? Hardly.

El hombre magico, the neighborhood kids called Pickett. The magic man, who amused them with his tricks and thereby made life a little easier for their parents. Huddy doubted a single adult had ever taken the time to witness any of Pickett's tricks. They were for children, after all. Even if they had, what would they have seen? A little stage magic, that's all.

But Huddy wasn't so easily fooled. What about the niece, this Wendy? Could she perform parlor tricks too? There was no indication of it in the records, but then there'd been nothing of the kind of Pickett either. It wasn't the sort of thing information gatherers would bother to report.

The Ramirez family lived in the town of Port Lavaca. That meant nothing to Huddy, who was much more familiar with the suburbs of London and Hong Kong. The fact that Port Lavaca lay on the South Texas coast between the cities of Houston and Corpus Christi meant more to him. CCM had considerable interests in Houston.

He switched to a different body of information. Yes, there it was, the big refining plant that was part of CCM's petrochemical division. It was located south of Houston on Matagorda Bay, not far from Port Lavaca itself. Interesting, but not particularly useful.

He studied the screen as he reactivated the intercom. "Shawna, try Ms. Somerset's office for me again, will you?" A longer pause than last time before a new, familiar voice sounded over the speaker. It was cool and polite, all business.

It had to be. Others were listening.

"Mr. Huddy? Ruth Somerset here."

Huddy smiled to himself. "I have some questions for your division, Ms. Somerset, that I'd rather not discuss over the intercom. I know you're busy, but could you possibly spare me a minute or two?"

"You're certain it's important?" There was a sigh of exasperation. "You're right about my being busy."

"I'm very sorry, but I need your services urgently." He could see her grinning at the other end of the line.

"If it's really urgent, then. I'll be right up."

He contemplated procedures while he waited for her. It wasn't long until she strode into his office. Neat and formal, as always. Black skirt, off-white blouse and black vest. Ruffled sleeves, dark hose, single gold necklace. Black shoes. Professional as all get-out. He wondered what his colleagues, who considered Somerset something of the local ice queen, would have thought if they could have seen the kind of underwear the assistant chief of computer operations usually wore beneath her business suits and dresses.

Her gaze shifted quickly to the still lit terminal. "Found something in my files?"

"I can always find something in your files." He forced himself to turn serious. "Have a seat."

"Really, Benjy, this had better be important." She pursed her lips. "I have a lot to catch up on."

"Important's not the word. I'm preparing to sound the abyss. To run out on a limb and see how far I can go before it breaks under me. Getting ready to make a three-meter dive into a bucket of murky water."

"You're also being obscure."

"Not intentionally. It's just that I'm a little overwhelmed by some recently unearthed possibilities."

"What kinds of possibilities?" She crossed perfect legs, waiting for him to get to the point.

"You recall the one possible troublemaker I was concerned about when we were up at the site several days ago?"

She thought a moment, then shook her head.

"His name was Pickett. Jake Pickett."

"Oh yeah, now I remember. You were going to check him out in person."

"That's just what what I did. Went up to offer him a job that would get him out of the area and away from the nosy. He refused the job again, but he was so pleased with the clean-up work that I didn't feel he presented a real threat. He's sharper than the average site-proximate citizen, but it's more native cunning than real intelligence."

"If he's no problem, why bring him up now?"

"As I was leaving, Pickett performed a few little tricks for the neighborhood delinquents. Then he did a couple especially for me."

Somerset didn't look quite so pretty when she was confused. "The point of which is what, Benjy? I don't see where you're going with this."

Huddy took a deep breath before continuing. "I have reason to believe that the proximity of the Pickett family to the dump site and continuous exposure to its contents has, over a period of time, resulted in a genetic mutation which has manifested itself in the person of Jake Pickett in the ability to utilize that paranormal ability commonly known as telekinesis."

She stared at him. When she was sure he wasn't kidding around she burst out with the high, delicate trill that was Somerset laughter. Huddy didn't join in, simply waited patiently.

"You *are* serious! Benjy, you've got to stay away from science-fiction films. They're a bad influence on you."

"Most people are quick to laugh when anyone brings up the subject of parapsychology," he murmured. Since he'd expected it, her reaction did not upset him. Indeed, he would have been disappointed if she'd reacted in any other way. "What about that Israeli, Uri Geller? The one who bends spoons by looking at them? What about those people who develop film simply by thinking pictures onto the negatives? What about Kirlian photography? And there are other examples."

"I watch the news, read the papers," she responded. "Explanations exist for every example you mention."

"And maybe there's one I'm not seeing for what this Pickett can do. Come on, Ruth, you know me. I'm the strictest pragmatist you've ever met. I'm not given to flights of fancy and I require hard evidence before I'll believe a plane can fly or a new employee can do the job. But dammit Ruth, I *saw* this! It *happened*. It happened right in front of my eyes. I hadn't been drinking and I wasn't high."

"You saw what happen?" Her voice was calm now, careful. She didn't want to antagonize him, and he was so *positive*.

"I saw him remove bottle caps from tightly capped beer bottles without touching them. I was holding the bottles, and I'd tried the caps first. They were on tight."

Somerset leaned back in the chair. The white blouse and black skirt were suddenly pulled taut over a deceptively voluptuous body and for a moment Huddy had another kind of tight on his mind.

"Bottle caps. For bottle caps you drop everything and run around shouting that the sky is falling?"

"Not just that, no," he said, unmoved by her sarcasm. "After that he asked if I wanted to see another trick. I said that I did. So he cleaned my car."

"What?" She frowned at him.

"He cleaned my car, the Eldo," Huddy repeated, pleased by her reaction, "without touching it."

For the first time there was a hint of real interest in her voice. She wasn't patronizing him now. "He did *what?*

Huddy rose and began pacing back and forth behind his desk. As he talked his hands stirred the air like those of an Italian traffic cop. He was full of nervous energy and excitement and managed to convey some of both to Ruth.

"I stood there and he volunteered to show me another trick. He said, 'Your car's dirty,' and I said yeah, and the next time I looked at it there wasn't a speck of road dirt on it. Even the wire wheels looked like they'd just come through the wash. I couldn't have turned my attention away from it for more than a few seconds. A few *seconds*. I'd just climbed a filthy dirt road. The underside of the Eldo was all gunked up. This old man grins at it and it's showroom neat.

"He didn't wash it off, somehow. I checked for that right away. It was as dry as morning. God knows where any water could've come from anyway. I'm thinking about this, thinking hard, all the way back on the Freeway. And the only explanation I can come up with is that somehow he moved that dirt without touching it. So help me.'' He stopped pacing and stared at her expectantly.

"It doesn't make any sense," she said slowly.

"Very clever. Move two squares forward. Do not pass Go."

"Shut up and let me think, lover. You said there were a lot of kids around and that this Pickett plays with them a lot. Maybe they had something going together. Maybe the kids jiggled the car somehow when you weren't looking."

"That road grime was caked on, Ruth. To knock it loose you'd have had to drop the car from ten thousand feet. But your choice of words is propitious. Only I don't think the car was jiggled. I think the dirt was."

She considered his attitude as well as his words. She knew Benjamin Huddy pretty well by now. She doubted he was playing some kind of elaborate trick on her. He wasn't the practical joker type and even if he'd been so inclined, this wasn't the kind of joke he'd choose to perpetrate.

"I studied all the medical records relevant to site-proximates," she reminded him. "There are no suggestions of, uh, paranormal abilities in any of the personal histories."

"Maybe not, but there's plenty of mention of other kinds of abnormal developments. Premature deaths among children born to site-proximate parents. Physical deformities. Why not mental deformities as well? If Pickett's the only one, it's hardly surprising that nothing would appear on his chart."

"Funny," Somerset murmured, "if anyone was likely to develop paranormally, Pickett's family would be the likely place to look for one."

"Exactly," said Huddy. "Both of his parents and his sister developed cancer. I'm surmising that the same carcinogens that killed them also affected Pickett, but in a non-fatal and highly unique fashion. He has heart trouble. That's probably traceable to site exposure. He also has something else."

"You really think this is worth pursuing, Benjy?"

He nodded slowly. "And then some."

"Alright. How do you intend to proceed?"

"First I need to make arrangements to have Pickett

watched. Particularly when any of the local kids gather around him. We should be able to monitor him fairly tightly even at a distance. Use Foraker's people. They're pros and they're patient, and they won't ask unnecessary questions.''

Somerset nodded, making mental notes. "What am I supposed to tell them to look for?"

"Parlor tricks. Sleight of hand. Anything out of the ordinary. I want anything he does for those kids videotaped. This is all superficial anyway. We'll really find things out when Pickett arrives for his tests.''

"He agreed to submit to testing?" Somerset's eyebrows lifted.

"He thinks he's coming in for a free medical exam. Which he'll receive. Only it'll be a lot more extensive and sophisticated than he thinks. Why shouldn't he come in? There's no reason for him to think we have an unusual interest in him.''

"You said he was sharper when he first appeared. Native cunning, you called it. What if he gets suspicious? What if he finds out that you're interested in him because you think living next to the dumpsite has had some kind of permanent effect on him? Perhaps he already suspects it may have had something to do with the premature deaths of his parents and sister. You do anything to reinforce that belief and he's liable to go looking for someone official to complain to.''

"You're right. We'll have to be careful about that. I wouldn't worry about it. If he learns too much and it looks like he's going to make trouble and he's not worth hanging onto, he can always have a convenient heart attack. He may have one anyway. It shouldn't be a problem. None of his neighbors are what you'd call close friends. His only relatives live halfway across the country and there's no indication that he has frequent contact with them. We should be able to do pretty much what we please with him.''

"I'll do what I can to help, Benjy. You know that. I also want you to know that I don't buy a word of what you've said.''

"Think what it could mean, though, if I'm right about Pickett. If his mind has been altered somehow and it's connected to his living conditions, we might be able to replicate them in sufficient detail to reproduce the results. Not here, of course, but some of our South American facilities could handle the work. Sure, it'd be dangerous. We'd probably lose some Indian 'volunteers.' It'd be worth all the trouble and risk, though, if we could isolate a specific which could induce the same talent in others."

"*If* Pickett possesses any such ability," she reminded him skeptically.

"Sure, sure. It would take several generations to appear. I'd bet that the DNA of Pickett's parents was affected first, and then the mutation intensified in Pickett and maybe his sister as well. Other factors intervened in the case of the sister. She was a dead end."

"What good to us is a discovery that may take generations to confirm?"

"All we have to do is prove that Pickett has the ability. We'll have anything we want while we work to confirm it. Our own division, maybe, autonomous within the corporate structure. All the money and freedom anyone could desire. Our own company. How'd you like living in South America?"

"I'm not sure. I hadn't given it much thought lately."

"Think about it. You could be a queen down there."

"Royalty doesn't appeal to me. And you'd better slow yourself down until we have some facts to show around. Nothing's proven yet, remember?"

"So I admit to being enthusiastic. Can you blame me?" He put both hands on the desk. "I take full responsibility. But I need your help, sweetness. We can handle most of it on our own time anyway. The company doesn't have to know a thing until we decide it's time to tell them. In fact, it's better the company doesn't know. If this turns out to be as important as I think it will, we may want to shop it around.

"That's another reason why I want to use Foraker on surveillance. He'll report directly and solely to you." He came around the desk, put both hands on her shoulders and spoke with quiet intensity.

"This could do it for us, sweetness. Every dream we've ever had, every wish you've ever made, could all come true. It's all tied up in some freak talent an old man has, and I don't think he even knows he has it. Best of all, if I'm wrong, neither he nor the company is likely to hurt us."

At the board meeting later that afternoon, Shapeleigh, the Senior Vice-President in charge of general operations, surprised Huddy and everyone else by making a brief but formal speech commending him for his work in the "Riverside matter." It was one thing to receive commendation on your record, something else to have it spelled out in front of all your colleagues. Huddy enjoyed every word.

Apparently the county inspectors had been all over the dumpsite. They'd evidently expected to find a real sore spot. Instead they'd been forced to leave puzzled and frustrated, much to the delight of the properly outraged company representatives who'd accompanied them. All those reports of terrible smells issuing from the little valley had evidently been exaggerated or plain falsified by the largely immigrant population living nearby.

Oh, there'd been some evidence of soil contamination, but nothing serious. Nothing life-threatening. As for the presence in the area of chronically ill children and adults, well, there was no way to prove their diseases were the result of living next to the valley. Not without spending a lot of money, which Huddy and others within CCM had correctly surmised the county did not have.

There was one inspector who seemed inclined to pursue the matter further, but he was too busy planning his extensive South France vacation to quibble over such minor troubles. No point to beating a dead horse, especially on such slim evidence of wrongdoing.

As for questioning those people who lived near the site, the inspectors had departed in such a disgruntled mood that the company representative who'd accompanied them reported it as unlikely that any questioning would ever take place.

Yes, Huddy and Ruth Somerset were owed the thanks of Consolidated Chemical and Mining's entire organization. Shapeleigh beamed paternally across the long table at Huddy while delivering this corporate benediction, and Huddy's colleagues and competitors gnashed their teeth in private frustration. They'd missed this chance and Huddy hadn't. It grieved them deeply.

Later, when the others had departed, Shapeleigh drew Huddy aside and offered his personal congratulations. There was talk of large amounts of money as well as hints of vacancies to be filled in the near future. Huddy listened politely, appreciatively, but only with half a mind.

The other half was intent on bottle caps and dirt and a certain old man. . . .

Jake Pickett watched the water sink into the ground around the old rose bushes. Soon it would be time to cut them back for the winter. The old hose became a neatly coiled green snake beneath the water spigot. Pickett prided himself on the neatness of the little yard. It wasn't much work, what with only the roses and irises needing attention. The big scrub oak that grew next to the brick pathway required only an occasional soaking.

He walked around the house to enjoy the sunset. Off to the west the sun was hunting for a resting place in the distant Pacific. Despite having spent his whole life in Southern California, he'd been to the beach only twice, both times as a child. He recalled liking the ocean; the play of the surf, the hot sand between his toes, the gulls crying raucously overhead as they swooped and dove for garbage; but not caring for the people who frequented the beach. It was too crowded for him.

He preferred his house and his little hillside. For company he had the attendance of the laughing, brown-skinned children. Their parents were nice to him, and if he felt like any real change of pace he could always drive down to the city park or up to Arrowhead. For Jake Pickett familiarity bred content. No one bothered him.

Entering the kitchen through the back door he checked the small pot of pork and beans simmering on the stove. After stirring briefly with a wooden spoon to keep them from sticking he tried a sample. Done, he thought, and hot. A wife probably would have improved his diet, but somehow he'd never felt the need for permanent companionship. Just a crusty, dull old bachelor, that's me, he thought, undismayed by the image.

He poured the beans out of the pot into a large dish, using the spoon to scrape the last of them and making sure he didn't miss any pieces of pork. He twisted a couple of hunks of bread from the big round loaf on the counter, put the sealed bag back in the refrigerator, and headed for the living room.

The pork and beans went down well with the evening news. Both were basics of Pickett's lifestyle. Sometimes it bothered him that he didn't understand a lot of what the honey-voiced correspondents said on the evening news. It wasn't that they used such big words. They didn't. It was just that some of the subjects they discussed were completely alien to him. He regretted not having progressed past high school.

Circumstances, life, had interfered and made any higher education impossible. He'd always had to work to bring in money, especially after mom and pop had died so young. Things had gotten a little easier after Catherine had moved off to Texas. He'd always managed to make enough to support himself. With social security he was actually better off than he'd ever been. It made him feel good, confident. Of course, it helped that he'd never had much and therefore never expected much. He didn't feel particularly deprived.

The pork and beans went down warmly. As usual, they were much more nourishing than the news. He rose and re-entered the kitchen. Carefully he washed out the dish and put it in the yellow rack to dry, then returned to the television.

Outside, the sun had finally set. It was cooling off daily. Soon it would be winter and the rains would come; short, vicious downpours that were typical of Southern California. The ridge on which his house was built had more rock in it than most hillsides. Mudslides would occur elsewhere and he would read about them and cluck his tongue. People in this part of the country would build in the damndest places. It always amused him.

He enjoyed the rain, although for the last few years the cool weather had begun to affect him at the joints, as if his heart trouble wasn't cross enough to bear. Better count your blessings, you greedy old man, he admonished himself. You might be living in South Dakota instead of Southern California. Hell, you don't know what cold *is*.

He watched the bubbles fill the screen and listened to the music. Lawrence Welk was pleasantly familiar. After Welk it was time for sitcoms. Those he didn't much care for. It seemed like he'd outgrown the crude gags that were in vogue these days.

The documentary that followed on PBS was nice. All about the South Pacific. The TV was as close to Fiji as he'd ever get, not only because of his lack of money but because of his heart condition. Still, he enjoyed the vicarious traveling. It was the best thing about television.

The late news then, largely a reprise of what he'd already seen earlier. He watched it for the weather update. As he rose to turn the set off, he wondered if perhaps he should take some of his small savings and invest in a color console to replace the black and white. They were so damned expensive, though, and the images wouldn't come in any sharper or the words any clearer. Still, it was a thought he'd toyed with for months. Shows like the one on the South Pacific always gave the idea new impetus. He'd think about it some more, he decided.

He was half undressed when he walked into the bedroom. There was no television in there. Televisions belonged in dens and living rooms. He'd decided that when the new invention had first come onto the market.

There was a portable radio on the end table next to the bed, however. It was battered but serviceable. He flipped it on. It was preset at the local all-news channel. Despite the depressing nature of the majority of the news, Jake found it relaxing. As to many poor people, the day's litany of disasters and crises was more reassuring than debilitating to Jake, because it reminded him of how much better off he was than much of the rest of the world.

The anchorman/DJ currently working had a particularly pleasant voice. They both have something to offer, he thought. Television and radio. On the radio they didn't worry about making stupid jokes to each other or about how they looked. You could be a journalist instead of a movie star. The forced camaraderie, the bad ad libs (happy news, the stations called it) had nearly turned him off television news completely. For a while he'd taken to watching it without the sound.

The electric blanket had been on for several hours and the bed was nice and warm as Jake slipped beneath the covers. He got cold easier than he used to. That was a sign of aging, the doctor had told him, Funny, but he didn't feel like he was getting old. He didn't feel a day over fifty. Except for his heart, of course.

He didn't have to look to make sure the little bottle of nitroglycerine tablets was where it belonged, on the end table next to the lamp. The bottle and the tiny yellow pills it held had been part of his life for twenty years. He could find it quite easily without the lamp's aid.

A glance at the clock showed him that it was nearly ten. Midnight in Texas, he mused. He leaned back against the two pillows and closed his eyes. The moon cast faint illumination through the thin curtains. Jake didn't try to fall asleep. It was Thursday night. He always got a call from Amanda Rae on Thursday night. Their conversations were always the highlight of his day.

She didn't have to call so late, of course, but it was easier that way. Easier on her rather than Jake. After all, she did all the work.

It was funny how their regular conversations had begun. They'd been talking to each other so consistently over the years that Jake could almost call her. It was much simpler for her to make the call and for him just to wait, however. She didn't have as much trouble making the connection that way, she'd explained to him.

The first time she'd called him he hadn't known it was her. He hadn't even known what it was, much less who. There'd been only a mindless, wordless wailing inside his head. He spent hours scouring the house for the source, thinking that maybe one of the neighborhood kids had gotten stuck somewhere—in the narrow crawl space that ran beneath the floorboards, maybe, or on the slope that ran down into the dump.

This had gone on for days running into weeks before Jake had decided maybe it was time for him to go down to the Senior Citizens Center in Riverside and see a doctor. The doctor had given him some pills and some advice, neither of which had done any good.

It was only later, after the wailing became crude words, that Jake learned he was hearing his grandniece Amanda Rae. That first desperate, wailing call had come to him from her parent's house in Port Lavaca, Texas, more than sixteen years ago. He'd talked about it with Amanda lots of times. It took a while for them both to figure out that he'd been hearing her call out from inside her mother, because that first wail had reached him two months before she'd been born.

_____ VI _____

So as Jake snuggled back into the pillows and waited for his grandniece to call it made no difference that there was no telephone in the bedroom. He and Amanda Rae didn't need one. They had something better, much better. Jake didn't pretend to understand it, but Amanda thought she did. He was so proud of his grandniece. She was smart, downright brilliant her teachers had called her. It was all those books she read.

Jake knew that Amanda Rae was a lot smarter than he was, but it didn't intimidate him. You couldn't be intimidated by someone you were so close to. In their strange, secret fashion Jake and Amanda were much closer to each other than uncle and grandniece. They were more like brother and sister.

It was strange, but Amanda couldn't call anyone else. Only her Uncle Jake. They often speculated about that, to no avail. If it was true telep—Jake stumbled over the word—true telepathy, it was awfully limited. She couldn't talk that way to her mother or father or anyone else. Only Uncle Jake.

It became their special secret. Her parents didn't know about it, nor did her doctors, of which she had many. There was no reason for anyone to suspect it, because there was no evidence of it.

67

Jake smiled to himself as he lay there against the pillows. It sure saved on long-distance bills. This way he could keep up with Amanda's family; with his niece Wendy, with her hard-working husband Arri and with Amanda herself. And he could do more than just take, he could give. Maybe he wasn't book-smart, but he was sure world-smart. His commonsense advice had been of good use to Amanda on many occasions. It's important for a youngster to have an older person to talk to who's not immediate family. Jake made a sympathetic and safe, long-range father confessor.

Then he was there. In Port Lavaca. It was much more than just a silent two-way exchange of thoughts. Ideas could be exchanged as well, and sounds, and sometimes even smells. It was as though part of Jake's mind was suddenly shunted halfway across the country to sit behind strange eyes.

There was a dim, misty picture of Lavaca Bay. From the angle Jake knew Amanda Rae was staring out her bedroom window in the direction of the Aransas National Wildlife Refuge. For an instant they were one person, the tired old man and the immobile young girl.

It was a fair trade-off. Through her Uncle Jake, Amanda was still able to experience the sensation of walking, a lovely motile daydream. It kept the memory of what walking was like alive within her, and made her a little less bitter.

"Hi, Uncle Jake," a whispery voice said inside his own head.

"Hello, Mandy." He smiled with his mind. "The Bay looks awful pretty tonight."

"It is. Hot and sticky, though."

"That's no surprise. I wish I could feel it."

"I wish you could, too, Uncle Jake. I wish there was more moon, though. The moon is always so pretty on the water. You can see the fish jump."

"Haven't done any fishing in a while. I wish I could come and see them jump myself."

"You *are* seeing them jump, only through myself." She laughed inside his mind, *vox telepathica*.

"You know what I mean," he said, chiding her gently. "I haven't seen you in years. It'd be awfully nice to go out there for a real visit. In person. But I don't have the money."

Amanda was too polite, too understanding to suggest that her Uncle Jake might consider giving up his color television and spend the money he'd put away on a trip to Texas instead. She did go so far as to say, "You know mom and dad would love to see you."

"Not anymore than I'd love to see them, Mandy. Maybe I can manage it in a few months."

"Sure, Uncle Jake." It was a persistent fiction they both worked at maintaining. "Maybe in a few months. How's your heart? Any troubles?"

"Not lately," he assured her. "In fact, I feel better than I did this time last year. I haven't had a really bad spell since January, and then only briefly. Been taking pretty good care of myself." He chuckled at her. "Maybe I'm getting better, huh?"

"You never know, Uncle Jake." Amanda knew from her studies that several heart attacks had damaged her uncle's heart beyond possibility of improvement. He'd been fighting a holding action for the past five years and he'd continue doing so for the rest of his life. She worked very hard at not thinking about that.

"I've been walking a lot," he told her, "playing with the local kids. Having a pretty good time. Did you hear about the mine explosion in Bolivia yesterday?"

"Sure did. It's terrible what they do to those poor people down there, working them like animals year in and year out just for a little tin and silver."

"No wonder cocaine running's so popular, Mandy. It's a lot easier to work than tin ore. I really can't blame them. It's been that way all through history."

"I know, Uncle Jake. It'll probably be that way all through the future, too. How are your neighbors?"

He ran through the list of names that Amanda had become familiar with. "Oh yeah," he said, "I had a visitor the other day."

"That's nice. Who was he?"

"Nice fella. Well dressed. About your dad's age. He was with that outfit that wanted to give me that job guarding some empty building in San Diego."

"The one with the subsidized adult housing?"

"Yeah, that's the one."

"I thought that sounded kind of nice, Uncle Jake," she said noncommittally. "You turned him down again?"

"Sure I did, and you know why, too. I couldn't leave this place. What for? For a few years of lying around listening to a bunch of old people? I don't need the money, either."

"If you had more money," she said, "you could come visit us more often."

"That's true. I thought of that. But I couldn't leave this house, Mandy. Mom and pop died here and—"

"That's alright, Uncle Jake," she said soothingly. "I understand. I'm just teasing. You said the job involved guarding an empty building?"

"Well, a night guard in an office building. I was going to watch a bunch of blank television screens and yell if I saw any burglars."

"They came all the way up from San Diego and offered you subsidized housing for a job like that?"

"Plus salary and moving expenses too. It sure sounded like a good deal. If it wasn't for this house I'd have been tempted. Hey, what's wrong?" He hadn't heard anything but he could feel the disturbance in her.

"Subsidized housing? Moving expenses? A salary? Nothing personal, Uncle Jake, but you're not exactly the sort of person a big business makes a long-term investment in."

He chuckled. "Yeah, that's what I thought. But he said that his company liked to help out seniors and that my references checked out good."

"Uncle Jake, you haven't held a regular job in twenty years."

She was beating a dead horse, and Jake told her so. "It doesn't make any difference, Mandy, because I never really considered taking the job. So I didn't think about it all that much. You know," he went on, changing the subject, "they cleaned up the old dump below the house."

"I'm glad to hear that," she said. "That was long overdue. From what you've told me about the place it sounded like one of hell's cesspools."

"It wasn't no field of chrysanthemums, that's for damn sure. I worried all the time about the local kids playing down there. I used to do it myself when I was younger, until I learned better. Now it's nice and clean. Hey, you know I showed this visitor some of my tricks.''

"Now Uncle Jake,'' said Amanda warningly, ''you know what I told you about that.''

"Yeah, I know. But he saw me do the bottle cap trick for the kids. I don't get a chance to show off much. So I cleaned up his car for him. Took the dirt right off. Made it slipt.''

"Oh Uncle Jake, I've *told* you not to do that kind of thing in front of adults, and strangers especially.''

"It's alright, Mandy. This fella was real nice. He seemed to enjoy it. You should've seen the look on his face. Anyway, he said that I was entitled to a free checkup on his company, to show you what a nice guy he was. I don't like fooling with the hospital. You know how they can be about Medicare and Medicaid.''

Amanda was immediately on guard. "What kind of checkup?''

"Now Mandy, there's no reason for you to react like that. This fella was being real straight with me. I never asked him for a thing. He just volunteered as how they had the slot open for me that I might as well make use of it.''

"Did he offer it to you before or after you made the dirt on his car slipt?''

Jake had to think a moment. "After, I guess.''

Her voice was full of exasperation. "Uncle Jake, you like people too much.''

"Can't help it, Mandy. That's just me.''

"Uh-huh. So this joker offered you a job in San Diego. Moving expenses, salary, free medical exam. Uncle Jake, companies just don't do that sort of thing out of the goodness of their collective hearts. Sure you'd make a good night watchman, but not *that* good a night watchman. Surely not so good that they'd bring you all the way from Riverside down to San Diego. Not when they could find just as good a watchman *in* San Diego.''

"You're awful suspicious, Mandy. I'm not sure I understand. Why make me the offer if they didn't mean to follow through with it?''

"I'm sure they would have, Uncle Jake, but not for the

reason you think. You say they just cleaned up that dump?''

''That's right. You should've seen all them tractors and trucks running around here in the middle of the night. I guess they wanted to do it cheaply.''

''Sure they did, and quietly. They also probably wanted to get you and anyone else who might prove talkative away from the site.''

''Oh, come on now, Mandy. You've been reading too many of those spy novels.''

''Uncle Jake, have any people moved away from the neighborhood recently? In the past couple of weeks?''

''Well, yes. The Greens and the Gomezes. But that's no big surprise. People are moving in and out of here all the time.''

''How did they move, Uncle Jake?''

''What do you mean?''

''I mean, did they pile everything in the family car, or did professional movers come and take them away?''

''Now that you mention it, they used moving vans. Two different companies, but—''

''Doesn't that strike you as kind of unusual, Uncle Jake? From what you've told me, the people who live around you are awfully poor. Professional moving services don't sound like the kind of thing any of them could afford.''

''Well, I don't know for sure what kind of money people around here have or don't have,'' he replied a bit defensively. ''Although neither the Greens nor the Gomezes struck me as particularly well-off. Maybe they got new jobs someplace and their employers helped them move.''

''Exactly, just like the job for which this fellow was offering to help move you down to San Diego.'' Excitement began to compound her suspicions. ''Uncle Jake, this man wanted something from you. He sounds like the type of person who only wants things from people.''

Jake started to argue, hesitated. Mandy was very good at working complicated problems out. He'd learned to trust her opinions.

''He doesn't sound like the sort of person who comes straight out and asks for what he wants. He'd try to get it indirectly, the way they probably did with the Greens and the Gomezes.''

"Who's 'they'?" Jake wondered.

"The people who were responsible for the dump. Are you sure this man who came to offer you the job wasn't a representative of the outfit that owns the dumpsite?"

"He said he represented some security company in San Diego," Jake murmured.

"Names," she said, "just names."

There was quiet then. After a while Jake said, "Amanda Rae, are you still there?"

"I was just thinking, Uncle Jake. You know about all the reading I've done. Marty brings me books from the University bookstore, too. I've always been half convinced that a lot of unusual things like grandma's death, maybe your bad heart, my way of talking with you, your ability to make things slipt, all comes from the family growing up around all those chemicals out there in California. The old well you used to use before you got piped water was probably contaminated, and you've told me lots of times how you and grandma Catherine used to play in the dump. Just breathing the air around there probably had a lot to do with it."

"Amanda, we don't know that any of that's true, and there's no way to check on it."

"Of course there isn't," she agreed. "But I'll bet somebody was getting around to checking on it and that's why whoever was responsible finally cleaned the place up and why they did it so fast and at night."

"I really can't go along with all that, Mandy. I'm sure whoever's responsible for the dumpsite is part of some responsible outfit. People don't let poisons just sit around like that. Sure, it didn't smell none too good, but—"

"Uncle Jake. Dear sweet Uncle Jake. You're too nice for your own damned good."

Jake thought about reproving her for the cussing, but he'd done enough of it at her. He could hardly forgo her the use of an occasional damn or hell. Besides, kids these days thought no more of swearing than they did of spending ten bucks on a movie.

"Uncle Jake, I don't think you should take up this stranger's offer of a free medical exam. What was his name?"

"Mr. Huddy."

"Yeah. I don't think you should go see this Mr. Huddy, and I don't think you should submit to his exam. And I want you to promise me that you're not going to make anything slipt for him again, no matter how much he pleads with you or how much money he offers you."

"Amanda, it's just a harmless little trick."

"I've tried and tried to explain to you, Uncle Jake, that you're the only person in the world who we're sure can do that little trick.

"Please don't do what this Huddy guy wants. Don't go with him and don't take his exam and don't show him any more tricks. If he asks you about it tell him it was a real magician's trick. Tell him you were a semi-professional magician when you were younger. Tell him anything, but don't tell him that you've always been able to make things like bottle caps slipt. This is important, Uncle Jake."

"Alright, Mandy," he said, trying to calm her down. "If it means that much to you, I'll do it, but I don't see what you're getting so all-fired upset about."

"That's okay, Uncle Jake. You don't have to see. Just promise me, okay?"

"Okay, Mandy. But I'm only doing this to please you, you know."

"Isn't that the best reason in the world to do anything? Now tell me, how did the Dodgers do yesterday?"

"Real well." Pickett warmed quickly to the new subject. "They creamed the Pirates. That Mexican kid was pitching. . . . I never can pronounce his name aright."

"Just think it," Mandy told him. He did so, and she knew.

He was up to his wrists in ground round the next morning when the doorbell rang. He sighed, wondering who it could be, and wiped his greasy hands on a towel. The meat loaf would have to wait.

He moved into the den and opened the door. It never occurred to him to check first to see who was on the other side, for all that he lived in one of Southern California's more violent neighborhoods.

The neighborhood knew. So did the street and the rest of the barrio. Don't mess with the old man who lives up on the hill. He's good for the *niños*.

Jake pulled back the door. Standing there smiling at him was the nice young man he'd talked to before: Benjamin Huddy. There were two other younger men with him this time. Both were impressively large.

Jake wondered at their presence and decided that a man like this Mr. Huddy might have assistants with him sometimes. It occurred to Jake that Huddy had never explained in any detail just what it was that he did. Jake had assumed he was a personnel recruiter because that's what he'd come to see Jake about. But Huddy had never actually said anything like that.

It wasn't part of his nature to be impolite, however. "Come on in, Mr. Huddy. Nice to see you again."

"You too, Jake. I can call you Jake, can't I?"

"Don't see why not. Come in, though I don't know if there's chairs enough for everybody." He moved to his easy chair. Huddy sat down on the couch.

"That's alright, Jake. Drew and Idanha don't mind standing. Do you, boys?"

Neither of the large young men responded. They just took up positions next to the doorway and watched quietly. It bothered Jake a little because he didn't know what they did. Then the answer came to him and he relaxed. Probably they were just traveling with Huddy on their way to other business and rather than sit in the car and wait they'd decided to come inside. That made sense. It was hot out.

"Well," murmured Huddy. He had a little booklet of papers he was thumbing through. "How are you this morning, Jake?"

"Feeling real fine, Mr. Huddy, thanks."

"Call me Benjamin, please. I'm glad to hear that. Do you remember me asking you about that medical exam? The one we'd like to give you free for considering our offer?"

"I didn't really consider your offer, Benjamin. It don't matter anyhow. I've decided against taking your exam."

Huddy's expression slid away for an instant, revealing something other than pleasant innocuousness before the mask was put back in place. Jake didn't really notice the brief transformation.

"I don't understand, Jake. You seemed so enthusiastic about taking the exam when we talked about it before. The tests are perfectly free. They won't take very long. If it's the long drive that's troubling you, we'd be happy to drive you into town for the exam and bring you home."

"Sorry, but I've changed my mind, Benjamin. I don't feel like having some doctors poke me around just now. Maybe another time."

One of the younger men who'd accompanied Huddy stepped away from the door and said politely, "If you'd like, Mr. Huddy sir, I'm sure we can convince Jake here to come along with us." Jake didn't miss the angry stare that Huddy threw the heavy-set assistant.

"Back off and let me handle this, Drew."

"Sure, Mr. Huddy. Whatever you say." The big man resumed his position, looking hurt.

Huddy smiled reassuringly at Jake. "You have to excuse my companions. They're trainees and they're anxious to be helpful."

"Sure, I understand," Jake said. If they were assistants, then what did they do for Huddy? It didn't make sense. They just stood around and watched.

The noise of the neighborhood children playing out in the street occasionally reached the men in the house. Huddy had seen the kids on the way in. He didn't want any trouble, not now. Such considerations were premature anyway.

"Really, Jake," he began, trying another approach, "I don't understand you. This exam is only for your benefit. I've never had anyone refuse a freebie before."

"Well I'm real sorry, Benjamin, but I'd just rather not go into L.A. right now, and I'm getting a mite tired of arguing about it."

"I don't mean to upset you, Jake. I know you have to watch that because of your heart and all. Listen, will you do one thing for me? I'm going to look awfully silly when I tell them you're not coming in for the exam. Will you at least think about taking it? I can push it back another couple of days." He handed over a card. "If you change your mind before next Friday give me a call and I'll have the exam rescheduled. This is my local number."

Jake reached over and accepted the card, studied it briefly. "Consolidated Chemical and Mining?"

"Security is just one of our divisions. We're one of those big conglomerates, Jake. We have interests all over the world, not just in L.A. and San Diego." He stood. "Just think about it, Jake. That's all I ask. We've got a couple of days and I'd really like to see you come in for the exam. I'm concerned about your health."

"So are the boys down at the V.A.," Jake told him. "Okay, Benjamin. I will think about it. I promise."

"That's little enough to ask, Jake." Huddy glanced across to his pair of assistants and they responded by stepping out the front door. "So long, Jake." Huddy was smiling easily. "You have a nice day."

"You too, Benjamin." Jake watched them go until the Cadillac had turned itself around and started down the road, trailing dust and laughing bright-eyed children in its wake.

That fella is sure concerned about my health, alright, Jake thought, though Jake wasn't sure why. He hadn't had anyone take this much interest in his welfare since he became eligible for Medicare.

Could Amanda Rae be right? Could this exam that this fella wanted Jake to take have nothing to do with his general health? Naw, that didn't make no sense, he mused. Why else would he be offering Jake the free exam?

But he sure was being persistent.

Huddy extracted a bottle from the cabinet shelf that served as a bar and poured two fingers of the contents into a glass with ice. He added more liquid from another bottle, then filled another glass.

Somerset was sprawled decoratively across the curving couch, looking indifferently ravishing. Beyond her the floor-to-ceiling windows opened onto the lights of the megalopolis, the vast flat Christmas tree that was the Los Angeles basin at night. He handed her her drink.

"I just don't understand why he should do a complete turn-around like that," he muttered as he sat down close to her. "He seemed so enthusiastic when I made the proposal to him the first time. What could I have said to make him change his mind?"

"Take it easy, Benjy." She sipped at the drink. "Probably

you had nothing to do with it. He just changed his mind. You know how these old codgers can be."

"No, I don't know how they can be. I don't have many dealings with 'old codgers' and neither do you."

"Swell. So he changed his mind. He may change it again. You told me that you gave him two days to think it over and that he agreed to reconsider."

"I know, I know." Huddy rose and moved to replenish his drink. "But we can't afford to give him too much time. Suppose," he said earnestly, "suppose he's a little sharper than we're giving him credit for. Suppose he talks to somebody else about this. He noticed the CCM on my business card right away. Smart he may not be, but he's damn observant. I got out of the slip easily enough, but I kicked myself all the way back to the office. It was just reflex, handing over a card like that."

"Like you say," she soothed him, "it doesn't seem to have done any harm. He'd made up his mind before you showed him the card."

"Yeah, but if he talks to somebody else. . . . What if he's made the connection between his little magic demonstration and my sudden interest in his health?"

"That's hardly likely. He doesn't have the educational background that would enable him to make that kind of connection. If he did he probably wouldn't have done his 'tricks' for you in the first place."

"I know I'm worrying needlessly," he said tiredly, "but I can't help it. I'm a natural worrier. I wish he hadn't changed his mind about going in for the exam that day. If we'd just gotten him into the car everything could've been managed from then on. But there were too many kids around to try 'helping' him into the Eldo.

"You know, I'll bet I'm the first perceptive adult he's ever done those tricks for. He thinks they're just suitable for children."

"Which may be the case, Benjy. Keep that in mind. We still don't have any hard evidence for anything more than parlor magic."

"I know what I saw," said Huddy slowly, positively.

"Of course you do, Benjy. I'm not disputing that. I'm just

saying there might be other explanations for what happened besides magic and the supernatural."

"It's not supernatural. It's psionics and parapsychology."

"Which most intelligent scientists regard as falling in the realm of the supernatural. I've done some reading, you see."

"So have I, Ruth. You know me. I'm as much a realist as anyone you're likely to run into."

"I'm aware of that, Benjy," she said sweetly, "and that's the only reason I'm going along with you on this one."

"You know something," he said, suddenly excited, "his sudden refusal to take the exam, his abrupt turnaround, that tells us something in itself."

"Like what?"

"Like maybe he's aware of his own abilities and he suspects that I am, too. Otherwise why refuse to take a simple medical exam? Isn't his abrupt refusal proof that he has something to hide from us?"

She considered that one as the liquor warmed her belly. "Now that," she said evenly, "is an intriguing thought, Benjamin." She mulled it over further. "Yes, a very intriguing thought. Why refuse the exam if he has nothing to hide? Unless maybe he's talked to someone about this and gotten some advice."

"Who could he have talked to? If he knows he can do more than simple tricks, who could he confide that knowledge to with any assurance it would stay secret? No one in that neighborhood, that's for damn sure."

"Maybe it would be better just to pick him up," she suggested thoughtfully.

"That's why I had two boys with me today, but the presence of all those kids checked me. Besides, when he said he'd think it over again, I thought it best to give him another couple of days. Naturally it'll be easier if he comes in of his own free will. Hell, maybe he only refused because he was constipated or something. Old folks ailments. He may call tomorrow and ask to come in. If he does I'll go get him right away, before he has time to change his mind again.

"If we do have to pick him up it's the sort of thing that'll be better done in the middle of the night. And I'd rather use something besides my own car. A van would be better. Something with a plumber's or electrician's insignia on the side. How did Navis react when we didn't show today?''

"Philosophically," she told him. "I just told him the project had been put back for a few days. He complained about having to juggle his precious time, but that's all."

"Good. Navis is a good man. He'll keep his mouth shut. When he sees what's to be gained from this, he'll be so busy with his tests he'll forget that what he's doing is illegal."

"We may have to cut him in," she observed.

"I'm prepared for that," Huddy told her. He sipped at the liquor. "It'd be impossible to exclude the doctor running the tests from participating in any benefits. Two more days. He changed his mind once, maybe we'll get lucky and he'll do so again. If not, I'll have another chat with Drew. We'll go ahead and make arrangements for the van, just in case. We may have to go with a hot one."

"Surely that's not necessary."

"Might be simpler and safer than trying to disguise a company vehicle, and any rental could be traced. Damn," he frowned. "This isn't my department. The clean-up was one thing. This sort of deal is petty."

"Would you like me to handle it?" she asked. "You've been working awfully hard. First the clean-up, now this, not to mention your regular work."

"That's alright. How can I ask you to take over details when you don't really believe in what I'm doing? You don't, do you?"

"Not really. Not yet, no."

"Then I can't ask you to take risks for something you don't feel strongly about. Look, you're right. I'm worrying too much. We're dealing with one solitary old man."

"What happens to him when you get him into Navis' hands?" she wondered. She recrossed her legs, showing smooth tanned skin all the way up to her silk.

"He'll be sedated, told he's been transferred temporarily to a hospital ward. That's no problem. An old man like that with heart trouble could expect to wake up in a hospital bed anytime. Then Navis can begin his tests. I expect if there's anything to my suspicions Pickett will be with us for a long time."

"Suppose he doesn't cooperate?" Somerset asked. "Suppose he decides he doesn't want to perform his little tricks for Doctor Navis?''

"Oh, he will," Huddy murmured softly, "he will. I've already talked to Navis about that possibility. He isn't worried about getting Pickett to cooperate."

VII

"Mandy, I don't understand. So much fussin' over my health. Even the people at the hospital don't show that much interest in me."

"Uncle Jake," Amanda said inside his head, "don't you understand yet? That card that man gave you proves it. Consolidated Chemical and Mining. That's a big corporation, Uncle Jake. And you showed one of their representatives how you can make things slipt. A man who probably has a good background in science and engineering. A man who'd know right away that you just don't make things slipt."

"It wasn't much of a trick," Jake murmured innocently. "All I did was—"

"I know what you did. Bottle caps and road dirt. It was obviously enough. I've warned you about this before, Uncle Jake. You should've known better."

"I'm sorry, Mandy, but what's done is done. Still, it seems like a lot of fuss over some dirty hubcaps and beer. I wish I knew more about how I make things slipt. I know you've tried to explain what you think it is." He rolled over in the bed. "I just don't—"

"Don't apologize, Uncle Jake. I don't really understand it. I'm just making guesses. Medical exam, huh? These people aren't interested in how your heart's doing. They want to look at your head."

"Well, would that really be all that bad, Mandy?" said Jake a little belligerently. "What if I went ahead and took their exam? Maybe they could tell me how I make things slipt."

"Uncle Jake, I've *told* you, people like this, if they get interested in you, they're going to want to make use of you and your ability. For money."

"But how can they do that?" he whispered into the darkness. "I don't know how I do it. Besides, there are easier ways to open bottles and clean cars."

"How do you know that's all you can do, Uncle Jake? You've never tried anything else. These people are going to make you try, whether you want to or not. How do you know you can't make something else slipt?"

"I don't, but. . . ."

"It's something you should think about," she murmured to him. He could see that she was sitting by the window again, because he could see the light on Lavaca Bay in his own thoughts. "The exam doesn't worry me that much, Uncle Jake. What does worry me is that big corporations rarely care much for the well-being of the people they use. These people only care about your ability. They're going to push you as far as they can in their tests, and with your heart. . . ."

That got to him. Jake Pickett was a strong man, tall and full of compact, wiry strength, but that damn bad engine he carried around inside his chest made him vulnerable.

"I told you," he said, "this fella Huddy seems like a nice sort." He could hear her sigh mentally.

"Uncle Jake, in some ways you're an awfully smart man, but you haven't had to deal with people much. I've spent a lot of time in hospitals. There are good doctors and bad doctors. There are medical people who want to help you and those who look at you like you're something to be cut and sliced and put under a microscope. I haven't met this Mr. Huddy, but from what you've told me he sure sounds like the microscope type."

"Well, I told him already that I'm not going with him or his people for any exam."

"His people?"

"He brought a couple of others with him last time. I think they were his assistants. I guess they were."

"Two of them," Amanda muttered.

"Yeah. Come to think of it, they were pretty husky fellas. Neither of them said much."

"That settles it, Uncle Jake," she said decisively. "I want you to leave. You get out of that house. You get out right now."

"But I told them I wouldn't take the exam."

"Oh, you'll take it if you stay there, Uncle Jake. That 'nice sort' will see to that. I know it. I can feel it. You get out of there right now before they come back for you."

"Get out? But. . . ." This was not at all how he'd expected the conversation to go. He sat up in the bed, seeing nothing in the dark room. "Get out where? This is my home. Maybe I can talk to these people."

"You've already talked to them, Uncle Jake. That's part of the problem."

"You really think they'd try to hurt me if I didn't cooperate with them?"

"No. No, they won't *try* to hurt you, Uncle Jake. Not that that makes much of a difference when they do. They'll smile and apologize as they run their tests. This man Huddy won't try to hurt you. He just won't care if he does."

"Then I won't do a damn thing for him and his friends. I won't take their tests no matter what they do to me."

"You'll take the tests whether you like it or not, Uncle Jake, if they get their hands on you. You can't talk to these people. You must get away from them. Leave. Run away."

Jake could not have said at what point he became the child listening to the adult Amanda. "But you don't understand, Mandy. Running away's not as easy as just saying it."

"Uncle Jake, even I can see you doing it, and I can't even run. We'll figure out a way to keep these people off your back. But you have to get out of there now, before they come back for you. I need time to think about what to do. You said they gave you some time to turn over the exam?"

"Two days," he told her.

"Then you'll have a full day's head start. I know," she said, delight momentarily overcoming concern, "why don't you come to Port Lavaca? You haven't visited us in years and years. I've been trying all this time to get you to come. Now you have a good excuse."

"Mandy, if you feel that strongly about it, then I'll do it. I'm still not convinced you're right about Mr. Huddy or his company, but if it's going to worry you that much. . . ."

"It would," she assured him.

". . . . Then I'll come visit. Mighty sneaky way to talk me into coming down, though." He tried to turn the situation into a joke. "You ought to send Mr. Huddy a thank-you note for giving you the means for talking me into this."

"I don't think I ever want to meet your Mr. Huddy," she replied humorlessly. "Get yourself together fast, Uncle Jake. I know you won't need to bring much. Once you're here we can figure something out to discourage Huddy from bothering you. He won't try anything around a busy household. Mom and dad will be here to help, too."

"I'll leave first thing in the morning," he promised her.

"Can't you leave right now?"

"No, I can't." He slipped back down under the light covers. He was tired these days, so tired. He hadn't always tired so quickly or easily, he remembered. Getting old was no fun. He didn't *feel* old. He just didn't work as well as he used to. "Not tonight, Mandy."

"Please, Uncle Jake? Please?"

"Give your Uncle Jake a break, Mandy." He was already half asleep. "You've already talked me into coming to see you. Isn't that enough for one evening? You know that your poor old Uncle Jake gets worn out easy. I'll run away a lot better if I do it on a good night's sleep. Huddy gave me two days, remember. I have plenty of time."

"Okay," she said worriedly, "but don't dally around in the morning."

"Me, a dallier?" He smiled to the empty room. "I'll leave here first thing tomorrow morning. I'll be up with the sun like usual and I'll leave. But a good night's sleep is important."

"Alright, Uncle Jake. I can't make you leave now. But you make sure you get away before they come back to check on you."

"Don't worry." Her thoughts were already fading. "I will.
I will. . . ."

There was only a dull, empty echo of vanished consciousness in Amanda's mind, like the wind that sweeps under the
door of a tightly closed closet. She knew he was asleep.

Pushing away from the window she turned the wheelchair
and rolled over to the bed. Using the armrests for support she
lifted her upper body onto the mattress, then picked up her
legs and pushed them under the covers. She snuggled down
into the warm bed.

Worried, she was so terribly worried for him. She'd read
the histories of less than ethical medical experiments. That's
surely what this man Huddy wanted to do to her beloved
Uncle Jake. Experiment on him. Benignly if possible and
otherwise if not. He'd want to find out how Uncle Jake made
dirt and bottle caps slipt.

She'd worry all night long, until she knew he was safely out
of the little house in California. In a way it might all be for the
best, though she couldn't look at it as lightly as her Uncle did.
It would be *so* good to see him again. He was such a warm,
easygoing person, a second father really. They had something
in common no other two people in the world could have,
something only they could share.

No, she wouldn't stand for anybody mistreating her Uncle
Jake. Everything was going to be alright, though. All he had
to do was slip away without being seen. He could make this
visit a long one, maybe. She knew that her mom and dad loved
Uncle Jake almost as much as she did. They'd be overjoyed to
have him stay. There was plenty of room in the house. She
wouldn't worry about him because he wouldn't be living
alone. It wasn't good for him to be by himself, the Huddys of
the world notwithstanding.

Maybe her mom and dad could even persuade him to stay
with them permanently, here in Port Lavaca. They'd tried to
do that before. Maybe now he'd listen. His heart wasn't getting any better. Yes, everything might turn out for the good.

She turned on the pillow, smiling to herself now. She felt
much better knowing that he was coming to her. As she relaxed she thought about what she hadn't told him.

It was something she'd come to worry about as a result of

all her readings and researches. She'd never managed to learn what gave Uncle Jake the ability to make things slipt or what it might mean. Of course, no one else knew about such things either.

The worry was that although he'd only made little things slipt, like bottle caps and dirt, he might be able to make other things slipt if he was pushed hard. She didn't worry about what might happen to Uncle Jake if those circumstances ever arose.

She worried about what Uncle Jake might do to someone else.

The ambulance moved silently through the near-deserted neighborhood. Most of the children were away at morning sessions. Those parents who held jobs had been working at them for hours. Only a few housewives remained to stare curiously at the dimly marked old ambulance as it squeaked to a halt next to the barrier at the far end of the road. It backed up carefully and turned around to point back toward the city.

One man, tall and clad all in white, waited patiently behind the wheel. Two others emerged from a side door and started up the narrow trail leading to the house at the end of the dirt path.

This was better than stealing around in the middle of the night, Huddy thought. Much better. Leave it to Ruth to think up a solution to an awkward problem. Her mind was as devious as her thighs.

"Remember, Drew," he told his subordinate quietly, "I want as little noise and activity as possible. This man has a bad heart and he's no good to us dead. That's ostensibly why the 'ambulance' is taking him in." He nodded toward the bigger man's shirt pocket. "The dosage should be just right. I made sure the doctor measured it out carefully."

Drew grinned, tapped the pocket where the loaded hypodermic waited. "Old man shouldn't give us any trouble, sir."

Huddy nodded, turning his attention back to the house they were approaching. He didn't like Drew much. Drew was dumber than he looked: a crude, ignorant, brutish specimen. Unfortunately, the primitive qualities of such types were sometimes required.

"I'm still hoping none of this will be necessary and that he'll agree to come with us voluntarily." Huddy self-consciously straightened his white physician's smock. "If not, I'll engage him in conversation while you slip around behind him and put him out."

"What about finding a vein that way, Mr. Huddy? Wearing this ice cream suit doesn't make me a paramedic."

"You forgot," said Huddy irritably. "The hypo's loaded with a general sedative. You don't need to inject a vein. Just jab it into a muscular area."

"Didn't look like the old bastard had any muscular areas. Skinny old dude. If you can get him to stand up while you're talking to him I'll try hitting him in the butt. That way I can get an arm around him in case he tries struggling or crying out."

"Sounds like a good plan." Huddy found the mental image distasteful. It was one thing to arrange a covert operation to clean up an inanimate chemical dump, quite another to take away a human being against his will. Go on, say the word, he ordered himself. Kidnapping. Kid-nap-ping. There, that wasn't so difficult, was it?

Not that he'd be that blunt with Pickett. There were a host of excuses he could use on Pickett if the old man required explanations. Necessary for his health, and so forth. Personally he would have prefered to be directing this operation from a distance, just as he had with the dump clean-up. Unfortunately, he couldn't trust anyone else to do this properly. Drew and Idanha were directly responsible to him, and he had to be along to make certain everything went precisely as planned. This wasn't like shipping barrels of waste to Baja. He intended to deliver the old man to Doctor Navis personally.

He'd even prepared excuses should something go radically wrong and the entire operation blow up in their faces. Maybe the police would stop the ambulance for some inexplicable reason. Sorry officer, this man's sick, have to get him to a hospital. No, we don't need an escort, thanks, not critical. We'll just be on our way, thanks.

He didn't think it would come to that. It shouldn't. His preparations had been meticulous. Even the old ambulance had been doubly checked for bad brake lights and such. All they had to do was move a tired old man to a doctor's office for a couple of days of testing. An hour and a half drive and he could dump everything in Doctor Navis' lap and get back to his own work.

Against the resources Huddy had mustered there wasn't a lot Jake Pickett could do.

"What if he tries to run on us before I can get behind him, Mr. Huddy?"

"He won't," Huddy assured him.

"I dunno. I've seen some old guys could really move when they had to." Huddy tried not to look too exasperated. Drew had the brain of an uninquisitive teenager. Be easy with him, Huddy thought. You need this man. He's no better or worse than the rest of his class.

"He can't run. He has a bad heart, remember?"

"Oh yeah." Drew frowned slightly. "Forgot that for a minute. Naw, you're right. He won't be doing any running."

"The worst he'll do," Huddy went on, "is refuse to go with us and protest a lot. That we are prepared to cope with. You won't have any trouble carrying him?"

"Are you kiddin', Mr. Huddy?" Drew laughed, short and sharp. "Him and you both. One in each arm. I've had to muscle guys lots bigger than this one."

The little stucco house was quiet, the single sprinkler sitting out front cool with morning dew. Huddy gestured for Drew to stand off to one side and out of immediate sight as he rang the doorbell. When no reply was forthcoming he thumbed the button a second time, then rapped sharply on the door with his knuckles.

"It's early yet, Mr. Huddy," said Drew thoughtfully. "Maybe he's still asleep."

"Maybe." Huddy was frowning to himself. They walked around to the back of the house. The curtains were drawn over the bedroom window. "Can't see a damn thing." He rapped on the glass several times. Still no response from within.

"Old people can sleep really hard," Drew observed.

"I know that, you idiot." Huddy was starting to get worried.

There was a back door overlooking the now sanitized

hellhole that had been the dump. Huddy knocked on it once, then tried the knob. It refused to turn. There was no sign of a deadbolt. He stepped aside and gestured to his companion. Silently Drew moved to the door. He pulled a ring full of keys and blanks from a pocket and worked on the lock for about two minutes before it turned.

Stepping back, he smiled and gestured broadly. "After you, Mr. Huddy."

Huddy smiled thinly in reply and pushed the door open. It led to the living room. "Mr. Pickett? Jake? It's me, Benjamin Huddy." The only sound in the house was the distant ticking of a clock.

"Maybe," suggested Drew, peering over Huddy's shoulder, "the old boy already had his heart attack. That'd be funny, wouldn't it, with us waiting on him with an ambulance."

"You're a riot, Drew. How come you haven't done Vegas yet?"

"I have, but not with jokes," said the younger man meaningfully. "We go in?"

Huddy nodded, led him inside. It didn't take them long to thoroughly check out the little house. Jake Pickett was not there, alive or dead. He wasn't on the bed or hiding under it, wasn't lying limply in the bathtub or slumped over the kitchen stove. They checked the bedroom drawers but Huddy couldn't tell if there was clothing missing. He hadn't the faintest idea what the old man's wardrobe normally looked like, except that he was pretty sure it wasn't very extensive even when everything was cleaned and put up.

Drew was waiting for him near the back door when Huddy finished his inspection of the laundry closet. They'd checked out the half attic and found nothing up there but wasps' nests and old newspapers.

"What now, Mr. Huddy?"

"I'm thinking, dammit. Back to the ambulance." They hurried back down the trail.

The driver looked up curiously. Drew glanced at him, said, "The old man's split."

"We don't know that yet," Huddy pointed out. "He may have gone visiting. I don't see his car but it could be in somebody's garage. At worst maybe he's gone shopping.''

"I remember you saying that local people hereabouts did that for him," said Drew.

"Not all the time, I'll bet. Let's check the neighbors first. They know when we're coming. They ought to see when Pickett's going."

It took three tries before they found a house with someone at home. The plump, dark-haired woman had a dish in one hand, a rag in the other. She stared expectantly at them, wondering at the white coats. A little girl no more than four or five clung to her mother's dress. She sucked on her thumb and stared at the strangers out of wide eyes, naked as a guppy.

"Excuse us, *Señora*," said Huddy pleasantly. "We're looking for Jake Pickett." No response from the woman. "Pickett?" He took a step back from the doorway and pointed up the road. The woman smiled understandingly.

"Ah, *Señor* Pickett, si. *Yo miro.* . . . I saw him yesterday morning."

"Yesterday," Huddy murmured. "Could you please tell us where he went?"

"Why you want to know?" asked the woman suspiciously.

"I'm one of his doctors." Huddy expanded his smile, tried to look understanding. "He was having some problems with his heart." He tapped his chest. "We were supposed to take him in to the hospital for observation."

The woman frowned. "That's funny. My husband saw him yesterday on the way to work. It was very early and he asked because *Señor* Pickett, he never go out much."

"I know." Huddy forced himself to remain calm. "Can you tell me please where he went?"

"My husband tell me last night that *Señor* Pickett say he going fishing."

"Fishing." Huddy struggled with the word, as if it were alien to his tongue.

"*Si*. He go sometimes. Sometimes with other old people from the Citizens Center, sometimes with people from the hospital, sometimes by himself."

"Do you happen to know where he was going fishing?" Huddy asked desperately.

"Sure," the woman said. "Sierra Nevada."

"Sierra Nevada," Huddy repeated dumbly. "Did he happen to mention where in the Sierra Nevada?"

The woman frowned as she thought. "No, my husband not say. So I guess *Señor* Pickett not say." She was suddenly concerned. "Hey, *Señor* Pickett, he not bad sick, is he? He's a nice man. You know, he has an orange tree in his yard. Every year when the oranges are ripe he let everybody in the neighborhood go and help themselves. Nice man."

"Yes, I know he's a saint," said Huddy intensely. "Please try to think, *Señora*. Are you sure you don't know where in the mountains he said he was going fishing?"

"No, I would remember. If he's bad sick I hope you find him. Maybe he forget you coming for him?"

"Yeah, it looks like it. Don't worry, *Señora*. We'll find him." He hesitated, then handed the woman one of his business cards. "Listen, this isn't my hospital number but I can be reached here. If *Señor* Pickett shows up, would you call me and let me know? I'm Benjamin Huddy."

"Hoody?" She stared at the card.

He nodded. "Please call me. But don't tell *Señor* Pickett about it." He smiled again. "I don't want him to worry. He doesn't really like doctors and hospitals."

"*Si*, I'm the same way myself, *Señor* Hoody. Nothing against you."

"I know. Thank you, *Señora*. You've been very kind. Good-bye."

"*Vaya con dios, Señor*." She closed the door on him.

Huddy stood thinking on the doorstep, then spun and headed back for the waiting ambulance.

"What's the next step, Mr. Huddy?" asked Drew, keeping pace like a big dog with its master. "You think he's onto us?"

"I don't know. I don't know. Mighty funny, though, him suddenly taking off like that."

"Maybe he planned on going fishing all the time," Drew suggested. "Maybe that's why he decided to cancel out on the exam in the first place. Didn't want to miss his fishing trip."

"Maybe," murmured Huddy, "but if that were the case I don't see why he wouldn't have told us about it. I know he could have forgotten, but he didn't seem senile to me. No, something stinks, Drew." They piled back into the ambulance. The driver looked laconically at his partner.

"Well, man?"

"The old guy's gone fishing up in the Sierras."

"Oh boy." The driver didn't sound enthusiastic. He had some idea what was coming. "That's a lot of mountains to check out, Mr. Huddy. You sure you don't just want us to wait until he gets back?"

"He may not plan on coming back. Damn." Huddy pounded the dash with an angry fist. "I don't see how he could have gotten onto us!"

"Maybe it's like the fat taco said," Drew murmured. "Maybe doctors and hospitals just make him nervous."

"Yeah, I'll bet they do," said Huddy tersely. "But that doesn't mean you have to run away fishing to cancel an appointment. He said he'd think about the exam. I don't see him just picking up and taking off to make sure he gets out of it. He had no reason to suppose we'd try to force it on him."

"So what now?" the driver wanted to know. "We start combing the Sierras for him?"

"We start looking for him, yeah," replied Huddy, "but not by hand-searching the Sierras, and certainly not in this hunk of junk. Remember the Seven-Eleven we passed coming up the hill?" The driver nodded, turned the key. The ambulance started off down the bumpy, filthy road.

He had made the call collect. As soon as Somerset was on the phone he started in. They didn't have time for casual banter.

"It's Benjamin. Pickett's gone."

"What do you mean, gone?" asked the puzzled voice at the other end.

"Gone, as in vanished, disappeared, evaporated. *Now* do you believe that he's got something to hide?"

"I don't know," she said. "The whole thing still strikes me as more fantastic than likely. But if he's really run off somewhere. . . ."

"One of his neighbors," Huddy continued, "says that her husband saw him yesterday and that Pickett told him he was going fishing in the Sierras. I wouldn't see him taking his old clunker up there, but it's gone, too."

"Do you know what kind of car?"

"I never took a good look at it. He pointed it out to me once but it was parked *way* down the hill from his house. I didn't think it would be *necessary* to have a good look at it."

"Well, it doesn't matter. I'll check it out."

"From back in the office?" Huddy was only mildly surprised. Nothing Somerset did really surprised him. "How are you going to manage that little number?"

"Let me worry about that. You just get your ass back here fast. I'll find out not only what kind of car he owns but where he's taken it to. Relax, Benjy. Everything's well in hand. This is only a temporary setback. Just leave it to me."

Huddy found himself looking at the ambulance. Drew and his partner had emerged from the Seven-Eleven. Each was sucking on a garishly colored slurpee. The sight was as disconcerting as seeing Bozo the Clown with a sawed-off shotgun. It verged on the surreal. But then, so did this whole morning.

"I wonder what could have made him suspicious," Somerset was saying. "I can't understand his sudden change of mind about the exam."

"Yeah, me too," said Huddy. "Maybe he just doesn't like tests but was too macho to admit it. This way he doesn't have to tell me he's afraid in person. But I don't think that's it. I don't like this development one bit, sweetness."

"Are you sure you didn't say anything the last time, Benjy, to make him suspicious, to give him an idea why you really wanted him to take your exam?"

"I can't imagine what I might've said," Huddy told her honestly. "I didn't allude to his magic tricks at all. I don't know why he'd suspect my motives."

"Then," said Somerset from the other end, "maybe he really has gone fishing."

"Maybe," said Huddy reluctantly.

"It doesn't matter. We'll track him down anyway. It'll be simpler if he has gone fishing."

"What if he has?"

"Then we wait for him to finish his vacation, catch his limit or whatever, and come back home. I know you're impatient to have Doctor Navis start in on him, Benjy, but maybe it would be better to wait."

"No, it wouldn't," Huddy insisted. "If he's sitting on the

shore of some half-empty lake up in the mountains I'd just as soon send the boys up there to pick him up." His spirits rose slightly. "Come to think of it, that'd be even easier than what we were going to try today. Yeah, maybe the old boy's done us a favor, even if he's inconvenienced us some in the short run."

"Suit yourself, Benjy. This is your party. I'll find out where he is. If we're lucky I'll be able to tell you by the time you've changed your clothes and checked out your office."

"Good." He didn't inquire further how she was going to manage all that. He'd learned to trust Somerset. When she said she was going to do something, she usually did.

Ruth Somerset put down the phone and adjusted the bra strap that had been giving her trouble all morning. Her mind was trying furiously to adjust to this new set of circumstances.

The old man had gone fishing. The old man *hadn't* gone fishing. Only one thing was certain. He was gone, and he'd evidently left in something of a hurry. According to Benjamin he'd said nothing about any incipient fishing trip during Benjy's previous pair of visits to Riverside. That might have been an oversight on Pickett's part, but she didn't think so. According to Benjamin the old man had a bad heart but all his other faculties were operative, including the mental ones. Despite her better judgment she was starting to wonder if there might not be a bird at the end of her lover's wild goose chase, and if, just maybe, it might lay golden eggs after all.

"Ms. Somerset, can you check these figures, please?"

"What?" She turned from her contemplation to see an eager young man standing before her desk. Neatly dressed, good worker. A name registered: Olson. Been with her section for nearly a year. His teeth gleamed and he wore just the right amount of cologne. Nice scent, too.

Her mind was only partly on the work he handed her, but it was enough to run the necessary check.

"Everything here looks fine, John." She returned the papers along with a scintillating smile.

"Thanks, Ms. Somerset." He smiled back at her, unsure how personal to take it, then beat a nervous retreat.

Cute little puppy, she mused. Sadly, she had to put him out of her thoughts.

There were only two explanations that made any sense. The

first was that Pickett still suspected nothing, that he was nothing more than a forgetful old man who really had gone fishing for a few days.

The second was that he was suspicious of Benjamin's motives in spite of Benjy's assurance that nothing had been done to provoke such suspicions, or else something as yet unknown had made him nervous about the exam and he'd fled for reasons as yet unfathomable.

Understanding would have to come later, she told herself. The first thing to do was to find him.

She made the preliminary, obvious checks herself. No, neither the Trailways nor Greyhound offices in Riverside or San Bernadino had recently sold a ticket to a Jake Pickett. It added up, what with his car missing. She inserted a non-company diskette into a minidrive, activated a blank screen, and found a name and matching phone number which the machine autodialed.

"Hello? Lieutenant Puteney?"

"Yeah. Who's this?" The voice at the other end of the line sounded puzzled.

"This is Ruth Somerset. Of Consolidated Chemical and Mining? Surely you haven't forgotten me already, Lieutenant?"

The tone changed quickly. "Ruth Somerset! You're damn right I remember you! How the hell are you?"

"Reasonably content," she informed him. "How about yourself, Don?"

"Aw, same old routine. The usual ax murders, drownings, arsons and assaults-with-intent. Hey, when are we going to get together again?" The eagerness in his voice made her want to laugh, but she controlled herself.

"Now Don, you know that's not easy. Besides, what would the little woman think?"

"Hey, cool it. This is only a semi-private departmental line. Somebody else could cut in on us."

"Nobody has," she assured him, after a quick glance at the empty LED readout set atop the phone.

"How can you be so sure?"

"My little bug killer tells me so."

"Oh, secure phone, huh?"

"That's right, Donny. This is my office. We don't tolerate industrial espionage at CCM."

"You've probably got more worth stealing than the LAPD," he replied with a chuckle. "C'mon, Ruth, we can get together. I can manage things from this end."

"Well, in that case, maybe within the next couple of months. I'm pretty busy."

"A couple of *months?*" His disappointment was palpable.

She was enjoying her little telephonic tease. She'd first met Lieutenant Donald Puteney when he was running security for a corporate get-together at the Century Plaza. It was an easy way for the men in blue to supplement their income. All they were likely to catch was a spilled drink. Better than a bullet out on the street.

Puteney had done even better. He'd managed to catch Ruth Somerset, though she'd done most of the netting. She'd found him mildly attractive. Her primary interest, of course, had been in acquiring a potentially valuable contact. Now she'd put that contact to use.

"Sooner, if I can manage it, Don. But first I need a little favor."

"Uh-oh, here it comes."

"Take it easy," she said, pouting over the phone. "You haven't even heard what it is, yet. And no favor, no date."

"You haven't given me a date yet."

"That's right, I haven't, have I?" She paused, letting him stew in his own smart remark.

"Okay, I'll try, Ruth. It depends on the favor."

"Jake Pickett." She spelled both names. "Two 'T's. Seventy-one years old, lives at—" she punched a key on one of the several terminals that lined her desk—"three thousand Hermosa Lane. That's just outside the city of Riverside's east limits."

"What about him?" Puteney wanted to know.

"I need a description of his car and I need to know where it is right now. He'll be with it."

"You want me to put out an APB on this guy?" Puteney asked her curiously. "What's your interest in him?"

"Private. Company business."

"I sure as hell didn't think it was personal. Seventy-one."

"We have to locate him," she continued, adding thoughtfully, "it's for his own good. We have reason to believe he may be in some danger from exposure to dangerous chemicals. Company wants it kept quiet. You understand."

"Sure I do. Exposure to dangerous chemicals, yeah, that'll cover me if there's any trouble. I shouldn't have any problems with this. You want me to have him picked up?"

"No," she said quickly, "that won't be necessary. He's no danger to anyone else." She gave him her office number. "As soon as you run him down let me know where he's gone to, will you? I can handle the rest from here."

"What makes you so sure this old guy will be with his car?" Puteney asked her.

"He will be. He seems like a fairly conservative type, not the sort to go around abandoning cars."

"If you could give me a better description of him we could look for him as well as the car."

"That's alright. Just find the car for me and he'll be around. Can you get right on it?"

"Can I?" She could see him leering over the phone, resolved to put off the meeting as long as possible. "I'll put the request through to Sacramento right now. I can't say how long it'll take. Depends on how fast the information gets out and where he's gone to."

"I know it won't take you very long, Don." She was practically cooing into the receiver. "You can move fast when you want to."

"Any speed you like," he assured her confidently. "How about a place and time, now?"

"As soon as you find the car. See you, Don." She hung up. Always nice to have friends, she thought. At least this one wasn't a sicko, like some she'd made use of in the past. If she'd had access to the Highway Patrol registry and computer she could have located Pickett's car herself. Access to official records like auto registration was usually not granted to strangers, however, so she'd have to be content to let acquaintances like Puteney do the legwork.

She'd never doubted that he'd help her. If the prospect of another meeting with her hadn't been sufficient to induce him, the mention of a little chat with Mrs. Puteney would have done the job. She was glad it had worked out this way, though. She disliked a mess.

Besides, she might have need of Lieutenant Puteney's services again some day. Catch more flies with honey. She eyed the wall clock. There was still plenty of CCM work to be done. She had no more idea when Benjamin would return to the office than she did when the lieutenant might call her back.

At least today was a weekday, she mused. Not that the police department shut down on weekends, but it would be easier to deal with Puteney through office channels, where she had the advantage of on-call computer information as well as built-in excuses for not talking to him at length.

She'd always enjoyed working with computers and had gravitated naturally to the profession. They were always so responsive, she thought. Predictable, never emotional or dangerous. Not like men. Of that more mobile and exasperating group she'd found Benjamin Huddy by far the most interesting and reliable. Some day, of course, it might be necessary to discard him. She hoped it wouldn't come to that. She genuinely liked Benjamin and he obviously felt the same way about her. There was a definite affinity between them. Nothing as ennervating as love, but rather a mutual admiration and willingness to work together to obtain mutually desirable ends.

She was examining a long train of statistics as it unscrolled on one green screen. Part of an upcoming report she would be putting together on CCM's African operations. She reached for a file and extracted a single disk, which she inserted into the empty drive. Men were like software, come to think of it. She enjoyed being able to plug them in and out of her life.

Benjamin, Benjamin, she sang to herself, whatever have you stumbled onto? His enthusiasm had almost won her over, though the whole business she still found too absurd to believe. Telekinesis, indeed! The stuff of bad horror films, for all the scientific gobbledygook he'd quoted in support of it. Rationalizations and nothing more.

Of course, he'd been the only one to witness the old man's miraculous demonstration. That was a pity. Bottle caps popping off beer bottles, dirt vanishing from the underside of a car; hardly the raw material from which great careers were fashioned. She'd gone along with the whole silly business this far because Benjamin always seemed to see opportunities where others saw nothing. If he felt this matter worth pursuing, she was bound to help him follow it through to the end. She wasn't sanguine as to what that end would be.

But why had the old man disappeared?

It wouldn't hurt her to stick with the project to find out. She wasn't directly involved the way Benjamin was. Her machines provided her with distance and protective space. For example, she didn't have to deal with people like those two horrible men Benjamin was compelled to employ. Drew was one name; she couldn't recall the other.

Much better to let Benjamin deal with such types. It was a disturbing side of the business. Large, brutal, uncouth individuals, long on brawn and short on brain. Beneath the smart yellow dress her legs moved against one another.

"This won't do," she murmured to herself, concentrating harder on the central computer screen. "There's work to be done."

VIII

She spent the rest of the morning and a large part of the afternoon alternating work with replies to Huddy's anxious inquiries. He called every fifteen minutes.

"No, Benjy," she'd tell him repeatedly, "there's nothing yet." She could visualize him fuming away in his office upstairs, unable to work. He didn't have the inner discipline she possessed.

At last, a call, not from him this time, but via her secretary's outside line.

"Ms. Somerset? I have a Lieutenant Donald Puteney of the LAPD on the line for you."

"Thank you, Sandy. Go ahead and put him through."

A brief pause, then, "Hi, gorgeous."

"Hi, yourself. You have something for me?"

He allowed himself a single sinister ha-ha before getting down to business. "Your man Pickett drives a 1961 blue and white Ford Galaxie, license number ay-dee-six, four-two-eff." Her right hand worked with a pencil as he relayed the information. "Bought it new in October sixty-one from—"

"Never mind that," she interrupted impatiently. "Where is he now?"

"Highway Patrol finally located him heading east out of Blythe. The ID was made at the border station and since my office was the one that put out the request, I was notified. You said that you didn't want him stopped so they let him through."

"That's what I wanted." She was trying to picture a map of Southern California. She rarely drove anywhere outside L.A. "Going *east* from Blythe, you said?"

"That's right. On Interstate Ten."

"Thanks, Don. That's what I needed to know."

"Hey, wait a minute! What about . . . ?"

"Call you back." She hung up on the disappointed officer and hastily buzzed Benjamin's office. He made it downstairs in record time. Meanwhile she took a quick geography lesson.

"Blythe," he muttered as he strode through the doorway. "Going east out of Blythe." He sat down opposite her. "That's way south of the Sierras. Even for someone who might like to take the long way around." He shook his head. "No, he's running, Ruth, and not into the Sierras, either."

"What's east of Blythe?" she asked him.

"Nothing. Not a damn thing. Not until you get to Phoenix. After that on I-10 there's Tucson and then nothing until. . . ." His eyes widened slightly. "Texas. You remember?" He leaned over her desk. "The only relatives he has, the niece and grandniece, down by Houston?"

"That's a hell of a drive," she observed, "for an old man with a heart condition to attempt solo in an old car."

"But why else would he be going that way?"

"Maybe he knows somebody in Phoenix who's not in our records," she murmured. "Maybe he's headed someplace we haven't imagined."

"Well, I'm not going to wait to find out. I wish to hell I knew what I'd done to make him suspicious of me."

"Too late for that now," she pointed out. "What are you going to do?"

"Have him picked up, of course. Who do we have in the vicinity of Blythe?"

"Company, you mean?" She raised her eyebrows, swiveled in the chair. Her fingers danced over a keyboard. A moment later she was shaking her head discouragingly.

"The nearest company facilities are in Perris. That's practically around the corner from Riverside. Nowhere near the border."

"Nothing in Blythe itself?"

She shook her head again. "Not even a drugstore."

"I know people in Vegas," he said softly, "but even that's too far. And the roads in that part of the country stink."

"What about the Phoenix-Tucson area?" Her fingers moved again. "Here we go. Southwest Phoenix Division, Eutheria Plant and Products."

"What do we have there?"

"Potash, mostly. Some borates. The General Manager's name is Frank Lasenby."

"Right. Get ahold of this Lasenby."

"Get ahold of him yourself," she told him. "I'm not your secretary, Benjamin."

"Come on, Ruth," he said tiredly, "not now, huh?"

"Just reminding you." She instructed her own secretary to make the connection.

"What have we got on this guy Lasenby?"

"Twenty-one years with the company," she said, reading off the screen. "Family man. No evidence of misconduct, no history of bribe-taking. Seems pretty straight." She touched a couple of keys, activating a code and releasing a lock within the system. Information appeared on the screen that wasn't contained in the general personnel files.

"Here we go." She shifted in her chair. "Suspected homosexual activity. At least two incidents. One dating back to his college days."

"That'll be enough," said Huddy, sounding satisfied. "Hopefully we won't have to use that."

"Hopefully," she agreed. "Still, it's always nice when you need something from somebody to be able to carry a knife in the hand you're not shaking his with."

"Yeah. Lasenby will help us pick Pickett up before he gets into Phoenix. I don't want to have to fool with him there. It's not our territory and we don't know the ground."

"Not only that," she said, "but I don't know anyone in Phoenix. This information on Pickett comes through my California source. He's out of that range now. We might be able to work something with his Arizona contacts, but I wouldn't want to have to depend on that. Besides, I don't know if I'd try working this source any further." She thought of the disappointed lieutenant. "From here on we're going to have to track Pickett with our own resources."

"That's no problem. We'll have him in custody in a few hours. There's only the one interstate running from Blythe through to Phoenix."

"I've been checking the maps," she told him. "If he's on his way to Texas he doesn't have to go through Phoenix. The interstate's not quite finished all the way into the city. There's a cutoff that runs down through the town of Gila Bend and swings across to Tucson where it links up with Ten again. He's an old man in an old car, and it's hot out there. Bet you he doesn't go through Phoenix."

"Where's the best place to cut him off before he hits the turn-off?"

"According to the map, the junction for Gila Bend is at a town called Buckeye."

"I didn't know you were such a geography buff, sweetness," he told her.

"Just during the last few minutes."

"Right. I'll put out the word to this Lasenby and his people to look for Pickett's car at Buckeye. Surely he hasn't gotten that far yet."

Somerset shook her head, smiled prettily. "The Blythe sighting was at"—she checked another glowing screen—"ten thirty. Assuming he maintains the same rate of speed from Blythe to Buckeye he won't arrive there for an hour or so yet. That should be plenty of time for this Lasenby to organize things."

"I just wish Pickett wasn't quite so frail. I'm getting tired of handling him with kid gloves."

"Don't let it get you all worked up, Benjy. Keep your real objectives out where you can see them. You're going to need this old man's cooperation."

"No," he said, "I *want* this old man's cooperation. According to Navis I don't necessarily need it." He sat there quietly, thinking.

"Something else, Benjamin?"

"There are a lot of dirt roads, back country roads, farm tracks in that part of Arizona. We can't be sure we haven't missed him, or that Lasenby's people won't. I think we need to prepare for that possibility."

"Benjy, you're always overcompensating."

"I know. That's how I've managed to get where I am. Life's like a spacecraft, sweetness. You have to have backup systems ready to take over for your backup systems." He was looking hard at her.

"Come on, Benjamin, say it."

"He's heading for Texas, right? There's just an outside chance he might make it. His car might break down and he'd get on a bus, or a plane, and we'd lose track of him completely. We have to consider that possibility."

"I'm not sure I like the way you said 'we.' What have you got in mind?"

"CCM has a major installation down south of Houston. It's very close to the niece's home in Port Lavaca. I think it would be a good idea if you made arrangements to run an inspection and check out of the computer facilities down there."

"Oh no, Benjamin. Not South Texas."

"It's late summer, almost autumn," he told her. "The weather won't be too bad."

"No. I'll just melt, that's all. Unless the occasional hurricane blows me away."

"Please, sweetness. I have to be here to monitor things at this end. If this Pickett should show up at his relative's place, if we should miss him somehow, we need to know immediately so we can take steps. I know it's highly unlikely that he'll slip past our people at Phoenix, but we have to be ready for any eventuality."

"Alright," she said, sighing and giving in. "If you think it's that important, Benjy."

"I do," he said vigorously.

She knew how he could be once an idea fixed itself in his mind. "Maybe it would do me good to get away from the office for a while. I'll be closer to the Bahamas, anyway."

"If you need justification from my section," he began.

She shook her head. "I have enough independence and discretion in my own. I won't be missed here for a couple of days, especially since I'll be gone on company business. I can always find something to check at any installation. Houston won't be any different." She shook a warning finger at him. "But as soon as they pick him up, you let me know."

"I'll contact you at your hotel, first thing," he promised her.

"If there *is* a hotel near Port Lavaca."

"That's coast country. There's probably motels and resorts all over the place. As for setting a watch on the niece's family, we have plenty of people in Houston who can handle that. All you'll have to do is give directions, guzzle seafood and wait for word from me."

"I'd enjoy it more if it was New York," she muttered.

He rose. "It won't be for long, sweetness. I know you'll handle it just right. I've got a lot of confidence in you."

"Maybe even as much as I have in you, Benjy?" She pushed back her chair and made her way around the desk and into his waiting arms. "We'd better have confidence in each other, because if anybody in the company gets wind of what we're up to and there's trouble, we're going to need all the confidence both of us can muster."

"Now don't you worry, sweetness." He kissed her gently. "This is all going to work out fine. Pickett's just delayed matters a day or so, that's all. But this is important to me. It could be damned important to us."

"I know," she murmured. "I know how important it is to you or I wouldn't be involving myself in it." His hands were moving. She leaned back, smiled at him. "Hang on and let me lock the door." He let her slip reluctantly out of his grasp. She wasn't free of it for long.

"AD6 42F." Royrader leaned back in the pickup and glanced at his companions. It was crowded with the three men in the front of the cab. The one in the middle, Archer, pulled a piece of paper from his left shirt pocket and stared at it.

"That's it, alright. Sixty-one Galaxie, blue and white. We've got our man." Royrader stared at the car, sandwiched in among the others in the dusty parking lot. "Hell, that wasn't hard. What do you suppose the company wants with him, anyway?"

The driver gave a noncommittal shrug. "Ain't none of our business." Corked and potent, a ready hypodermic rested in his breast pocket. In its way it was no more lethal than the sheet of paper resting on Archer's lap.

"What do we do now, Ed?" Archer carefully refolded the paper and replaced it in his pocket. "It's lunchtime." He nodded toward the restaurant. "Place'll be full of hands in from the cotton fields. We can't just walk in and drag him out whether he's conscious or not."

"I've got an idea." The driver pulled the big pickup as close to the Galaxie as he could manage, blocking the driver's door. The three of them exited the truck. They had to wait a moment while an elderly couple came out of the restaurant and entered their own car. As soon as they'd pulled out of the lot Royrader used a key to make a nice long gouge in the passenger side of the old car.

"That oughta do." He stepped back to admire his handiwork. "We can tell the old boy we got the license number of the outfit that scratched his heap up. While we're all staring at this we ought to be able to put him out and slip him in the pickup before anyone comes questioning." He looked to the restaurant entrance.

"Let's do it. I've got other work to do."

"Yeah, me too," said Snyder, the last member of the trio.

The cafe had two sets of doors, a common Arizona barrier against the heat. Inside, the distant whine of the highway gave way to the gentle hum of the air conditioner. Archer was right about the hands. The cafe was packed, from the tables set out in the center of the floor to the booths back in the only half-private section.

Most of the diners were men: rough-faced, burnt dark by the sun. They wore boots and jeans and cowboy hats, not out of any care for current fashion but because they were the most practical work clothes for the kind of hard field work these men performed. They drove harvesters, repaired fence, poisoned weeds and cared delicately for the thousands of acres of cotton that occupied the desert floor for miles east and south of the town.

Waitresses darted to and fro from table to table like tick-birds working a herd of hippos, neatly dropping off or picking up plates and glasses and only rarely entering into the conversations. These were always brief and concerned with women, money and crops, not necessarily in that order.

"There he is," said Archer confidently. They'd all familiarized themselves with the description of their quarry and no one disagreed with him. "That's got to be Pickett."

Sitting alone in a back corner was an old man. There were older men seated in the cafe, but all were accompanied by friends or wives. Furthermore, this old man didn't wear a hat and there was no sign of one on the nearby rack. That immediately marked him as a stranger. His footgear confirmed Archer's guess. The old man was wearing sneakers. That made him the only one in the cafe except a pair of younger tourists who wasn't wearing a set of worn, mud-encrusted boots.

"Yeah, that's him for sure," murmured Snyder. He took a step toward the back table.

Royrader put out a hand and held him back. "Take it easy. We're in no hurry. We've found the guy. Let's let some of this lunch crowd leave. Besides, I don't know about you guys but sitting out in the truck all morning hunting for this bird has given my throat a real solid tickle."

"I could go for a beer myself," Snyder confessed.

"Fine." They found an empty table and sat down. A tired-looking waitress with her hair piled high up over her head like a big basket of redwood shavings came over and waited patiently for their order.

"What've you got on tap?" Royrader asked her.

"Bud and Michelob."

"Three Michelobs," Royrader told her.

"Yeah, three for me too," said Snyder. The waitress smiled politely.

"That's all for now," said Royrader.

"Nothing to eat? You boys aren't hungry?"

"As a matter of fact, we are," said Royrader, "but we've got business first."

She gestured with her pad. "Okay." The crowd swallowed her up.

"Nice ass," said Snyder, watching her go.

"Keep your mind on your business, Frank," Royrader admonished him.

Archer had the best view of the old man. "Looks like he's eating a club sandwich." He glanced at Royrader. "You sure we haven't got time for lunch before we have to pick him up?"

The older man smiled. "Let's not push our luck. We found the guy like we were supposed to. We can eat later. As soon as we finish our beers we meet him outside and give him our scratch story. Then we pile him into the pickup and hustle him down to the plant. From there he's Lasenby's problem and we can go have an early supper."

"I wonder what they want him for?" Snyder reiterated. "He don't look like much."

"Old guys like that don't ever look like much," said Royrader. "That's how they can get away with stuff. Maybe he's an embezzler or something." He glanced over his shoulder at their quarry. "Look guys, Lasenby didn't tell me anything. All I know is that he called me into his office and gave me the dope on this old guy and told me to get some people together and pick him up. Then he pushed the envelope on me."

The other men knew about the envelope. It held three thousand dollars in nice fresh hundred-dollar bills and it sat folded in one of Royrader's pockets. A thousand for each of them as soon as they delivered this guy Pickett to Lasenby. So they hadn't asked too many questions.

"Hell," Snyder muttered, peering at Pickett over the heads of the other diners, "if they want him so bad, why didn't they just come out and pick him up in person? Old codger like that's not going to give Lasenby or anybody else any trouble. He sure has some folks upset about something."

"Yeah, well, keep in mind that's none of our business, right? We just do our job and forget it."

"I know," said Synder, a little hurt. "I'd just like to know what's going on, that's all."

"So would I, Frank, so would I," said Royrader. "But we're not likely to find out, so let's not kill ourselves worrying about it, okay?"

At that point the beers arrived and the conversation turned to the NFL game of the week and how the Bears had managed to blow yet another lead. Snyder was originally from Chicago and the discussion was of more than academic interest to him.

Across the room, Jake Pickett had started in on the second

half of his club sandwich. He'd noticed the trio the instant they'd walked into the cafe, had subsequently observed them staring at him, particularly the little one in the middle. Now, there was nothing especially noteworthy about Jake Pickett's appearance. Except for his footwear there was nothing to mark him as exceptional among the other diners. So there was no reason for a bunch of strangers to spend an inordinate amount of time looking at him.

He also noted that the new arrivals were a lot cleaner then the rest of the men occupying the cafe. They hadn't been spending hours out among the dirt and bolls. They apparently hadn't ordered any food. Only beers.

They continued to take turns glancing back toward him, apparently unaware that their interest was being noted. But since they seemed content to sit and drink, Jake figured he might as well finish his lunch. He didn't think they were likely to try anything outright. Not in the crowded cafe. If they were so inclined they would probably have tried it already.

It was confirmation of all Amanda's suspicions, as far as Jake was concerned. Sweet suspicious little Mandy. Thank goodness for her, he thought.

It wasn't that Jake hadn't suspected that fellow Huddy's motives. He'd seen plenty of television. It was just that he was such a nice young man. He'd seemed genuinely concerned about Jake's health. According to Amanda he *was* concerned about Jake's condition, but not in the way he'd indicated, or in the way Jake had hoped.

Now Huddy had apparently gone so far as to send people out after Jake, to bring him back. For what? For an "exam." The images that conjured up in Jake's mind weren't pretty, and they certainly weren't healthful. He wondered how Huddy had tracked him down. Not that it mattered now.

What did matter now? His mind was a whirl. Normally he didn't have to deal with anything more complex than the heating instructions on a frozen dinner. Surely he couldn't just get back in his car and head down the highway toward Gila Bend. No, the first thing was to get out of here quickly and quietly. He would have to change his driving plans. The highway between here and Gila Bend was busy but rural. Once he made Phoenix, however, he thought he could shake these people easily. After all, it wasn't the CIA that was after him, only the hirelings of some fanatic young executive. He glanced surreptitiously at the three drinkers. They didn't look too sharp. Surely he could lose them.

He finished all but the last couple of bites of his sandwich, rose, wiped his mouth. As he did so he saw two of them turn to look sharply in his direction, as quickly look away. At the same time their waitress arrived with another round of beers. Maybe that would hold them for a couple of extra minutes, he thought.

Putting one hand rather dramatically against his stomach, he turned and walked slowly toward the sign marked Rest Rooms. A couple of the little gold stick-on letters had fallen off. The men at the table relaxed, started on their fresh beers.

Inside the john, Jake waited until its only other occupant finished his business, zipped his fly and departed. Then he closed the simple latch lock on the door.

There was the necessary window at the back. It was open, but a screen kept Arizona's small winged wildlife outside. Jake inspected it quickly. It balanced loosely on a couple of snaps. He tugged at them with his fingers, but they were tighter than they looked. He couldn't budge them. His pocket knife, however, made short work of them.

He pushed hard with one hand and grabbed with the other, managing to catch the screen before it fell to the ground; not that anyone in the busy cafe was likely to hear anyway, but he didn't see any point in taking unnecessary chances. He let it drop carefully. It landed soundlessly outside the john.

Putting one foot on the nearby urinal, he grabbed the sill with both hands and pulled himself up and through. Twenty years ago it would have been easier. Now his belly held him back for a minute. He'd worked hard all his life, however, and that accumulated tolerance paid off now as he worked his way through the opening.

A minute later he was standing next to the side of the building, quietly thanking the architect for complying literally with the law that required bathroom ventilation. Windows were superfluous in most South Arizona buildings; an antagonist of air-conditioning. So there were none facing the dining area, and no way for anyone inside to see him race around the structure and into the parking lot.

He slid behind the wheel of the Galaxie and fumbled with the ignition. His eyes shifted constantly from the keyhole to the cafe's front door. The gouge on the side went unnoticed. He turned the key and the engine made a sound like a tired lawn mower. No burst of energy came from beneath the hood.

Phoenix, he thought frantically, just get me to Phoenix, old blue. Then we can both rest. But not here. Don't die on me here.

"Hey, Ed?" Archer pointed toward the back of the restaurant. Two farmhands stood in front of the door to the men's room. One had been trying the handle. Now he stopped and started pounding on the door with the flat of one hand.

Royrader rose and led his companions away from the table. The half-finished beers were quickly forgotten.

"What's the problem?" he asked the frustrated farmhand.

"Hell, I don't know." He nodded toward the door. "Some joker's been in there for ten minutes. He's got the door locked, and I've got to pee like a Russian racehorse." Turning away from Royrader, he resumed his pounding on the door. "Hey man, come on out of there! Your time's up!"

Royrader exchanged a look with Archer, then Snyder. The latter pushed the irritated hand aside and kicked out hard with one boot. Other diners looked up and there was a faint protest from the vicinity of the cash register which the three men ignored.

"Hey, partner, I ain't *that* desperate," said the startled farmhand.

The door flew inward with a slam. Snyder went in first, followed quickly by Royrader and Archer. They saw the gaping window right away.

"Dammit," Royrader muttered under his breath. They piled back out through the john and back into the cafe, ignoring the comments of the other diners and the protest of the woman manning the register.

Then they were outside again, squinting through the glare and heat of the late summer sun. The Galaxie was gone. Archer pointed to his left, up the road.

"There he goes!"

"Christ," Royrader snapped as they headed for the pickup.

"If he gets into truck traffic we'll have a helluva time trying to pull him over."

It was at least ten miles from Buckeye to the point where the Los Angeles-Phoenix traffic began to bunch up on its way into the valley of the sun. Once he entered real traffic, the old man would be surrounded by eighteen-wheelers and tourists, not to mention the ubiquitous highway patrol cruisers. At least they had one thing in their favor, Royrader thought as they piled into the pickup. The quick look-over they'd given the old man's car indicated he didn't have a CB. He couldn't call for road help.

The pickup roared, sending dirt and ants flying as it rumbled out of its parking space and tore out onto the street.

"Take it easy, Ed," Archer advised him. "We'll catch him."

"Yeah," said Snyder, leaning out the opposite window, the wind making him squint as he tried to see up the road, "that's no four-barrel he's pushin'."

"It's not that." Royrader's expression was grim as he gripped the wheel hard. "I just don't like being taken for a sucker, especially by some dumb old geezer out of L.A."

"Don't get your ass in an uproar," Archer advised him. He was staring through the dusty windshield, trying to see up the road. "We'll be all over him in a minute. Just think about the envelope and all that sweet green stuff."

"Yeah, the envelope." Thinking of the money did make him feel better. He was a lousy third-string foreman at the plant. His days were spent clad in hardhat and coveralls, white gunk and choking grime. Of course, dirty as it was, that work was still a lot cleaner than what he was into right now.

Hell with it. Too late for second thoughts. If not him and his buddies, Lasenby would've found three other guys for the job, and in less than five minutes. Times were tough.

He tried to blot out thoughts of anything but the over-stuffed envelope heavy against his chest.

IX

Jake held the accelerator pedal to the floor, but the old Ford didn't respond the way it used to. It had been a long time since any real speed had been required of it. Jake didn't know much about cars, but he did know that you couldn't coax rpm's out of an engine that no longer had the strength to manufacture them.

He could see the pickup coming up fast in his rear-view mirror. Its occupants' identity was masked by the glare off the glass, but it didn't take much guessing to imagine who they were. They'd discovered the trick he'd pulled on them in the washroom. That wasn't so bad. What was bad was that they'd discovered it about ten minutes too soon.

He strained to see a possible refuge, but there was nothing here. No gas station to pull into, no motel, nothing but scrub and pavement. He was trapped on a desert road only a few miles from the safety of big-city traffic.

A few dirt roads and narrow side streets branched off the main highway, pointing toward neat frame houses and distant cotton fields. He could imagine what would happen to him if he turned off on any of those. His only hope was to bury himself in traffic, lots of traffic. A highway patrol car was too much to hope for.

For an instant tiny flashes of fire danced behind his retinas and he winced. The little men were at work inside his chest again, banging away with their chisels and saws and hammers. But he couldn't spare a hand away from the wheel to dig for the nitro bottle in his breast pocket.

His morning dose of calcium blocker had done its job so far, but it wasn't designed to protect him from the kind of stress he was subjecting his mind and body to now. Keeping his foot on the accelerator and his eyes on the road ahead, he clung grimly to the wheel and tried to shut out the pain.

Despite the Galaxie's best efforts the big pickup truck loomed steadily larger in the rear-view mirror. Inexorably, it pulled up on him. Then it was cruising alongside. The man who leaned out of the window and shouted at Jake tried to keep a smile on his face. He only partly succeeded.

"Hey, old man, pull over!"

Jake didn't answer him, didn't look at him, continued to stare resolutely straight ahead. Where were the police? Where was the highway patrol? Jake didn't even consider what kind of story he'd tell them. If they arrested him he was bound to be better off than he'd be if he gave in and pulled over. Or would he be better off? Cops could be manipulated too. He'd read about what some of the big corporations could do. How far did young Huddy's reach extend?

"Come on, old man!" The man in the truck was shouting insistently. "Just pull over. We just want to talk to you, that's all."

"You go away!" Jake yelled out his own half-open window. "Go away and leave me alone! I'm not bothering you fellas." A soft pounding had started inside his chest. It was a warning, a throbbing internal siren, a signal flashing at the railroad crossing. Not dangerous, it said. Not yet, but slow down, be cautious, take it easy. Which was the one thing he couldn't do right now.

"Look, old man," said the one leaning out the pickup's window, "there's just some people who want to talk to you, okay? We don't even know who they are. Pull over and we'll talk about it, okay?"

"Go away!" Jake shouted, rolling up his window all the way. The man who'd been yelling at him gave up, pulled back inside the pickup's cab. He glanced meaningfully at the driver.

Royrader considered the road ahead. Four lanes, an occasional car going the other way, otherwise still mostly deserted. He checked the speedometer. They were doing seventy-five. Either the old man's car couldn't make any more speed or else he didn't dare risk losing control of it. It was fast enough, though. At this rate they'd run into traffic within the next few minutes.

"Hang on," he warned his friends.

"What are you gonna do?" Archer wanted to know.

Royrader glared at him. "Run him off the road, what d'you think? We can't just keep running parallel with him."

"He might roll that old car," Snyder observed.

"Tough. We've got to do something." He turned the wheel to the right. The front end of the pickup leaned into the Galaxie. Rubber from the big front tires squealed against blue steel, sending paint flying.

They're going to do it, Jake thought wildly as he felt the Galaxie being pushed toward the shoulder. They're going to do it! The pickup carried twice the weight of his old Ford. The shoulder was all sand, scrub and sagebrush spotted with ocotillo and jumping cactus. He'd be okay if he didn't turn over, but that would be the end. They'd drag him out of the car and take him off to wherever they'd been ordered to. Jake knew where that would land him eventually; in Huddy's clutches, strapped to a doctor's bench. Little pieces of metal, poking him, prodding him, tiny wires running into his head, no, no!

Why didn't I go to college? he wondered. I had the chance. Maybe I'd know more about myself now, about what I am, about how to protect myself, even if Amanda insists nobody else knows anything about what it is that I do. Too late for that now. Fifty years too late. Bottle caps and dirt and mystified children.

He'd never tried anything else, never tried to make anything else slipt. It was no more than a game, a trick to make kids laugh. That's all it was, all he ever wanted it to be. But this fellow Huddy thought differently. Mandy had done her best to warn him about the possibility. Too late now. Too late. He didn't know what to do next.

"Tell me what to do, Mandy!" he thought wildly. "Tell me what to do!"

But Amanda couldn't help him. She wasn't talking to him now and she was the one who had to make the long reach out, make the connection. The phone always rang at his end.

Truck. Gotta stop the truck. But he didn't want to hurt anybody. Even during the war he'd been spared that necessity. As a welder he'd worked out the duration in Los Angeles, building Liberty ships.

The pickup rammed into him again. For a second or two the tires on the right side of the Galaxie kicked up sand. The Ford slid crazily, its back end gyrating like a go-go dancer. Then it was back on the pavement and the pickup moved toward it yet again.

The steering wheel . . . what about the steering wheel? That was kind of like a bottle cap, wasn't it? No, not really, and they'd lose all control and they'd crash and it would be all his fault. He didn't want to hurt anybody, not even a little. What was familiar, what could he do for sure, what was just like a bottle cap? The big right front wheel slid toward the hood of the Ford and then he knew.

It was funny when he tried it. It was as if an old friend had been there all the time. A real good, close, intimate friend, the kind you can call every five years and ask, how are ya doin' and not worry about making small talk or not having written. He'd never tried to make use of his friend before because he'd never had reason to. But he did now, for his own sake.

Really it wasn't any different from making the bottle caps slipt, though it made him feel funny inside. Not in his heart, which always felt funny and was beginning to slam against his ribs with agonizing force now. Somewhere else. Inside his head, and it made his head hurt a little bit too. It always hurt a little bit whenever he made things slipt, but this time it hurt more than usual.

But it was just like the bottle caps.

"Jesus Christ!" Archer threw his hands up to protect his face. A low moan came out of Synder as he clutched reflexively at the sill of the window. Royrader fought to bring the suddenly berserk wheel under control. The air around him was full of sparks, chewed-up pavement, and dust. The cab was filled with the odor of something burning and a terrific screeching that drowned out their panicky curses.

Somehow Royrader managed to keep them level until the pickup finally ground to a halt.

"Christ," Archer was murmuring over and over, "Jesus H. Christ."

"It's alright," Royrader told him. He was holding the wheel so tightly his fingers were white up to the knuckles. It kept the rest of him from shaking. "It's alright now, we've stopped. We're okay."

Ahead of them the thin outline of the old Ford had already vanished into the distance. "What the hell happened?" Synder asked shakily.

"I don't know." Royrader ran the rapid sequence of events back through his mind, did not stumble across an explanation. "I don't know. I just lost control, that's all. She just went crazy on me." He yanked on the door handle, pushed outward. The door didn't move. Holding the handle down he rammed his shoulder against the door, enjoying the pain that shot up his arm. The door gave, opened with a creak.

He half stepped, half stumbled out of the cab onto the pavement. Other cars slowed as they came up behind the pickup. Their passengers gaped at the accident, but no one stopped to help. That suited Royrader just fine. He wasn't much in the mood to answer questions just then. Already he was debating how he was going to explain their failure to Lasenby. Worse than that was the image of hundred-dollar bills floating away like parakeets on the desert air.

Slowly he made his way around to the back of the pickup. One of the rear tires was visible off to the right, just rolling to a stop far out in the brush. It bumped up against a saguaro, tumbled over, and worked itself to a halt like a coin tossed on a table.

Royrader's companions were slow to regain control of themselves. Eventually Synder and Archer both worked their way out of the cab. The last of the dust and dirt was beginning to settle around them.

"I thought you had this truck in top shape," Archer said accusingly as he inspected the undercarriage.

"First time I've ever had any trouble with it." Royrader

spoke absently. He was absorbed in an inspection of the rear axle. "Never anything like this, for sure."

"Hell." Synder was staring down the highway in the direction the Ford had taken. "Nobody's ever had any trouble like this." He turned his attention to his superior and drinking buddy. "You get the feeling, Ed, maybe there was something about this little job Lasenby didn't tell us?"

"I don't know." Royrader didn't know what to think. He was confused and angry and not a little frightened. "I just don't know what to think. Come on, let's pick everything up and try and put this heap back together."

They started back down the highway, leaving the pickup sitting motionless on its fenders and axles. All four of the big off-road tires had slipped their axles simultaneously. That didn't make much sense to Royrader. The pickup was his baby, his companion on many a fishing and hunting expedition. He'd taken it across wild creeks and lava-bedded ravines and never lost a wheel. Now he'd lost all four at the same time. He still didn't know how he'd managed to keep the truck from rolling. In fact, if all four wheels hadn't fallen off at precisely the same instant, that's exactly what would have happened.

It took the three men most of the rest of the day to track down the four wheels and roll them back to the truck. It took the rest of the evening to locate all thirty-two lug nuts. They were scattered on the shoulder and across the highway. Fortunately every one of them appeared to be undamaged, save for minor abrasions of the chrome and a few corners.

Snyder inspected them one by one as Royrader and Archer worked to jack up the rear of the truck. Snyder could understand losing one lug nut, or maybe two, or even having a whole wheel come off what with the way they were banging up against the old man's car. But thirty-two nuts off thirty-two screws, at the same time? That was worse than crazy; it was fucking scary.

Suddenly the loss of the thousand dollars he'd been promised didn't seem so devastating. Suddenly all he wanted was to go to Willy's Bar and get drunk and get ready to go back to work tomorrow morning. Suddenly he didn't want to see that frightened old man ever again.

"Tell Mr. Huddy here what happened one more time," Lasenby instructed Royrader.

"Look, Frank," the driver of the pickup said to his boss, "I've already told you what happened." He glanced once at his two buddies seated behind him, for moral support. "We *had* this old guy. We had him. But he refused to pull over, refused to stop. You said do what was necessary to bring him in. So we started to edge him onto the shoulder, real gentle like, and all of a sudden the bottom drops out of my truck. All four wheels coming off at the same time like that. Man, I never heard of anything like that happening to anyone, even in an off-road race. You want answers? Me and the guys would like a few ourselves."

Huddy sat behind and to the left of the plant manager's desk. He had his legs crossed and his fingers steepled as he listened intently to the story. It took an effort to contain both his disappointment and his excitement.

True, they'd temporarily lost track of Pickett, but picking him up again shouldn't be too difficult. This time, once they'd located him, they'd wait until the time was just right before trying to pick him up, and he'd have real pros on the job instead of what was available locally.

But the forthcoming delay didn't disappoint him because the failure of these men had provided him with something almost as valuable as Pickett himself: proof. He knew what had happened to this man's pickup, because he remembered the bottle caps. He saw them popping off their rims as vividly as if the old man had given him the demonstration yesterday.

This was much better than bottle caps, however. Much better. Idly, he wondered if Pickett could do the same thing to, say, the gears that held tight the treads of a tank, or maybe the bolts attaching an airplane's wing to its fuselage. In their failure these three sods had opened up a universe of wondrous possibilities, and every possibility had the same name: Jake Pickett.

For that reason as well as reasons of security he was inclined to be kindly toward them.

"It's alright, you tried your best. It was an accident, that's all."

"Accident, hell," said Royrader. "It wasn't no accident."

"And by way of compensation," Huddy continued smoothly, "I think it only fair that you receive your promised bonuses anyway, for trying your best."

"Excuse me, Mr. Huddy," Lasenby began, "but are you certain that you . . . ?"

"I'll give you an authorization through my own office, if you prefer, Frank."

"Whatever you think best, Mr. Huddy." The manager was puzzled, and not a little envious of his three employees.

Royrader's anger had dissolved instantly at Huddy's words, though the confusion remained. "Thanks, sir. Look, if we can, we'd sure like to know if, well, if there's something we ought to know. I mean, it was mighty funny what happened to my truck out there and—"

"You are to receive your bonus money, Mr. Royrader," said Huddy softly.

"Yeah, but . . ." Royrader broke off as Snyder approached him and put a hand on his friend's shoulder. Snyder smiled thinly at the neatly dressed representative from the coast, then looked down at his companion.

"You heard the man, Ed. Let's get out of here, huh? We've got our own work to do."

"Sure, but we should—"

"Yeah, let's split," said Archer, heading for the door. "Like the man said, we did our best and we blew it. We're through with it, right?" Together he and Snyder hustled their reluctant companion out of the office, closing the door loudly behind them.

Lasenby guessed the reason behind Huddy's unexpected largess. "You think they'll keep their mouths shut about this like you want them to?"

"I think so, Frank. The money should do it, but even if they get drunk and start spouting off about it in some bar, no one's likely to believe a word they say."

"*I'd* sure like to know what went on out there, sir," the manager said.

"It's all part of a CCM experiment that's gone a bit awry." Huddy spoke as though confiding some important secret. "We've been having a few problems with it. Nothing drastic. Part of it's due to recalcitrant employees not honoring the terms of their contracts."

"Like maybe this old man?"

Huddy just sat there, let the manager draw his own harmless and inaccurate conclusions.

"Well," Lasenby said, "if there's anything else I can do to help, sir, just let me know. The home office can always count on Frank Lasenby."

"You've shown me that, Frank." Huddy rose and the manager rushed to match him. The two men shook hands. "I'll be sure to let Headquarters know how helpful you've been."

"Thank you, Mr. Huddy." Lasenby escorted him from the office and walked him through the plant back out to his waiting rental car. Only after Huddy had disappeared through the plant gates did Lasenby begin to wonder seriously about his employees' story. For a moment he thought of calling them back in and asking them to repeat it one more time in the absence of the intimidating presence from the West Coast. Then he shrugged, decided against it. There was his own bonus money to consider, not to mention the favorable recommendation Huddy had promised to turn in, and there was plenty to be done around the plant today. So he quickly forgot all about it.

Huddy could hardly contain his excitement as he drove back toward Phoenix. He couldn't keep from checking out every car he passed to see if it mightn't be a sixty-one blue and white Ford Galaxie.

He blamed himself for the failure even as he congratulated himself on what it had taught him. He'd been too anxious to get Pickett back, still envisioning the old man as a harmless quick pickup. Next time he'd plan more carefully.

There was the possibility, of course, that the three men had made up the whole story to cover their failure, but Huddy had discounted that likelihood early. The tale was too fantastic, too unbelievable to be a lie. Besides which, the three didn't have the intelligence to make up anything so incredible.

Privately he saluted Jake Pickett, wherever the old man might be. It was nice of him to have confirmed what until now had only been Huddy's suspicions of his potential. Out of respect for that potential, Huddy intended to see that the old man was recovered quietly and professionally this time. Maybe he'd even fly Drew out from Los Angeles. They had plenty of time in which to not make any more mistakes, and he'd feel a lot better if people he knew personally were on the job. They'd handle the recovery so that Pickett wouldn't even have the chance to pull something like that trick with the wheels a second time.

Give the old man a day or two, let him start on his way out of Phoenix thinking he'd made good his escape. Let him relax a little. Maybe he wouldn't even make the connection between the men in the pickup truck and CCM. Pickett didn't strike him as much of a chess player. His other talents more than made up for that deficiency. They were talents which Huddy intended to put to his personal use.

"They tried to get me, Mandy." Jake lay on the bed in the Motel Six and tried to convey his fear to his grandniece. "They tried to run me off the road."

"Oh Uncle Jake," the voice whispered sympathetically inside his head, "I'm so sorry. I warned you, though."

"I know you did, Mandy. But it'll be alright now. I lost 'em. Scared them a little, I think. I tried not to hurt anyone and I don't think I did. It'll be better when we're together. We'll work things out, just the two of us."

"Yes we will, Uncle Jake. How did you get away from them?"

"I didn't know what to do, Mandy. There were three of them and they were in a big truck. I couldn't think of what to do. I tried to ignore them and that's when they tried to run me off the highway. I thought of the bottle cap trick; you know, the one where I make the bottle caps slipt on the kids' sodas? I did it with the caps holding their wheels on. They came right off and I got away from them clean. They're not following me anymore, either. I've checked. I checked several times before I found this motel."

"Calm down, Uncle Jake. It's good that you got away from them. Where are you now?"

"In a motel. Oh, you mean what town. I'm in Phoenix. I'll leave here early tomorrow morning. If they try to bother me again I can do the trick with their wheels. It'll be easier next time because I've already done it once. Mandy, it was so easy, but it hurt me a little. In the head. I'll be in Port Lavaca in a couple of days, if the old clunker holds up.''

"Uncle Jake?"

"What is it, Mandy?"

"I've been thinking about this a lot, Uncle Jake. Maybe it would be a good idea if we didn't meet here. Port Lavaca's so small and quiet. Maybe it would be a good idea if we met where there were lots of people around. You remember me telling you about our vacation last year?''

Jake strained in his half-sleep to remember, tossing fitfully on the sheets. "It was . . . in Dallas, wasn't it?''

"No, no, Uncle Jake, that was the year before last. Remember, we went up to spend some time with my brother Marty?''

"Oh yeah, at Marty's college, that's right.''

"Maybe we should try to meet there, Uncle Jake. Just to be on the safe side.''

"Whatever you think's best, Mandy. It's up to you.''

"Let me work on mom and dad and see what I can work out at this end, then. I'll keep you posted.''

"Okay, Mandy. You just let me know what you want to do.''

"I will, Uncle Jake. Good night.''

"Good night, Mandy.'' He relaxed and rolled over in the bed. A thousand miles away Amanda Rae drifted into her own sleep, more afraid for her Uncle than he was for himself.

"Mom?"

Wendy Ramirez was a cheerful, slightly plump woman in her mid-thirties; still blonde, still attractive, but not nearly as beautiful as her daughter. Wendy Ramirez could only lament the fact that wheelchair-bound contestants weren't eligible for the local beauty contests. Amanda could outshine any of the other local girls even while sitting down.

"What is it, darling?''

Amanda wheeled herself into the kitchen. It was a nice, large country kitchen and her favorite room in the house. It gave her plenty of space in which to maneuver her chair, and she could help her mother prepare meals at the butcher block and table, both of which had been modified to accommodate the wheelchair.

"Mom, why don't we take a vacation?''

"A vacation?" Wendy frowned. "Amanda, it's going to be fall soon."

"I know, mom, but couldn't we go up and visit Marty in College Station? Just for a few days. I miss him so much."

"I know you do, darling." Wendy put a serving dish in the wire rack to dry. "Your father and I miss him, too. But in a few months he'll be home for the holidays and he's only just gone back to school. Our showing up would upset his routine at the beginning of the semester."

"That's just it, mom," Amanda pointed out. "The holidays are so far away. Couldn't we, just for a couple of days? Just for a weekend. Maybe this weekend! It'd be a wonderful surprise for him."

"I'm sure it would, but it's hardly the best time," Wendy pointed out. "We've already had one hurricane, and your dad's got a lot of work to do on the boat."

"They're not shrimping now, mom."

"I know that, Mandy. You know why, too. Now's the time for them to fix the boat up and have it ready for when they *do* go out. Also, your father told me only yesterday that he and the Sanchez boys and Jim Grissom are thinking of going out after some halibut. Jim thinks he knows a place and with the drag net they could make some real extra money."

"Oh mom, that's not really fishing. They're just guessing. They're really going out to drink beer and have fun."

"To a certain extent." Wendy smiled as she conceded the point. "But if Jim's not all mouth this time they could really bring in some nice change. It makes them feel like they're doing something in the off-season, and all the expenses are deductible, even if they do spend most of their time shooting the bull and drinking Lone Star."

"I'm just asking for a weekend, mom," said Amanda, trying pouting where enthusiasm had failed.

"Tell you what. I'll see what your father says tonight. Is that fair enough?"

"Oh mom, will you?" She wheeled close and reached up with both hands. Wendy leaned over and embraced her daughter, then watched as she spun the wheelchair neatly and rolled out of the kitchen. It was so hard for her to refuse Amanda anything. She was such a damn good girl, hardly ever complaining about not being able to lead a normal adolescence. She had her friends who came over and visited, of course, and she could roll to visit anyone who lived within a couple of blocks. And she'd been so exceptional in her studies. The junior class counselor, Mrs. Moreno, had practically promised her and Arri that if Amanda maintained her grades during her senior year at the same level as the previous three, she'd not only be class valedictorian, her scholarship would practically be guaranteed.

It was unfortunate that by the time she would be ready for college Martin would already have graduated. But maybe he'd go to graduate school at A & M. Then they could spend at least a year at the university together and he could show her around. That would be good for her. She really did miss her brother.

"What do you think, Arri?" she asked as they lay in bed that night.

"I don't know, *querida*." Arriaga Ramirez rolled over and used the remote to mute the sound on the TV. "I wonder why she wants to go all of a sudden now? She just saw Martin. Vacation's only been over less than a month."

"You know how Amanda is." Wendy enjoyed the cool air fanning across her body. The humidity had broken and the first hint of fall swept in from the Gulf. "Impulsive, sometimes."

"No, not usually," Arriaga argued. "Most of the time she thinks things through carefully, much more so than you or I. That's why I'm surprised. She knows I have to work on the boat."

"But it would be nice to see Martin."

"Sure it would," he agreed. "Phone calls and letters don't make a substitute son."

"And we could have lunch on campus one day, and maybe stop in Austin to go shopping on the way back."

"I don't know," he said thoughtfully. "I told you about Grissom's spot."

"The halibut? If it's that important to them the Sanchez boys and Jim can catch halibut without you."

"Sure, and they can sell it without me, too, and cash the checks without me."

"Now Arri," she said, "there are times when monetary considerations should be put aside."

"I wish the bank had the same attitude. Unfortunately, they want their house payments on time. What did you tell Amanda?"

"Just that I'd discuss it with you. She'll be bugging you before you get out the door tomorrow, you know."

"I know. Quite a gal, our Amanda Rae."

"That she is, Arri. And you're quite a man."

"That's about enough mutual compliments, *es verdad?*" They laughed together. "Okay, look," he said somberly, "I'll think about it. That's the best I can do for now. Grissom's been planning this for weeks. He thinks there's enough halibut in this canyon he's found to bring us a couple thousand apiece. That's worth taking a shot at."

"I'm not arguing about that, Arri. I'd like to have the money in the bank just as much as you would. Can't they wait a few days? Couldn't they wait just until after this weekend? They'd have more time to ready the boat. When they finally go out it'll be a week better off."

"Sure it would," Arriaga admitted, "and we'd be a week nearer wintertime."

"Since when did the weather ever bother you and that bunch of wetbacks and rednecks you run around with? Most of the time the bunch of you are so drunk you wouldn't notice if you were putting out in the middle of Hurricane Allen."

"Okay, okay. I can see that I'm going to have to listen to this all night, right?" She grinned and nodded. "Swell. Alright, I'll talk to Grissom and the Sanchezes tomorrow and see if I can't get them to postpone the expedition for another week."

She rolled into him, making him wheeze. "Thank you, Arri. Thank you." She nuzzled his chest.

"Don't thank me yet. I haven't made up my mind for sure and neither have the others. If Jim insists on going out, he's majority shareholder in the *Grouper* and we'll have to go. I'll give it my best shot. I can't promise any more than that. God knows the boat could do with more work. The new winch hasn't been checked out yet and we don't want to go out until it is, because if something goes wrong with it at sea, old man

Paxton will say it's our fault and won't honor the damn warranty.''

"Want to check out my warranty?'' She snuggled a little closer, which he wouldn't have thought physically possible.

Not only was it possible, it was perfectly delightful.

X

The man who stood outside the door to Ruth Somerset's room at the Best Western didn't say a word; he just quietly handed her the package of cassettes. He rubbed at his eyes as he waited for her. They were red from lack of sleep. No matter how long he stayed in his particular and unusual business he never got used to long night work. Still, that was what he was getting paid for. His eyes weren't so tired, however, that he couldn't focus sharply on the expansive cleavage so delectably held out for display by the sharp décolletage of her nightgown.

"The usual stuff?" she asked.

"Not this time, miss." He was small and muscular and exhibited all the intellectual range of a box kite, she thought. But he was good at his job. "Not the usual at all, I don't think." He pointed toward the stack of tapes, bound together with rubber bands. "Check out the first side of the second tape. Something on there that might interest you. 'Course, I can't tell if it means anything. I don't know what it is that you're looking for."

"That's right, Max, you don't," she said sweetly. "Goodnight." She bent to fix her slipper, giving him just enough of a look at what he wanted desperately to get his hands on to keep him bothered and awake for the rest of the morning.

That was nasty of me, she thought. She enjoyed being a little nasty now and then. Actually, it was a substitute for Benjamin. She missed him more than she'd thought possible. It wasn't much of a vacation without him. Of course, it wasn't supposed to be a real vacation. It was supposed to be work, and that was just what it was turning out to be.

She locked the door behind Max. It was post summer-vacation time and the motel was nearly empty. She had practically the entire upper floor to herself. The room commanded a fine view of Lavaca Bay and the bridge reaching north toward Houston. There were better places to stay farther south toward Corpus Christi, but she was supposed to be here to monitor programming at the Matagorda cracking plant and could hardly rationalize sequestering herself any farther from it. Besides, here she could maintain that fiction while being on top of the real reason for her presence on this isolated section of coast.

At least the motel restaurant was good; better than expected, especially the seafood. But she would have preferred a week in New York.

The technician was right. There was something of note on the second tape. Trouble. No crisis, but it would do nothing to improve Huddy's state of mind. She rewound the tape, reached for the phone.

"I don't like it," Huddy murmured after she'd played back the offensive section for him. "I want the grandniece and her family where we can keep close to them."

"We can monitor them if they go to this University too, Benjy," Somerset argued.

"Yeah, but if we should have to do anything. . . . " He let the ominous thought go unfinished. "Hell, I'm worrying over nothing again. Just keep monitoring the house. You're positive there's been no contact between Pickett and the family?"

"There's nothing to hint at it on any of the tapes," she assured him, eying the cassettes. "Nothing's gone over the phone and if they received a letter, nobody's said anything about it. There's no mention of Pickett in the daily family chitchat."

"I still wish they'd stay there. I'd rather do any necessary work in a small town."

"Where the cops are sleepy and the livin' is easy?" she chided him.

"Come on, Ruth. This is serious."

"I'm always serious, Benjy. You know that. It's your unwarranted concern I can't get serious about."

"Can't say that I blame you. But I won't be able to relax again until we have Pickett in custody and I've delivered him to Doctor Navis back in Los Angeles."

"The sooner the better, Benjy. I can only hold so many shrimp dinners."

"I thought you liked seafood."

"I do. It's just that I wasn't planning on making its consumption my life's work."

"Soon, sweetness. It'll be finished soon."

"How are you going to pick him up this time? You don't want to lose any more wheels." She shook her head, remembering the story he'd hastily and excitedly related to her. "I still can't figure out how that happened."

"Why won't you believe, Ruth? All this accumulated evidence and still you don't believe. First the bottle caps and the dirt on my car and now—"

"And now what?" she countered, interrupting him. "The word of a bunch of factory hicks whose truck broke down during a high-speed chase?" She leaned back against the headboard of the bed, cradling the phone. "It's you I miss, Benjamin, not evidence one way or the other involving Jake Pickett."

"I miss you too, sweet thing. I checked the three men out. Their stories are tight."

"I admit that it's funny, all four wheels coming off simultaneously like that."

"Funny? It's damned fantastic!" Benjamin insisted. "It proves everything I suspected about Pickett."

"I wish I was that credulous, Benjy."

"It's not a matter of credulity, sugar, but of observation. You'll see for yourself some day soon. We're going to pick him up tomorrow outside Tucson."

"Then my presence here isn't really required any longer."

"Just until we pick him up," he said firmly. "In spite of all the preparations there's still a chance we could lose some more wheels. Remember, we're dealing with an unknown quantity here, though I think Pickett's extended himself about as far as he can. I promise I'll call you as soon as we have him sedated and on his way back. Then you can finish your 'inspection' of the Houston installation and wing your way home. Maybe we can even take that vacation."

"So soon?" she said, surprised. "As excited as you are about this I'd think you'd want to be around while Navis is running his tests."

"The team will notify me when they know something," Huddy told her. "I've thought about it and decided it might be better for me to be out of town in case the old man buys it ... weak heart, remember ... and somebody asks questions."

"I won't argue with that, Benjy. See you soon." She blew a kiss into the phone.

"So long, sweetness. Meet you in a couple of days."

She put the phone back in its cradle. It was quiet in the room, far enough from the highway so that you didn't hear the traffic. The weather was calm and you couldn't hear the lapping of the water against the bay shore unless you went out onto the little porch. She stared at the lamps, the vinyl-covered chairs, the TV bolted to its table, and she wanted to scream.

But Benjamin thought her presence here was necessary, at least until they picked the old man up tomorrow. Then this foolishness would be at an end and she could return home to her condo, her lover, and some serious work. No telling what was piling up in her office.

But as she rolled over and considered what to have for breakfast she kept thinking about the story Benjamin had told her, about the truck and the three men and the four wheels all coming off at the same time, and she found her gaze returning regularly to the curtained windows as though there might be something there, peeking in on her. Something better left alone. . . .

Arriaga Ramirez's opinion of his daughter normally would have stood up to examination. Usually Amanda was clear-headed, did think things through. But that morning she had panicked a little. After all, she was only sixteen, and the sight of the bug unnerved her more than it might have an adult.

At least, she thought it was a bug. The legs which held it tight against the wall were made of metal. It's body was plastic instead of chitin, and it sent out its messages by methods rather more complex than rubbing hind legs together.

She wouldn't have seen it at all if she hadn't bumped the telephone with her hand the first time she'd reached for it. She was going to call Nancy Sue down the street and see if maybe she wanted to come over and gossip and do some homework together. Amanda was assigned the same homework as the rest of the kids. She had the option of attending class or working at home. She'd elected to stay home for the last several school days, pleading fatigue.

When she'd reached for the phone and bumped it the back part had slipped away, exposing the small strip of grey plastic. Leaning close she'd been able to see where it had been fastened to the wall behind the phone, had been able to see clearly the tiny wires that ran from the plastic to places she didn't think they were supposed to go.

She knew the plastic and wires weren't part of the phone system. She knew because she hadn't seen the grey plastic before. There were two other telephones in the house and when she found the plastic and the wires attached to them too, she started getting really worried.

Her mom was out shopping. Her dad was working on the boat. She was all alone in the house, a house suddenly filled with nasty little grey spies. The house backed onto a sidearm of the bay and fronted on a quiet, tree-lined street. There were vacant lots on both sides and it was a long walk to the nearest occupied home, Mr. and Mrs. Coxley's.

Being alone had never bothered her before. There was about as much crime in Port Lavaca as in the middle of the bay. But the two deputies didn't patrol very much, especially when it was hot out, and when they did make rounds they kept largely to the business district way out by the highway.

Everyone knew what went on in a small town like Port Lavaca, but that didn't mean they'd know when some strangers came slipping in through an unlocked back door or open window. And she was trapped inside the house, unable to call for help without a mysterious Someone knowing about it immediately because of the omnipresent grey bugs. . . .

Calm down, she ordered herself. You're getting all excited over nothing. No one was crawling through the window to get at her. No hand appeared around the kitchen doorway leveling a gun at her. *They* didn't know that she knew.

She made a thorough check of the rest of the house. In addition to the tapped telephones she found clones of the grey bugs in her mom and dad's bedroom, under the bed, and in the dining room under the lamp.

She was careful only to look and not touch. Any disturbance might alert whoever had planted the devices. She didn't want to alarm them. Her mother and father were out together much of the time, but she was almost always home. Still, someone had slipped inside and planted the bugs. The thought made her skin crawl. Someone had entered her sanctuary and done something illegal. Someone had invaded the privacy of her family. What was worse, she knew that if someone could get in to monkey with telephones and light fixtures, they could get in to do other things, too.

But why would anyone want to? Her father was a fisherman. Her mother worked part time at a dress shop. It didn't take an hour to figure out that it all had something to do with Uncle Jake.

Those people who want to test him must know about his family, she thought. About us. They must be worried about him coming here and them checking up to see what they can find out. What could she do about it? Not a damn thing.

Tears started from the corners of her eyes. What *could* she do? There was no place else for Uncle Jake to run to. This was the only family he had. She'd been right to suggest meeting him in College Station. But if they were watching the house, they'd see her leave with her mom and dad, and they'd follow, and it might not make any difference.

Should she explain what she knew to her mom and dad? Maybe they'd believe enough to at least alert the Sheriff. Would that matter to these people, as powerful as they seemed to be?

Just get here, Uncle Jake, she thought. Once we're together we'll work it out. I know we can. She loved her Uncle Jake like a second father, and he loved her like the daughter he'd never had. She wasn't going to let these mean people hurt him, no matter how omnipotent they seemed to be. As long as she had an ounce of strength left in her body they weren't going to get what they wanted. Uncle Jake didn't have much longer to live. He knew that and he didn't try to hide it from her. She appreciated that, his honesty. She appreciated everything about him. She wasn't going to stand by and watch somebody make a guinea pig out of him during his last days.

She told him so later that night.

"What do you mean," he thought at her, "your house is bugged?"

"Didn't you ever see any spy pictures, Uncle Jake? You know, bugs. Listening devices. They're on all our telephones and all over the house. I probably didn't even find all of them. Somebody's monitoring our house."

"I don't see spy movies, Mandy, but I watch the news. I know what bugs are. I just . . . it's hard to believe." Why should it be? He asked himself. That business outside Phoenix a while back, that was hard to believe, too. Stopping that truck the way he had was even harder to believe, but it had happened.

"Don't worry, Mandy," he told her. "I know how to stop them bothering me now."

Her reply was tinged with exasperation. "Uncle Jake, it's not that easy. These are smart people. They have money, and they want you. You're just one man."

"I'll take the wheels off any car they send after me." He was feeling pretty good about himself.

"Listen to me, Uncle Jake. You didn't listen to me. These people that want you, they're *smart*. They'll figure out you did that to their truck and they won't give you a chance to do it again."

"Then how are they going to catch me?"

"They'll be a lot more subtle the next time, Uncle Jake. Now that they know they can't run your car off the road, they won't try to."

The humming of cars caressing the nearby interstate reached him faintly, there on the bed in the motel room. "What else can I do, Mandy?"

"First off you've got to get rid of the car you're using, Uncle Jake."

"Get rid of the Galaxie? Mandy, I've had that car over twenty years. I can't just dump it. Besides, if I get rid of the car how am I going to . . . ?"

"You've got to get rid of it, Uncle Jake. That's how they traced you the first time."

"Well, I don't know, Mandy. I understand what you're saying about them not giving me the chance to do the wheel trick again, but I've had that car so long."

"Please, Uncle Jake. You've always listened to my advice before."

"I know, Mandy, but twenty years; that car's a part of me. How can I just abandon her?"

"What's he raving about?" The big man standing outside the back of the motel room tried to decipher the old man's moans as his partner worked on the window screen.

"Beats the hell out of me," said his partner. "You remember what Drew said, though. This guy's weird. Just ignore it."

"Suits me." The big man checked his watch. "Let's get him out of there and turn him over to the California people. I don't like running late."

"Hey, I didn't put the damn screen here. Wonder what they want the old guy for?"

The big man shrugged, watched as his partner carefully removed the screen and pushed gently but firmly on the sliding window. It held a moment, then skidded reluctantly on its runners.

"Listen to him babble." The smaller man's name was Degrasse. "Sounds like he's been drinking. That ought to make it easier. We'll have him out of here in a minute. How's the wife and kids?"

"Okay," said Nichols. "Marva's got her average up to one seventy. How about yours?"

"Julia's got some female trouble. Nothing serious."

"That's tough."

"Yeah." They both slipped into the bathroom, their rubber-soled shoes silent against the vinyl tiles.

They waited quietly until their eyes adjusted to the dim light filling the room. It was dark in the bedroom beyond. Now they communicated with gestures instead of words, one man pointing, his companion nodding in assent. They exited the bathroom. The mumbling from the single bed was louder now. They ignored it, concentrating on the business at hand.

Jake had said good-night to Amanda. Now he lay on the bed and considered his plight. Life shouldn't be so confusing. When he'd retired he had thought he'd left confusion behind. There were the incredibly complex missives that arrived regularly from the social security administration and the welfare department, but he threw most of them in the trash. They'd never given him any trouble about it.

But *this*. All his life he'd been able to get by without suffering. Because of his age and his talent as a welder he'd even managed to avoid participation in both wars. Now, quite unexpectedly, he found himself running from his warm, familiar little home. He was confused and uncertain and scared, and found himself relying for help in coping with an indifferent, cold world on the advice of his paralyzed grandniece. All because of some silly magic tricks.

She was reluctant to leave him. Her presence was still there: warm, comforting, loving.

"I have to go, Uncle Jake. I'm getting tired."

"That's alright, Mandy. I understand." Strange that their chats should put so much more of a strain on her than on his fragile self. Of course, she was doing most of the work.

"You mind what I told you now, Uncle Jake. You be careful and take my advice."

"I'm still not sure what I'm going to do about what you said, Mandy, but I'll think about it real hard."

"Alright, Uncle Jake. Good-night."

"Good-night, Mandy."

Degrasse glanced curiously up at his companion, whispered, "Who the hell's he saying good-night to?"

"Talking in his sleep."

"Drunk, like I said." He put his hand on Nichols' arm. "No slip-ups. Remember what they told us about the old guy's bad ticker. We've got to go easy with him. Don't break nothing, and let's not get him any more excited than we have to." Nichols nodded once. They'd been over all this before.

Taking the bottle and the rag from his coat, Degrasse

unstoppered the glass and poured the contents onto the thick piece of cloth. He was careful not to breathe in any of the resultant vapors. It was an old method; proven, quick, and efficient. It was also much easier to handle in the dark than a hypo. He didn't like hypos. He was no doctor. His specialty lay at the opposite end of the hygienic spectrum.

Nichols moved away, crouching low. Together they flanked both sides of the bed.

It was just as well, because the old man apparently wasn't as drunk or sleepy as they'd first thought. He started to sit up, staring toward Nichols.

"Hey, who are you fellas? What are you doing in my room?"

Their quarry might have a bad heart, but there evidently was nothing wrong with his eyes. Nichols hurriedly put two massive hands on the old man's shoulders, pushing him flat against the mattress. Degrasse pressed the pungent, ether-soaked rag over Pickett's face.

What's this, what's happening to me? Jake thought dazedly. The fumes from the rag, where are you Mandy, he was already starting to black out. They'd take him away, he knew, take him back to California. For testing. . . . No! He lashed out, kicked frantically. The man holding him down was young and strong, and the other one was using his weight against Jake's chest while holding the soporific rag tightly over his nostrils and mouth.

So Jake lashed out violently with the only other weapon he possessed. Half conscious, the reaction was more instinctive than planned, reflexive rather than thought out. He wasn't even sure what he'd done, but suddenly the peculiar, debilitating aroma which infested the rag was gone. So was the rag. He sneezed as a few of the fibers trickled into his nose.

"Son of a bitch." The man who'd been holding the rag over Jake's mouth gaped at his open hand, which was full of loose threads, and jumped backward off the bed as though something long and black and lethal had suddenly appeared in his palm.

Still unsure exactly what had happened, Nichols also pulled away.

Jake sat up in the dark bed and spat out fibers. "You fellas go away and leave me alone." He was still dressed, for which he was thankful.

The big man quickly got himself under control. "What the hell happened?" He was mad at himself for reacting like a dumb kid on his first job. Now they'd have to pin the old man and try again.

Degrasse was still in shock. "I dunno." He wasn't stupid, but neither was he a scholarship candidate. He was standing by the foot of the bed staring at his open hand as if his own fingers had somehow betrayed the rest of his body. "The rag came apart. And I don't smell the ether no more. The rag came apart. It's all gone."

"Shit." Nichols reached inside his coat. "We'll do it the hard way."

"Hey, no." Degrasse grabbed at his partner's hand but was pushed aside. Nichols pointed the .38 at the old man sitting up on the bed.

"Look, this is important to us. No offense, bud. We don't want no trouble with you and we ain't gonna hurt you if you just come along quiet-like."

"Nobody wants to hurt me," said Jake, still slightly dizzy from the effects of the ether. "Why do you people keep trying to take me away?"

"What do you mean, keep trying?" Nichols frowned.

It occurred to Jake that perhaps these two really knew nothing about the incident back on the highway the other side of Phoenix. Why should they? It's a big anthill, and it's not necessary for the ants on one side to know what the ants on the other are doing, even if they're working toward the same end.

He stared at the gun. It didn't look like a toy. It frightened him.

"Take it easy." Degrasse put a restraining hand on his partner's arm. "Don't get him excited. We don't want him to go and have an attack on us." He turned, tried to present a benign air to the trembling old man on the bed. In the dim light he was pale as a ghost.

"He don't look well at that," agreed Nichols. "Look, why don't I just crack him on the back of the head, real easy, and we'll haul him out of here."

"I dunno," said Degrasse. "If it upsets him. . . ."

"Shit, I'm getting tired of worrying about what's going to happen to him," Nichols grumbled. "We've been in here too long already." He nodded toward the front door. "They're going to be getting impatient out there."

"Alright, alright," said the frustrated Degrasse. "Go ahead, but don't hit him any harder than you have to."

Nichols started toward the head of the bed, grinning slightly. "I've never hit anyone harder than necessary, Phil. You know that."

"Stay away from me," Jake whined. "You stay away from me."

"Take it easy, old man." Nichols tried to sound comforting. "This'll just take a second. Then you can sleep."

The gun was coming closer. It ballooned until it filled the whole room. Jake couldn't see anything else. It was dark and black and the shiny gaping maw was pointed right at his chest.

There were two or three thumping sounds like rats jumping clear of the bed. Nichols froze, his gaze on the floor. The pistol's cylinder had rolled under the bed. The barrel lay near his shoes, the trigger off to the right, the hammer by the end-table. The protective plastic grips had split away from the handle and lay on the floor like the two halves of a shucked oyster. There was no sign of the bullets. The .38 had come apart in his fist, like a child's jigsaw puzzle suddenly kicked to pieces.

"God," the big man whispered. He swallowed hard. His expression, which only a second earlier had been one of complete confidence, had metamorphosed into something quite different. Slowly he began backing away from the bed. Jake stared at him, wondering at the abrupt change in his assailant. He hadn't done anything hardly at all. Just made the gun slipt a little.

Degrasse was staring at the sections of gun-puzzle lying on the carpet. "Just like the rag," he murmured huskily. "The gun came apart just like the rag."

Nichols had retreated until he was standing next to him. "Your gun. Use your gun on him, Phil."

"Like hell."

"What are we gonna do?"

"I duuno about you," said Degrasse, edging behind the

bigger man, "but they didn't say nothing about anything like this. This wasn't part of the deal. I don't give a shit what Drew says."

"They'll be angry." Nichols' voice was soft. His gaze never strayed from the suddenly spectral figure sitting up in the darkness on the bed.

"They can go screw themselves," Degrasse whispered. He was fumbling with the chain latch that secured the front door. "I'm telling you, this wasn't in the deal. When something comes up that's not part of the deal you have to get new instructions, right?"

"Yeah. Yeah, that's right." Nichols was crowding his companion. "Hurry up."

"I just want to be left alone," Jake said plaintively. He started to get off the bed. A low moan issued from Nichols' throat. He clawed at the door, nearly pulling it off its hinges in his haste to escape once Degrasse had the chain unhooked. Both men half fell, half sprinted out the open door. Jake found himself staring at the naked Arizona night.

XI

Slowly his fright and concern gave way to confusion and then more prosaic concerns. He knew that he had to get out of the room, out of the motel, and do it fast. He remembered the frightened big man muttering something about others waiting.

He fumbled quickly through his suitcase, taking only his razor and toothbrush and pills. Then he grabbed his wallet from the end table and debated which way to go.

Dimly he remembered the dark shadows emerging from the vicinity of the bathroom. He closed the front door and locked it, then made his way to the john. Warm air drifted in through the open window. At least, he thought wryly, he'd been practicing for this. Using the john as a stepstool he quickly boosted himself up and out the back of the building.

He stood there wheezing and trying to catch his breath. A glance to right and then left revealed only a moonlit vacant lot full of high weeds and old corn. Making up his mind quickly, he started jogging along the back wall of the motel. Crickets commented on his progress from their abodes in the corn.

It was a long building. The motel was one of several cheap national chains. His heart was beginning its first warning rumble as he rounded the far corner.

The office formed a brightly lit rectangle at the far end of the building, like the head of some giant nocturnal insect. Jack could see the buzzer which would summon the night clerk. Through the glass door and high windows he could also just make out several cars parked around his old Ford. Men stood there, talking quietly and occasionally glancing in the direction of his room. They were a fair distance off but there was enough light from the moon and the motel parking lights for him to make out the two men who'd been in his room. They were talking to the others and occasionally one or the other would gesticulate violently toward the building.

Leaning against the wall, he made a hurried, frantic survey of his surroundings. He could dash into the office and summon the night clerk, who could then call the police. But would they come quickly enough? This was a small town. And what reason could he invent that would make sense to a small-town cop? He stood there trying to sweat out a decision. A noise like an overwrought coffee pot made the choice for him.

The big Greyhound was idling in the parking lot of the restaurant next door. The restaurant backed onto a much more expensive motel than the one Jake had chosen. He pushed away from the wall and started toward the bus, trying to hug the darkest shadows between his motel and the next. His gaze was fixed on the open door of the bus. It could snap shut at any instant, he knew, stranding him there out in the open.

The two men who'd been sent in to bring him out had been startled by his little trick. He suspected neither they nor their numerous backups would be so easily startled a second time. The pain in his chest was a steady ache now, though the real throbbing still held off.

He forced himself to slow down as he neared the bus, forced himself not to look back over his shoulder for the heavy hand he expected to come down on him at any moment. But nothing grabbed at his shirt, and now he was so close to the bus that there would be witnesses . . . if everyone aboard wasn't fast asleep, he reminded himself.

Then he was mounting the steel stairs. They seemed six feet high to him. He was inside the bus, a warm metal cocoon. A hand touched his back and he jerked violently around, found himself staring down into the face of the bus driver.

"Hey, partner, what's wrong with you?"

"Nothing." He drank in the uniform, the insignia on the driver's cap. He'd never been so happy to see a picture of a dog before in his life. "I've just had a long night, that's all."

"Yeah, ain't we all. Pick a seat. We're leavin'." The driver stepped past him into his own chair.

"What's the first stop?" Jake asked him, allowing himself a quick glance out the windows and back towards his own motel. Still no sign of business-suited figures racing across the blacktop toward the bus. He decided they were still debating what to do next. He couldn't see his door but imagined several of them trying the lock.

Wasn't it amazing how bad a scare a little trick like that could throw into two grown men? It astonished him. It was a good trick, and he'd have to remember it if he encountered any more guns. It was hard to remember. He'd never made anything as complex as a pistol slipt before, or slipt that much. But he was fairly confident he could do it a second time. It seemed that he only had to do it once and then it became easy.

"Lordsburg," the driver said.

"What? Oh, next stop, yeah. Lordsburg." Jake knew he hadn't passed through a town named Lordsburg.

"New Mexico," the driver added helpfully as he scribbled something in his log.

"That's where I'm headed," Jake told him.

"Right. Well, you can pay the agent when we get there. You look like an okay guy to me, and I'm running late."

"Thanks." Jake worked his way toward the back of the bus, found himself a seat on an empty aisle. There were maybe eight other passengers and he had a fair amount of privacy, for which he was very grateful. He hadn't had much privacy lately.

The first thing he did was take the little vial from his shirt pocket. It was a fresh bottle and he neatly broke the seal. He swallowed two of the nitros, added a calcium blocker even though he knew he might be overloading his system momentarily, and then leaned back against the heavily padded seat and tried to relax.

The air brakes holding the bus in place let go with a wet hiss and it trundled out of the parking lot onto the main street. Jake allowed himself a look out the back window. The pavement was deserted. No one was running frantically after the departing bus.

It was still hard to believe, but then the image they had of him was of an old man with a bad heart. If they hadn't been in contact with the men who'd driven the pickup they might not envision him worming his way out the back window and running to freedom. As frightened as the two men who'd come into the room seemed to be, they might forget to mention that they'd left the bathroom window open. And with any luck they'd all spend several hours scouring the land surrounding the motel before someone thought about the bus that had been idling in the parking lot next door. With more luck, they might not think of the bus at all.

The nitro did its job. The calcium blocker would take a little longer, but would protect him all the way into tomorrow morning. Already the angina had faded and the pain was beginning to leave him. He was glad it was night and dark, glad that his few fellow passengers couldn't see the way the sharp fire in his chest twisted his expression. He put both arms across his ribs and squeezed. It did nothing for his heart but it helped him in the mind.

Mandy, Mandy, he thought tiredly, what am I to do? How are you going to help your Uncle Jake out of this? Right now final solutions didn't seem half as important as just getting to Port Lavaca. Just seeing Mandy again, holding his grandniece in his arms, that was a worthy enough rationale for all the trouble he'd been put through. She was the closest thing to a child he'd ever have. Maybe these awful people would hound him until his heart finally gave in, but at least he'd see his Mandy one last time. Wendy too, and that nice fella she'd married, Arriaga, and maybe his grandnephew Martin. It would be great seeing them all again, even if he'd been forced into it.

His heart was easy again. He wrestled with the lever that let his seat recline and snuggled down as best he could. He'd grabbed his coat on the way out, but he didn't need it. The bus was nice and warm.

Was a pretty good trick, he told himself smugly. Making the gun slipt like that. The rag, too. It never occurred to him as he drifted off into a sound sleep, lulled by the gentle vibration of the bus and the engine's steady hum, that the best trick of all had been making the powerful odor of the ether vanish completely.

"I'm not going back in there," Degrasse insisted.

"Look," said the well-dressed man leaning up against the flank of the Continental, "you and Nichols get your butts back in there right now and find out what's doing with that old man. Some very important people want to see him and I'm not leaving this burg without him. You catch my drift?"

"Yeah, and you catch mine," countered Degrasse. "You know how long we've done jobs for CCM? Long time."

Drew nodded patiently.

"You ever hear of us being afraid of anything before? You hear any stories of us backing down on an assignment before?"

"You come highly recommended to the Coast," Drew admitted. "That means nothing to me *now*."

"Well it damn well ought to mean something to you," said Degrasse, "because we—"

"Shut up," snapped Drew. "Keep it down. There are other people in this motel, you know." He pushed himself away from the Continental. "If you hadn't come so well recommended I wouldn't be so surprised at what I'm hearing from you now."

"You should have been there in the room with us," Degrasse told him. "You wouldn't be so surprised."

"Listen," said Drew placatingly, "I don't know what you guys think you saw in there, but—"

"*Think* we saw?" Degrasse glanced up at his companion. "Come on. Let's show him your gun."

"Oh, then you *will* go back inside?"

"Sure, we'll go back . . . if you and and some of the others come with us." He gestured toward the other half dozen strong-arm types spotted around the parking lot. Two sat in the back seat of the Ford Galaxie, waiting for a driver who wouldn't show.

"Real tough old man, is he?" Drew taunted them.

"Give us a break, man. At least until you see what we're talking about."

"That's about the only break you're going to get." Drew's tone was threatening. He waved to the others and they began to converge on the Continental. Once assembled, the little army advanced on room twenty-three.

It took only a minute to open the locked door. An empty room awaited their inspection. Jake Pickett was long gone now, wafted to freedom by a diesel guardian angel at sixty-five miles per.

They found an open suitcase, toiletry items, and a disturbed bed. They also recovered the component parts of a .38 special, along with a handful of loose threads which might once have formed a piece of cloth.

Drew differed from Degrasse and Nichols and the men who hurried out back to search the cornfield. He was intelligent enough to recognize the importance of something he did not understand, sensible enough to know someone else would have to come up with the missing answers. So he had the pistol pieces and rag threads collected and sealed in separate plastic bags.

Already he was composing the message he would have to deliver to his employer. Huddy was going to be very angry. Drew had had the opportunity to see how the executive reacted to disappointment, knew what to anticipate. A couple of plastic bags were a lousy substitute for the old man. Huddy never had explained the reason for his interest in the old man and Drew hadn't asked. It wasn't his place to ask. Going on what these two local stumblebums swore had happened and judging from the contents of the plastic bags, however, Drew was beginning to have some inkling. He didn't spend much time thinking about it because it didn't make any sense.

No matter. They'd get Pickett. Even if Huddy vacillated, they'd get Pickett. For Drew the business was becoming personal.

"I know she misses her brother." Arriaga Ramirez stood to the right of the sink, drying dishes. One of these days maybe they'd make enough to afford a dishwasher. He was an incongruous sight, standing there in the kitchen handling the dishware in his big hands. No one would dare joke about it, though.

He wasn't a tall man. Barely five-nine, but with the build of a professional wrestler. Coupled with a rough, almost brutal face, it gave him a wholly unwarranted threatening appearance. Arriaga Ramirez wouldn't hurt a fly. He commanded the quiet respect of his community, his friends and his fellow fishermen. A soft-spoken, deeply religious family man, he wanted nothing more than to be left alone to do his work and enjoy his friends and family. His aspirations were simple and uncomplicated, so he was rarely disappointed and often amazed at the surprises life sprang on him. He was trying to make sense of one of those surprises right now.

"It's just that it's an awkward time for me to suddenly take off."

"It's not really time off," Wendy argued. "It's not the season now."

"You know what I mean." He finished another plate and stacked it neatly atop the pile in the cabinet above. "You know what halibut's bringing these days."

"The halibut will still be there when we get back."

"I know that, but the weather may not be. I explained it to you before."

"Oh come on, Arri. It's a long way 'til November."

"The Gulf has her own seasons," he countered. "You know how capricious the weather can be." Capricious was Arriaga's favorite word of the week. He learned new words from his daughter. Arriaga had missed a lot of schooling in his youth, but he was damned if he was going to appear ignorant in front of his daughter's friends. So he would nod knowingly whenever Amanda Rae used a word he didn't recognize and then sneak off at night to look it up in the dictionary. He'd use it until he felt comfortable with it.

Amanda was completely aware of what her father was doing, of course, but she maintained her end of the fiction and he held to his. In that way daughter educated father without any damage to the latter's ego. It was a little game, full of secret love.

"That still doesn't help her forget her brother." Wendy dug at the skillet with the scrubbing pad. What she wouldn't give for some pots and pans coated with teflon or silverstone. But she was still short on the trading stamps and it seemed like the harder she saved, the faster inflation drove the price of the cookware up. It was a lot better than what her mother had had to cook with, though, she reminded herself. She bore down still harder with the scrubber.

"I miss him, too," Arriaga confessed. He was equally proud of his son and his daughter. In spite of her handicap they would soon begin making preparations for Amanda to go off to college. There didn't seem to be any question of her receiving a full scholarship. Martin wasn't quite as smart, but he'd qualified for work and grant programs and they were managing. None of the other fishermen had a boy in college, much less a daughter preparing to join him.

"We're going to need the extra money we can make from the halibut, for Amanda."

"*If* you catch any halibut," Wendy pointed out.

"If we do, maybe you won't have to use the trading stamps for those new dishes you want."

"The pots and pans can wait a while longer," she said, wincing as her knuckles scraped the pan. "It's Amanda's happiness I'm concerned about, not mine."

"You two are really set on this, aren't you?"

"Amanda is. And if Amanda is, then I am, Arri."

"Then I'll just have to work something out with the Sanchezes and Grissom, won't I?"

She put down her dishes and put her arms around him. "I guess you will. The halibut will wait."

"They say all good things are worth waiting for."

Decidely uninterested in the moans and groans of plebeian domestic bliss, Ruth Somerset sighed and shut off the recorder. These perople were puerile in outlook and boring in conversation, and she was sick of listening to their petty concerns and problems. She rested a long moment, then dialed a certain number.

"Benjamin?"

"Hi, sweetness. What's happening?"

"It sounds like the grandniece's family has decided to take

the coming weekend off. They've got that older kid up at Texas A & M and the grandniece is determined to visit him."

"Well hell," Huddy muttered. "Why'd it have to be this weekend? That's rotten timing."

"What difference does it make? Didn't your people pick the old man up last night?"

"No, they did not."

"What the fuck happened?" This would be over and done with by now if their positions had been reversed from the beginning, she knew. She should have managed the pickup while Huddy squatted in this hole monitoring tapes. But she wasn't in a position to say that sort of thing . . . yet.

"I'm not sure." To his credit her lover sounded just as fed up as she was. "I can't seem to get a straight answer out of Drew. You remember him, the guy I sent out from L.A. to supervise things.

"All he can tell me is that something spooked the two locals he sent in to winkle Pickett out of his motel room and that by the time he got things back under control, the old man had split. They still haven't found him. They will. It's a small town. But I don't like what's going on down there. Apparently the two who tried to take Pickett are still half incoherent. That's what Drew tells me, anyway."

"Did he do another wheel trick?" she asked.

"No. Nothing like that. It all took place in Pickett's motel room. No cars involved. That's part of what I don't understand. I'm going out there myself. This is the second foul-up and I'm sick of excuses. Drew's a good man, as intelligent as apes go, but I can see that I'm going to have to direct this pickup in person."

"But if you don't know where he is . . . ?"

"Like I said, it's a small town. The refuges available to an old man are finite. At worst we know which way he's headed."

"We *think* we know which way he's headed, you mean."

"That's why you're holding down the fort at the end of the hypothetical line, sweet thing. Take this sudden desire on the part of the grandniece to go visiting. From what you've told me that doesn't make any sense, even to her parents. You're *positive* the grandniece hasn't had a call from the old man?''

"No way, lover. We've got every phone and room in that house bugged. Everything comes through loud and clear. I suppose it's possible for her to have talked to him on a friend's telephone. The grandniece rolls around the neighborhood visiting girlfriends. I just don't see that as a valid likelihood. Pickett wouldn't know which friend to call and there's no way for the grandniece to know how or where to call him.''

"I agree. Look, I want that family kept there until we pick him up. I don't want them floating around some crowded university town. I know it's far-fetched, but if the grandniece has talked to Pickett they may be trying to set up a rendezvous outside her home town. Just keep them at home for another week.''

"You're still concerned that he might make it all the way down here?'' She made no effort to conceal her surprise.

"The way things have gone so far, nothing would surprise me. I'm just covering all the bases, sweet thing. You know me.''

"Yes, I know you, Benjamin. Very well. I'll see to it that they spend this weekend at home. How far do you want me to go to insure that?''

"Whatever's necessary. Just don't overdo it. Use local people. Houston should be able to help you out.''

Somerset replied somewhat testily, "I think I know how to handle it.''

"I never doubted that you did. See you, lover.''

"Good-bye, Benjy.'' She hung up absently, her thoughts elsewhere.

Wendy Ramirez rolled over in bed and frowned at the darkness. Strange hammering sounds had awakened her, and they weren't caused by the waters of the bay slapping at the seawall back of the house. They came from somewhere out front.

She sat there, supporting herself on one elbow, and listened. It might be a neighborhood dog at the garbage cans again, except tomorrow wasn't garbage collection day and everybody's containers would be locked away in garages. Some kids fooling around, probably, but . . . she nudged her husband.

"Arri?"

"Hmmm? What?"

"Arri," she whispered, "I hear somebody out in front of the house."

"You always hear somebody out front," he mumbled.

"No, not this time. I really hear something this time." She shook him so he wouldn't go back to sleep. "Please, Arri. See what it is."

He groaned as he turned onto his back, blinking at her in the near blackness. "Alright. What is it with women and noises in the night?"

"It goes back to the cave days," she told him. "Be glad it's not a saber-toothed tiger."

He smiled up at her, his teeth white in the dimness. "Probably a couple of milk-toothed kittens." He glanced over at the clock. "Three A.M." He added a half-intelligible curse in Spanish and slipped out of the bed. Legs went into underwear and jeans, feet into a pair of sandals. Wendy was sitting up, fully awake now, watching him.

Exiting the bedroom he staggered into the living room, scratching at his scalp. A glance out the front window showed nothing . . . no, wait a minute. He squinted toward the driveway. There was movement there. Port Lavaca was too small to be afflicted with such big city ills as car thieves, but Arriaga did not hold to the Pollyanna view of small town life that some rural inhabitants clung to. There was a first time for everything.

He felt under the couch for the steel pipe he kept there and quietly opened the front door. The moon was just enough of a lamp to allow him to see across the battered lawn and through the trees lining the long driveway. Someone was definitely fooling with the van. That van had cost Arriaga half a season's work because of the wheelchair lift and other special equipment installed for Amanda's comfort.

"Hey!" he called out. The movement ceased along with the faint knocking sounds. "Hey you! Man, if you know what's good for you you better get moving. *Comprende*?" No sign of activitiy or retreat.

The waterfront wasn't all quaint characters, camaraderie

and fish stories. Arriaga had learned how to handle himself at a young age. Now he started slowly toward the driveway.

"Look, man, I don't know who you are or what you think you're doing, but you've got five seconds to split before I call the cops to—"

Something hit him from behind. He staggered but didn't go down. As he turned he saw the tire iron coming toward him again and swung blindly with the pipe even as he was falling backward. The end of the pipe made contact with something yielding and a cry of pain filled the night. Wet stuff splattered his face, warm and salty. Blood, not mine, he thought as he collapsed to the driveway and rolled over. He fought to clear his eyes. Something hit him again, not as hard as the first time, but hard enough. Dream voices reached him.

"Let's get the hell out of here."

Then darkness.

The sheriff's sympathy wasn't forced, wasn't fake-professional. He'd known Arriaga and Wendy Ramirez for a long time. "You sure you never got a look at them?"

"No." Arriaga sat on the couch in the living room. The pipe he'd used the previous night lay on the coffee table in front of him. Wendy sat close to him, attentive and concerned. A cold compress rested on the back of her husband's neck. The sheriff leaned back in his chair.

"Doesn't make any sense to me, Arri. What would a bunch of kids want with—"

"Wasn't kids," Arriaga said curtly.

"How do you know, if you didn't get a look at them? Nothing personal, Arri. I'm not questioning you, but you have to look at this from my point of view."

"Look, Benbrook, that was no kid that hit me. Kids would've run like blazes the moment I stepped out the front door. These people didn't run."

"Kids could freeze if they were frightened enough," the sheriff argued.

"I'm telling you, Benbrook, these weren't kids. There were two, maybe three of them."

"Well, whoever they were, they didn't get away with anything. Frankly, I don't think theft was what they had in mind. That's why I tend to think it was a bunch of kids, Arri. I don't see why a couple of grown men would take the time or trouble to vandalize your van.''

"No kids from around here would do anything like that,'' Arriaga muttered. "You know that, Benbrook.''

"Sure I do. I'm just trying to make sense out of this, like you, Arri, and you're not helping me much.''

"I'm sorry. *Que lástima*.'' He winced, put one hand to the ice pack. Wendy squeezed his arm reassuringly.

"What about you, Wendy?'' said the sheriff. "Did you see anything?''

"Nothing,'' she confessed. "I didn't even leave the bedroom until some time had gone by and Arri hadn't returned. That's when I went outside and found''—she hesitated—"found him lying there next to the van. For a minute I thought he was dead.''

"Felt like it.'' Arriaga indicated the section of pipe. "I got one of them. In the mouth, I think. I hope he's feeling it this morning.''

"If it wasn't straight vandalism,'' the sheriff said thoughtfully, "then they were after the battery or something. If so, they were amateurs because they sure made a mess under your hood. Professional car thieves wouldn't be that sloppy or uncertain. Wires cut all over the place. The distributor's busted. Maybe they were trying to pry it out.''

"Maybe,'' said Arriaga, not much caring.

"Wendy, Arri, we'll get right on this. I'll shoot the information up and down the coast.'' He stood. "But without any descriptions of the assailants. . . .'' He shrugged. "Probably out-of-towners looking to pick up something to hock on their way through. You were unlucky enough to have the vehicle they picked on.''

"Yeah,'' said Arriaga.

"It could've been a lot worse, Arri. When you heard them monkeying around in your driveway you should've stayed in the house and called us.''

"I thought like you, Benbrook. That it was probably just a couple of kids I could scare away. Besides, if I'd called you, by the time some deputy could've showed up they might already have taken off with what they wanted. Nothing personal, Benbrook.''

"No offense taken, Arri. I've got two deputies and a lot of ground to cover. Sorry about the damage.''

"That's no problem. Insurance will cover it. It's Amanda I'm sorry for.''

"Amanda?'' The sheriff frowned uncertainly. He knew the Ramirez's daughter. Everyone knew everyone in Port Lavaca.

"We'd sort of decided to take the weekend off to go up and visit her brother at A & M.''

"Can't you still do that?''

"Not really.'' Arriaga shook his head, but only slightly because of the pain it produced at the back of his neck. "First off, I don't feel much like driving right now. More importantly, it's almost impossible to stuff her wheelchair and accessories into the back of the VW. It wouldn't be a very comfortable weekend wrestling with that, either for us or Amanda. Anyway, the doctor says no driving for me for a few days. No fishing, either, but I can work on the boat if it doesn't mean moving around too much.'' He glanced apologetically at his wife. "Sorry, *querida*.''

"That's alright, Arri. Amanda will understand. The important thing now is for you to get well, and for the sheriff to catch those awful people before they hurt anyone else.''

"We'll do our best, Wendy. You know that.''

"I know you will, Benbrook. Are you sure you can't stay for some coffee and muffins?''

"Believe me, I'd like to.'' The sheriff shrugged. "What the hell, why not?''

As they started toward the kitchen Amanda hurriedly backed her wheelcahir out of the hallway and rolled into her own room. She was more than just concerned now. At first she'd been terrified for her father. Now she was afraid not just for him but for her mother and herself as well.

If her father was right and the people who'd vandalized their van the previous night weren't kids, then she had a pretty good idea where they'd come from. She conjured up an image of the bugs and listening devices she'd uncovered, sucking at their privacy. The people on the other end knew everything that went on in the Ramirez household. They knew about the plan to go up to College Station to see her brother. It was clear now that they suspected some sort of collusion between her and her uncle, or else they just wanted his only relatives where they could keep tabs on them. Yés, that made sense.

His only relatives. . . . She'd read lots of spy novels. Relatives could be used to force someone to do something he didn't want to do. Threats. . . . It was getting more and more complicated. She'd never thought of herself and her family as being in danger from the people who were after her Uncle Jake. Everything was changing too quickly for her to adjust to, too fast to anticipate.

Her confidence was beginning to evaporate, her determination to falter. After all, she was only sixteen. Maybe what she'd read in books and seen in movies wasn't enough to enable her to outguess the sort of people she was up against. Maybe real life was full of nastier surprises than she'd believed possible. Last night was a good example of one.

She sat there in the chair, listening to the faint conversation coming from her parents and the sheriff, and chewed worriedly on her lower lip. She had to tell her Uncle Jake about what had happened. She didn't want to. It would only worry him more. But he ought to know, should know.

Several passengers turned to look toward the rear of the bus. The old man in the back was twisting awkwardly as he moaned in his sleep, talking to something unseen. Such sights were common enough on transcontinental buses. The passengers gradually returned to their own business. The old man gave no indication of getting violent, and he was obviously no wino. His moans weren't strong enough to reach to the front of the bus. The driver kept his attention on the road.

The motel wasn't as accessible as the potash plant outside Phoenix, but Huddy insisted on visiting the exact spot where Pickett had slipped past his people for the second time. An old homily persisted in taunting him: If a man does thee once, it's his fault. If he does thee twice, it's thy fault. Huddy felt responsible for the failure. There weren't going to be any more failures.

The motel manager stared through his office window at the

conclave surrounding room twenty-three. When one of the neatly dressed, solemn-visaged men assembled there threw him a warning look he quickly returned to watching the soap opera unspooling on channel ten. He vaguely recalled the last occupant of the room which was attracting so much unusual attention: old man, balding in front, pleasant and friendly. What had he done to attract the notice of such people?

Well, it was none of his business and he wasn't likely to find anything but trouble by inquiring further. He submerged himself in the maudlin antics onscreen.

On inspection Huddy saw nothing unusual about the motel room. There was the bed where the two hired hands had confronted Pickett. He inspected the bathroom, the window through which the old man had escaped, the cornfield out back. The two locals who'd missed the pick-up stood near the foot of the bed and waited. They seemed competent enough . . . until Pickett's name was mentioned. Then they turned surly and reticent.

Feeling slightly self-conscious without knowing why, Huddy sat down on the rumpled bed and listened while Drew spoke.

"I had the town searched half a dozen times. No sign of him. Nobody's seen him, either."

"How about the Tucson motels?" Huddy asked.

"Can't say. If he's retracing his route he'll be hard to run down. Our people up there can only do so much, Mr. Huddy. Big-city cops get suspicious when strangers start asking the kinds of questions the police like to reserve for themselves. Even here we've had to be damn careful. So it's possible he could still be here in town."

"Okay. Keep on it." Huddy nodded, dismissing Drew. Degrasse and Nichols moved to join him, but Huddy stopped them sharply. "Not you two. I'm not through with you yet."

They halted irritably. Huddy let them stand there and stew in their own worries while he turned his attention to the two bath towels laid out on the foot of the bed. One supported a tiny mound of threads. They weren't half as intriguing to Huddy as the disassembled .38 Special that was spread out on the other towel. It looked as if it had been broken down by a small-arms expert. They still hadn't found the hollow-point shells.

He tapped the barrel. "This just fell apart, you say?"

The locals exchanged a look. Huddy prodded them. "Come on, guys. I know a helluva lot more about this old man and what's really going down than Drew does. I'm a lot more inclined to believe anything you say than he is. *Anything*."

Nichols hesitated, then said quickly, "There wasn't any doubt about it, sir. The gun just came apart. *He* did it. The old man. I don't know how he did it, but he did it. I'm not sure I'd want to know how he did it." He was eyeing the pillows as if Pickett's ghost might suddenly materialize to give them another demonstration.

"And after that, you panicked."

"Hey, look . . ." Degrasse started to protest.

Huddy raised a calming hand. "I'm not criticizing you, just trying to establish a sequence of events. They gun fell to pieces, and you panicked."

"Okay, so we panicked." Degrasse still sounded resentful. "You would've too, if you'd been there." Huddy didn't comment.

"Excuse me." A very thin young man was leaning through the open doorway.

"What is it?" Huddy was irritated at having been interrupted.

"Well sir, it's only that. . . . You are the man from California, aren't you?"

"Yes, yes. Spit it out, man."

He stepped all the way into the room, eyed the other two men uncertainly. "I was on duty at the far end of the motel last night, when everything went down. Over by the manager's office."

"What about it?" Huddy didn't like people wasting his time, especially now that he had no time to waste.

"It's not like I actually *saw* the old man get on the bus, but I—"

Huddy instantly forgot about the pistol and the pieces of rag. "Wait a minute. What bus?"

"There was a Greyhound parked over at the Ramada Inn

next door. I checked it out, sir. It's the regular Benson stop.''

"That's it," said Huddy with grim satisfaction. "That's got to be it. The old man has a heart condition. He's in no shape to be running any marathons. I don't see any tourists stopping to pick him up in the middle of the night. That's it. What's your name, kid?''

"Jason, sir.''

"Well, Jason, you hustle your ass over to the Ramada Inn and pick up a copy of the Greyhound schedule. Find out where that bus was coming from when it stopped here last night and where it's going. You two." Degrasse and Nichols all but snapped to attention, relieved to be subject to something like orders instead of unanswerable questions. "Start checking all the towns along the interstate where that bus stopped between leaving here last night and now. They're mostly all small towns between here and Texas."

Huddy's mind worked furiously. Of course the old man could work to confuse his trail. He could get off anywhere. Change buses, change systems, take a roundabout route; only he didn't credit Pickett with that much imagination. From the first the old man had struck Huddy as a simple, uncomplicated type. For now, anyway, they'd proceed on that assumption.

"If he's still aboard the same bus, then we've got him."

"Yes sir." Degrasse and Nichols moved to follow the young man out of the room. They were glad to be rid of the snooty executive from the Coast.

Alone in the room, Huddy let himself lean back on the bed. Sure, Pickett had snuck onto the bus last night. No wonder Drew's people hadn't been able to find him. This next time they wouldn't charge in early in the evening. They'd wait until they were certain he was asleep. Surely he couldn't do his little tricks in his sleep. Now where would be the best place to pick him up?

There were several maps crammed into his jacket. He found the one he now had to use. It covered the Southwestern United States. On it a number of towns had been circled in red and had code numbers inscribed next to them.

The particular map Huddy was studying showed Consolidated Chemical and Mining's America. The coded, encircled communities boasted CCM facilities. He traced the likely route of a cross-country bus. It might veer south toward Houston, or it might go into Dallas. If it did terminate in Houston, then it would have to pass through this town, this one, then . . . Fort Stockton, he decided. A medium-sized city in central Texas where CCM maintained a small distribution facility. It was just large enough to have the people he'd need, yet small enough for the business to be carried out in anonymity. A good place to confront Pickett.

He'd fly on ahead of Pickett's bus and make the necessary preparations out of CCM's regional office in San Antonio. Ruth could join him there. That ought to please her. She'd been pestering him to get out of that coast town for days. Yes, she could replace Drew and he could send the big man down to Houston to take over her responsibilities for a while. Let the neanderthal listen to dumb household conversations. She could return to complete her "inspection" of the Matagorda computer facilities after the business with Pickett was all wrapped up. Then, the Bahamas. Somerset and himself on a deserted beach, nude and alone. He resented Pickett for putting off that vision yet again. He had no more sympathy left for the irritating old man.

Valuable old man, though, he reminded himself. Yes, Ruth would be better company in mid-Texas than Drew. He didn't need the big man from L.A. anymore. He would be on the scene himself.

There would be no more mistakes.

_____ **XII** _____

As always, Ruth Somerset turned heads as she strode down the corridor in CCM's San Antonio office building. She ignored the inevitable stares, the whispered comments. Even if she'd been inclined to reply to the yokels admiring her, she was too happy to be out of that damned motel to take unbrage at the lewdest comment. San Antonio wasn't New York or London, but it was one hell of an improvement over her surroundings of the past week.

Surveillance of the Ramirez household continued without her, under the supervision of Huddy's pet ape, Drew. Now that the family was effectively stuck there for a while, her decision-making presence wasn't required.

Finding Huddy turned out to take longer than anticipated. She eventually located him outside the building's basement laboratory. The outer office was familiar. There was one beneath CCM's Los Angeles complex that looked just like it.

He was sitting on a couch, puffing absently on one of those silly small cigars he affected.

"Hi, Benjy!" She rushed over and threw herself into his lap. He grunted, responded half-heartedly at best. She pulled back and frowned at him.

"What's the matter? Aren't you glad to see me?"

"That's a rhetorical question and you know it. Of course I'm glad to see you, sweet thing."

"I see," she said flatly. "I don't *know* how I could have questioned it. I guess I was just overwhelmed by the fervor of your greeting."

"Sorry." He manufactured a small smile. "I really am glad to see you, even if I'm not showing it much. What's new at your end?"

"Nothing you don't already know. You told me to keep the niece's family in Port Lavaca. That's where they are, and that's where they'll stay for at least a week. Drew can watch them now. We did have a little trouble. You heard?"

"Not the details."

She sighed. "The father decided to play hero. One of our Houston people lost a few teeth, suffered a minor concussion. Nothing that can't be repaired. They did get their job done before super-spic showed up. That van won't be going to College Station or anywhere else for a while."

"They only crippled the van? I thought you told me the family had two cars?"

"They do, but the other's a VW bug. They can't get around with the grandniece in it. Not easily, anyway. The van has a wheelchair lift and other special facilities for her."

"You say they'll be stuck there for a week?"

"More or less. No way to say for sure. If the local garage gets the replacement parts in earlier, they could be fixed up that much sooner. Doesn't look like it, though.

"The local fuzz think it was just a bungled rip-off job by a couple of city boys intent on swiping the van's battery and stuff." Her expression changed. "We've got another problem now, though."

"Great." He pushed back his hair. "What?"

"I was upstairs for a while and took the time to check in with my office. You know Hank Moorhead?"

Huddy nodded. Moorhead was a second vice-president in charge of general West Coast Administration. About five, six years older than Huddy, straightforward, unimaginative but persistent. Like the other younger executives at CCM West he'd reacted morosely to all the acclaim Huddy and Somerset had received as a result of the successful Riverside dump cleanup.

"What's that turgid bastard been up to?"

"The two of us have been moving around a lot lately. You especially, Benjamin. It's been relatively simple for me to cover for my movements. Checking up on Houston's cogitative facilities, remember? You suggested that one yourself.

"You, however, have been bouncing around too much. First back and forth to Riverside, then Phoenix, then some small town in southern Arizona. . . . What the hell's the name?"

"Benson," Huddy reminded her.

"Yeah, Benson. Now here. Anyway, Moorhead's sticking his nose down to where he's beginning to smell stuff. I can't fend him off because my department doesn't interact with his. He has his own computer section."

"Now who's worrying too much?" said Huddy coolly. "Don't worry about Moorhead. I can handle him."

"Of course you can, Benjy." What's he so uptight about, she wondered? "There *is* something bothering you. Tell mama, Benjamin. I know you too well."

"Too well for what?"

"Don't fence with me, lover, and don't try changing the subject. Your mouth says one thing, your manner another." She had a sudden, distressing thought. "Don't tell me that you've suddenly decided all this trouble's been for nothing? That the old man's a goof trickster after all and that there's nothing to any of your suspicions?" All of her initial skepticism came flooding back.

"Oh, there's something to my suspicions, alright," Huddy assured her. "But you're right about the old man not being exactly what I thought. At least, I think he isn't."

"You're confusing me, Benjy. I don't want more confusion." As she'd done on several previous occasions she wondered briefly if perhaps she hadn't thrown in her lot at CCM with the wrong man, his apparent intelligence and good looks notwithstanding.

"I'm just not sure of anything anymore," he muttered. "Especially if it involves an old man named Pickett." He stood, turned from the couch.

"You're not letting him make you paranoid, Benjy? I'm the only paranoid allowed around here." He didn't smile at the sally. "You don't look so good either, lover."

"I don't feel so good." He gestured toward a door. "Come on inside."

They had to utilize their company identification cards twice, inserting them into slots set next to thick doors, in order to gain admittance to the lab itself. Most of CCM's facilities were constructed above such subterranean lab complexes. Burying the labs enabled the company to insure secrecy as well as helping to contain any dangerous explosions or chemical leaks.

There was one particularly elaborate research complex interred just outside the city limits of Madison, Wisconsin. That facility was built like an iceberg, nine-tenths underground. CCM did work there for the Pentagon on chemical and bacteriological weapons systems. The fact wasn't advertised because if the local dairy farmers had been aware of what was developing in their midst they would have raised bloody hell all the way back to Washington.

"Hello, Mr. Huddy." A soft-faced man in a white lab smock strolled over to greet them. He glanced questioningly at Somerset. Huddy ignored the unspoken request for an introduction.

"Where are the materials, Monsey?"

"Over here, sir. We've just set them aside for a little while. We're working on graphic analysis right now." He continued to stare at Somerset until Huddy could no longer reasonably ignore him.

"Monsey, this is Ruth Somerset from the Los Angeles office. Ruth, Kendall Monsey."

"Hello, miss."

"Morning." She took an instant dislike to the researcher. Many men, sometimes consciously, sometimes otherwise, undressed her with their eyes. She didn't mind being admired, but there were other things people could do with eyes and expressions. Bejamin looked at her admiringly. This Monsey had little fingers attached to his eyes, and when he stared at her they went crawling greasily all over her.

He turned to lead them down a spotlessly clean, wide aisle

between two long lab benches. Others labored at benches farther away. All were clad in white.

"Can I answer any questions for you, sir?" he asked as they halted opposite the middle of the workbench.

"Not right now, Monsey. Thanks."

"You're welcome, sir. If you have any questions, miss, Mr. Huddy can show you to my office."

"I'll call you," she assured him. She waited until he was out of earshot. "Filthy little man, Benjamin."

"I don't like him either, but he knows his business. Have a gander."

She turned her attention to the workbench. Carefully laid out on the formica were the components of a .38 police special. Resting in nearby petrie dishes were the fragments of rag taken from Jake Pickett's Benson motel room. She recognized them instantly.

"You told me what happened at the motel. Why show me the results? Am I supposed to draw conclusions from looking at this stuff? It means nothing to me."

"It didn't mean anything to anyone, until Monsey and his people took a close look at the stuff. A real close look. I never thought to have the Phoenix pickup truck inspected closely. First off, it wasn't a company vehicle. Besides, what was there to check? The wheels came off. That's all. Only it's not all.

"This time I thought maybe it might be a good idea to have someone go over the objects that Pickett"—he hesitated— "affected. I thought we might be able to learn something. Well, we have learned something. Maybe. Look closer, Ruth."

She leaned over the table, squinted at the display. The pistol appeared to have been disassembled by an expert. The pieces of cloth might have come from any disintegrating section of fabric.

"I can't say about the gun," she finally decided, standing straight. "As for the threads, maybe the rag your people used was old and rotten. It could've come apart in a fight."

"It came apart, alright, but not in a fight," he told her. "And not in the way I thought it would have, either." His voice was soft, his tone indifferent. He turned to stare down at the workbench and his mind seemed a million miles away.

She couldn't fathom his attitude. Why was he so upset? If Pickett had done these things in the fashion described by eyewitnesses, then events seemed to be confirming all Huddy's initial guesses concerning the old man's peculiar abilities. He ought to be delighted.

That was when she decided to dump him the moment the opportunity presented itself. As soon as she could get out clean she'd start putting some distance between them. If he was going to sink into deep depression every time something happened he hadn't planned for she sure as hell didn't want him around when the time came to make quick, career-crucial decisions.

Her mind worked rapidly. If she watched herself and moved carefully enough to keep him from becoming suspicious, she might be able to claim all the credit for anything beneficial arising out of this Pickett business. If the operation was a complete bust she ought to be able to divorce herself completely from the consequences.

Thus comforted in her own mind she considered her future. Hank Moorhead wasn't quite the dumb flake Huddy insisted he was. Maybe he wasn't especially bright, but he was solid. If he thought he stood a chance of learning something that would take Huddy or Somerset down a notch or two, he'd dig for it like a wildcatter in shale. Huddy, of course, was the fatter target of the two. Yes, Moorhead could be enemy or ally.

She was trying to determine how best to approach him when she returned to L.A. when Huddy said, "Jake Pickett's not telekinetic, Ruth, like I thought . . . like I hoped he might be. He's . . . something else."

"Hmmm? Sorry, Benjy, I wasn't listening. You were drifting, and I was waiting on you."

"Come here." He took her arm, escorted her down to the far end of the workbench. Locked into the lowest shelf was a rack of large test tubes. Each glass cylinder held a differently colored powder. The quantities were very small.

"What do you think those are?" he asked her.

"Really, Benjy," she chided him, "you know I'm not the twenty questions type."

"We found all the pieces of the gun, and all the threads

from the rag. What we didn't find right away were the bullets that had been in the gun when it had come apart." He pointed toward the test tubes. "That's why it took us so long to find them. We had to vacuum the carpet."

She looked at the test tubes a second time, uncomprehendingly. "So they've been ground up for testing. What's that supposed to tell us, Benjy?"

"No, you don't understand," he corrected her patiently. "We haven't ground them up, for testing or for anything else. Pickett ground them up."

Hank Moorhead and intercorporate political machinations were abruptly forgotten. "If this is your idea of a gag, Benjy, now's not the time. I've just spent I forget how many days of utter and complete boredom squatting in a backwoods motel because of your infatuation with this old man."

"It's no joke, Ruth."

"Well then, if you're trying to see how easy I scare. . . ."

"Ruth, I wish it was just a bad joke. As for trying to frighten you, I'm not. Not intentionally, anyway. Myself, I'm already scared shitless." He thumbed a switch hidden beneath the edge of the tabletop. A concealed drawer slid open with a hum. It yielded a thick stack of paper.

"Here. These ought to be familiar to you." He handed her the computer printouts. "Analysis of the powders in those test tubes. When we extracted them from the motel carpeting they were all mixed together. See what they are?" He tapped the papers. "Lead, sulfur, copper . . . the proportions are all just right, even down to those composing the brass casings of the shells. Put them together in the right way and you get six slugs for a .38 special. There are no powdered alloys in those test tubes, either. Only basic elements."

She handed back the papers, waited quietly to hear the rest.

"What I think happened in that motel," Huddy told her softly as he replaced the readouts in the drawer and slammed it shut, "is that our two men entered Pickett's room as planned. This isn't difficult to reconstruct, you know. One of them put the ether-soaked rag over the old man's face. Pickett's whatever-it-is dissolved the rag. Probably broke down the ether as well, because one of the men insists that when the rag came apart the ether smell disappeared."

"I still don't know what you mean, 'broke down'. Benjy—"

"Let me finish, Ruth. Pickett caused the rag to come apart. Then our people improvised to the best of their limited mental abilities. One of them pulled his gun and advanced on Pickett, intending to knock him out. So Pickett had to react a second time, just like he did outside Phoenix.

"Only this time he went further than Phoenix. much further. He didn't just disassemble the threat the way he took the wheels off that pickup truck. He made absolutely certain the most threatening part of the object approaching him was rendered harmless. In this case that would be the bullets in the gun. He made sure that even if they put the gun back together again they weren't going to be able to use it on him." He led her back the way they'd come, picked up one of the pistol's hand-grips.

"See this?" He held it against the metal section of the handle. "They don't fit right anymore. We tried putting the gun back together again. It requires a closer tolerance than, say, slipping wheels back onto an axle. No part of this .38 fits quite right anymore.

"Monsey and his people put the parts under the microscope. You know what they found? There's a tiny layer of steel and/or plastic missing. It's only microns thick, but it's missing. From all around the gun. Pickett doesn't just cause things to come apart. That's what a telekinetic does. Pickett, he . . ." Huddy shook his head and looked empty.

"There's no name for it yet, for what he can do." He gestured at the workbench. "Monsey doesn't understand it either. He has no idea how those bullets were reduced to their basal elements or how that pistol was 'filed' down. But I do. I just don't know what to call it. I suppose you could say that Jake Pickett's a molecular disassembler."

Somerset favored him with a blank stare. She knew what the words implied, but she'd never heard them employed in quite that manner, and certainly never in relation to a human being.

"What we think it means," Huddy explained as he leaned back against the counter, "is that Pickett doesn't simply lift the bullet head off the shell or the barrel off a revolver. Furthermore, it's plain that he has no more idea how he does these things than we do. He's entirely innocent as to the process.

"When he utilizes this ability, when he projects it, he engenders a chemical breakdown at the most basic level in whatever he's concentrating on. The fact that the gun, for example, happens to come to pieces at the places where it's normally joined is apparently a reflection of Pickett's thinking. If he worked at it he could just as easily make the barrel come apart in the middle."

"Then what about the bullets?" she asked quietly.

"I'm not sure. One of two things happened there. Either he was so blinded by fear that he didn't relate to them in the way he did the gun and the rag—or for that matter, those pickup truck wheels or the bottle caps back in L.A.—or else this constant utilization of his ability is making it stronger and the treatment of the shells is the first manifestation of that intensified use.

"Pickett has the ability to destroy the molecular bonds that unite elements in chemical combinations. He can't affect atomic valences. At least, I don't think he can, because the elemental composition of the disintegrated bullets is normal. You know what this means to us?"

"I have a pretty good idea," she replied. "It means that you're going to have one hell of a time bringing him in for testing."

"Oh, we'll get him." Huddy sounded very positive. "He has this peculiar ability, true, but he doesn't know how it works and he's not quite sure how or when to use it. In the final analysis he's just an old man with a heart condition. The most valuable old man in the world, of course." His words quickened, his voice took on a note of barely controlled excitement.

"Don't you see what all this means, Ruth? What's at stake here far exceeds anything I ever dreamed of. Anything anyone's ever dreamed of. If Pickett can do that"—and he gestured down the bench toward the test tubes—"to a handful of bullets, imagine what he could do to a bomber in flight? Or to a nuclear plant in enemy territory?" Something more extreme than mere ambition shone in Benjamin Huddy's eyes. Something which comes within reach of few men and which only saints seem able to resist.

"We've got to keep this quiet, sweetness. I mean really quiet. Besides us only Doctor Navis back in L.A. knows what's really going on, and he's ignorant of recent developments." He gestured across the room to where a cluster of men and women clad in white were conversing in low tones.

"Monsey has suspicions, but at this point he's just guessing. His assistants don't even have suspicions. I think we can keep Monsey in the dark." He let out a short, nervous laugh. "It's not like anyone would believe the truth unless they had visible proof of what Pickett can do."

"Touché," she said sourly. "I still don't see how you're going to be able to pick the old man up."

"It's only a matter of the right time and place. Once we get him drugged he'll be easy enough to handle. The problem with both the attempts outside Phoenix and in Benson was that he saw his assailants and had time to react. We have to get to him when he's asleep. Everything will be worth it, though, when you take a moment to consider what we have here."

Something very dangerous, she thought. Yet the possibilities raised by Jake Pickett's awesome abilities were beginning to seduce her better judgment. Yes, much more than mere money and a few promotions was at stake now. Much more.

An exhausted Jake Pickett had no difficulty in sleeping on the bus. He drifted in and out of consciousness, luxuriating in the smooth ride and the chance to relax. Every time the bus made a stop he anxiously searched the loading dock for signs of men in neat business suits holding damp rags, but as the miles rolled by and none materialized, the tension slowly began to drain from him.

Maybe he'd finally succeeded in discouraging them, he mused. Perhaps they'd given him up as a bad job, or maybe they had lost track of him and were hunting him in Utah or Mexico.

Amanda wasn't nearly so sanguine.

"You're just deluding yourself if you think they've given up on you, Uncle Jake. These aren't the kind of people who give up on something they want. They're just laying back and lulling you into a false sense of security so they can surprise you once you've forgotten about them."

"But there's nothing I can do about it, Mandy." A woman near the middle of the bus turned to frown at his whispering, but said nothing.

"There might be something, Uncle Jake. This is what I think you ought to do. The bugs and taps are still here in the house, so I guess they're still worried about you coming here. There's no other obvious reason for you to come all the way to Texas."

"They can't be sure I'm making this trip to visit you."

"No, they can't be positive. And we're going to do something to really mess up that line of reasoning. Maybe they'll leave us alone and we can get up to the University somehow, where there'll be people around us all the time."

"What do you suggest, Mandy?"

"Uncle Jake, they've been right behind you if not ahead of you ever since you left California."

"Yeah," he admitted reluctantly, "but I lost them outside Tucson."

"Uncle Jake," she said with a sigh, "that's only temporary and you're just fooling yourself if you think otherwise. The thing you have to do is keep them from tracking you down again. You need to get off that bus. Don't get on any other buses, either. If they haven't seen you on the bus they can't be sure you're on it. There's still a chance to really lose them." She paused and he had an image of her rustling something. It was full of lines and colors; a map.

"The interstate forks outside a little town called Kent. Twenty goes northeast to Dallas, Ten comes into Houston. Get off the bus in Kent. I don't know if your bus stops there; it's a pretty small town, but I'm sure the driver will let you off. Don't come toward Houston. Go northeast and come down this way from Dallas. That'll take a little longer but it sure ought to confuse them."

Jake thought for a while, then nodded though she couldn't see the gesture. "That's a good idea, Mandy. Yes, that's just what I'll do." He fell asleep with a pleased smile on his face.

Up by the middle of the bus a plump woman turned to her companion. "Old drunks," she muttered. "They oughtn't to let them on the bus."

___ XIII ___

"You sure this is where you want to get off, mister?"

"I'm sure, son."

The young driver shrugged, brought the bus to a halt by the side of the road. The door opened with a hiss. Jake made his way down the steps, turned to look back up into the bus.

"I've got friends supposed to meet me here," Jake said cheerfully. He nodded southward. "Got a ranch not far from here. This is closer than town for them. Don't worry. They're expecting me."

"Hey, look, man," said an irritated voice from the back of the bus, "we're ten minutes late. I've got to make a connection in Odessa."

"Keep your shirt on," the driver told the anxious passenger. It was none of his business where the old man wanted to get off. But he still didn't feel good about it as he pulled back out onto the interstate. This was lonely country. He kept his eyes on the figure in the rear-view mirror until it had vanished from sight.

As soon as the rumble of the bus had been swallowed by the horizon, Jake turned to examine his surroundings. Getting off the bus outside of town had been his own idea. It was a precaution Mandy would have approved of.

Jackrabbits ruled this country, he suspected, along with coyotes and foxes and vultures. A trio of turkey buzzards made a circle in the sky off to the north, considering something dead. Not a good welcome, he thought. The landscape was flat in every direction, an endless gray plain of gravel, stunted brush and an occasional lonely mesquite. Even the road looked dirty. That made the blue sky appear all the more attractive.

It was warm but not too hot, breezy but not too windy. In another couple of months this barren desert would be transformed into a Gobi-like plateau of subzero temperatures and freezing gales.

The desolation didn't really bother him. Jake had always liked open places. His own home had stood alone among bare rolling hills for many years. It wouldn't be long before Riverside expanded to encroach on his little hill, he knew, surrounding it with modular housing (as the trailer people euphemistically liked to refer to their abodes), condominiums and industrial "parks." Especially now that the dump had been cleaned up.

He marveled at the presence of barbed-wire fencing on either side of the interstate. As if there was anything out here to protect. An occasional car or big truck emerged from the vanishing point at either end of the interstate to shoot past him in blurs of color and steel and fiberglass, all in a rush to come from someplace and get somewhere else. Those traveling eastward were uniform in their indifference to his out-thrust thumb.

He didn't relish spending the night by the side of the road. The weather could change abruptly out here. But at least no one could sneak up on him.

It was mid-afternoon when a big, boxy, four-wheel drive slowed and pulled over next to him. Bronco or Blazer or somesuch. Jake wasn't much on model names, not since the fifties.

The young couple inside looked tired, but the girl leaned out to give Jake a cheery hello. Her hair was jet black and her cheekbones were promontories below her eyes. Part Indian, how much and of what tribe Jake couldn't imagine.

"Car break down, old timer?"

He shook his head as he approached the truck. "Got no car. I was on a bus."

"Well you sure should have stayed there." Her husband sat stolidly behind the wheel, listening with interest. The truck idled roughly. "How the hell did you manage to get yourself dumped way out here?"

"Down on my luck," Jake told her, glad he didn't have to lie. "Had an argument with the driver, too."

"That's tough. Where you headed?"

Jake hesitated only briefly. If these were hirelings of those who sought him so intently they wouldn't be bothering with this friendly small talk. They'd have tried to yank him into the truck by now.

"East," he said simply.

"We're on our way into Fort Worth. See if Jim here can get a job. You can ride in back if you don't mind bouncing around with luggage, dirt and some oilfield stuff."

"Any port in a storm," he said gratefully. She slid forward on her seat and pulled the back toward her, making a path for him. He clambered in. Two suitcases made a serviceable if hard backrest, but there was enough room for him to stretch out.

"I'd like to offer you kids some gas money." The engine of the truck groaned as it shifted into a higher gear and they pulled back out onto the highway. He looked around. The road was empty in both directions. No one had seen him climb into the truck.

"Thanks," said the girl, smiling back at him. "We're okay cashwise. Jim's worked most of the fields between Van Horn and Beaumont. If we have any trouble we'll sneak off the road and scavenge some drip."

Pickett frowned. "Drip what?"

She laughed. "Explain it to him, honey." The driver began to enlighten Jake as to the nature of what flows out of the ground in west Texas and to what uses it may be put. He was a soft-spoken, intense sort. Jake liked him right off. He liked both of them.

Huddy rubbed first the left eye, then the right, then yawned and walked over to the soda machine. After staring at the selections for a minute he turned and walked away, deciding he wasn't really thirsty so much as he was impatient.

There was activity among the men around him. Across the street a bus was pulling into the Ft. Stockton station. Trailways. He considered the soda machine again, then checked his watch.

There was one other stop outside the city and it was also being watched, but if Pickett stepped off to get something to eat or just to stretch, Huddy suspected it would be here in town.

He'd sent Ruth back to Houston to wait for word from him and to check on the niece's family. Actually he just wanted her out of the way. She distracted the team he'd assembled, and he didn't want any distractions around when they contacted Pickett again.

There would be no overt approach this time. There were two men in the crowd milling around the back of the station who carried loaded hypodermics in their pockets. One or the other would surreptitiously slip up behind Pickett and inject him before he even knew he was being attacked. It should all be over in seconds. The liquid in the hypos was very powerful.

Huddy felt it was hours but it was only minutes later that Pickett's bus pulled into the station. Huddy checked the number on the side of the bus. Yes, this was the one they'd kept track of all the way from Benson. Around the station men shifted their positions, readying themselves as the word was passed.

Huddy tensed as the passengers began to disembark: a large black woman with a pair of hyperactive kids, an elderly couple, young men and women wearing backpacks and vacant expressions, one tourist couple who by their accents Huddy thought must be from Ireland. Then the driver.

The bus, as near as Huddy could tell, was now empty. Of Jake Pickett there was no sign. One of his people silently mounted the rear bumper and checked the bathroom in the back. He shook his head negatively. Not hiding in there.

The rest of the team watched him expectantly, waiting for a

hint on how to proceed. Huddy quickly moved forward and confronted the driver before he entered the station.

"Excuse me."

"Hey, this is only a ten minute rest stop for me, mister. You mind if I have my coffee?"

Huddy reached into a pocket, pulled out a wallet and extracted a twenty. "Have a coffee on me." He handed it to the incredulous driver. This kind of thing only happened in movies and cop shows; not in real life. But the twenty was real enough.

"I'm looking for an old man," Huddy explained as they entered the station and headed toward the cafeteria. "Slightly above average height, pot belly, deep voice. Talks short and concise. Not too bright."

The driver thought a moment, then said, "I know the guy you mean. Not with me anymore."

Huddy's eyebrows rose. "What do you mean, 'anymore'?"

"Hell, he got off way back up the highway. Hours and hours ago."

"Where?"

"That's funny, you know. That's why I remember him so easily." He entered the cafeteria, held the swinging door for his benefactor. "Hi, Marge," he said to the waitress. She nodded in recognition, automatically went for the coffee.

"It was just outside Kent, I think. Or maybe it was before Kent. Somewhere around there. I let him off on the side of the road. Empty country, mister."

"He didn't get off in town?"

"Nope. Said some people were going to meet him."

Huddy's mind fought to make sense of this utterly unexpected new development.

"Of course he might've been lying for all I know. None of my business why he wanted out right there. Maybe his ticket had run out and he didn't want to fight with the agent down the line. I wouldn't have hassled him, though. Nice old guy. But he wanted out, so I let him out."

"Shit," Huddy said tightly. He turned and rushed out of the cafeteria.

"Hey," the driver called after him, "don't you want some coffee?"

The waitress filled the upturned cup in front of the driver. "What did your friend want?"

The driver shrugged. "Beats the hell out of me, Marge. Some folks. You know. You still married?"

Huddy forced himself to slow down as he strode toward his command post. Members of his team eyed him curiously. Huddy ignored them. He was beginning to wish he'd never heard of Jake Pickett.

What the devil had made the old man decide to abandon the bus in the middle of nowhere? No witnesses in nowhere, of course. No one to see him flag down another bus or hitch a ride. Maybe the old bastard was smarter than they'd figured. That was a disturbing thought. A Jake Pickett without brains was threatening enough.

Slowly his people assembled around him. They didn't ask questions. Their job was taking orders. Huddy liked them for that. Now he had to decide what to do with them. All had come up from San Antonio for this pick-up. There wasn't going to be any pick-up. Nonetheless, everyone still had to be paid.

Huddy discovered he was beginning to hate Jake Pickett. If he'd had any qualms about harming the old man before, they were long gone now.

Jake woke up. The subtle vibration of the truck had changed, become softer and slightly rougher. They were pulling into a fair-sized city, rolling down an off-ramp. He blinked. The sun was gone and the moon already well towards its zenith.

"Where are we?"

"Abilene," said the girl. "You dozed off. Ever been here before?"

Jake shook his head.

"Town's grown like a terrier pup since the last time Jim and I came through," the girl continued. "Oil boom. There's a Motel Six on Main Street the other side of town." She spared a questioning glance for her husband, then looked back at Jake. "They all have two doubles in each room. You're welcome to one of 'em."

"No," he told her. "No, you've been good enough to me as it is."

"Well, you're welcome to go all the way into Fort Worth with us, but we can't spare the time to hunt you down."

"I'll take a room close to you," Jake told her. "I've got enough money for that. Not that I need much rest. I've been sleeping back here ever since you picked me up."

"What, in this thing?"

"I can sleep anywhere," Jake told her. "It's a habit I picked up in the shipyards during the war."

"Wish I could do that," she said wistfully. "Jim can do it. Comes from working graveyard on the rigs."

"One other thing," Jake said. "I want to buy you two your supper."

"Hey, that's not necessary," said the driver.

"I know it's not," said Jake. "That's why I'll enjoy doing it. Okay?"

"If you insist," said the girl.

His belly was growling. "That's settled, then. You know a decent place to eat here?"

"Lots of decent places to eat." She made a face. "The trick's finding one that's reasonable as well as decent. You like Mexican?"

"I'm from Southern California," he said. "What'd you have in mind?"

"Depends if the place I remember is still here. These little spots, they go in and out of business by the year in these oil towns."

They cruised southward, soon turned east on the main street. The city still had railroad tracks running through its center. Main street was a melange of neon signs, fast food restaurants and gas stations. It was several minutes before the girl let out an exclamation of recognition and they pulled into a garishly lit parking lot beneath a huge old sign that said Taco Something.

Jake enjoyed watching them order, delighted that someone else would be picking up the tab. It would double the pleasure of their meal. The food, when it finally arrived, was typical for this part of the country: huge portions hotly spiced accompanied by quart-sized glasses of iced tea. Jake dove into it with as much pleasure as his younger companions.

None of them noticed the woman seated across the room. She'd been staring at them since they'd entered. She wasn't thinking about her own meal, however. Her mind was on something else entirely—a five-letter word for money received in excess of normal salary. Word had been spread around. A phone number accompanied the word.

"You sure it's him?" said the man on the other end of the pay phone.

"I'm positive." The woman licked hot sauce from her upper lip and leaned out of the booth to stare into the dining room. The man who'd excited her attention was still there, sifting through a fried burrito. "His picture's all over the place. He's not alone, though. Seems to be with a young couple."

Huddy frowned. He knew that the Ramirezes were still in Port Lavaca. That left a single likely alternative. The couple had picked up an elderly hitchhiker and he was sticking with them.

It was late. That didn't mean Pickett's benefactors didn't intend to drive the rest of the night. He'd have to work fast. Maybe he'd get lucky for a change. He certainly was due.

He gave the grateful woman at the other end a number to call to make arrangements for her reward. Then he made some quick calls of his own.

Yes, it could be managed. Yes, it would be expensive. The best people wouldn't be available on such short notice. They'd have to go with what was available in the area. Yes, they could be ready to track them if they kept driving.

Huddy received a return call a half hour later. It caught him just as he was heading out the door. They'd taken motel rooms, clearly intended to spend the night. Huddy smiled. At last things were shifting in his favor. It was about time.

"Are you sure we can't convince you to share our room?" the girl asked him.

"No. The one next door is better for me," Jake assured her. "I like my privacy."

"I understand. We'll see you in the morning, then."

"I'll be up, don't worry." He shook each of their hands in turn. "And thanks, kids. Thanks a lot."

He turned and went through the door that connected both rooms, closed the one on their side behind him, then closed and locked his own. He tried the front door to his own room, making certain it was fastened securely.

"Two twenty-six," said the raised numbers on his room key. They'd had no trouble getting adjoining rooms. That would make it simpler in the morning. He tossed the key onto the spare bed. It was going to be nice to sleep on a real mattress for a change. The bus hadn't been kind to his back.

Outside the motel the word was passed. The tall man who'd been put in charge of the operation cursed as the description of the sleeping arrangements was given to him. He'd been summoned from a warm bed, no, ordered out of it, and he wasn't in a pleasant mood. They'd be stuck outside the damn motel for hours, waiting for the loaded hypodermics to reach them, before they could move in. Now the situation was complicated by the presence in the old man's room of these two kids.

"So he's sharing a room with them," said one of his associates. "Shouldn't make things much tougher."

"Look, this is kidnapping, Sanford. Not extortion, not fire-for-hire, not any of our usual stuff. And we can't botch this because the orders come out of Houston. From top people. I tried to tell 'em this kind of things's out of our league, but they wouldn't listen. Said they didn't have time to send more than a few of their own people up and they didn't know if they'd get here in time to be in on it. So we've got to do it ourselves, you and me and Wallace and the rest of the boys. Could be good for us, though."

"It'll be dark in the room and we ain't going to bust in until early morning," Sanford pointed out.

"Yeah, but these kids could still get a look at us."

"That's true." Sanford shrugged. When he did that he looked like one of those old toy figures where you push a stick protruding from the bottom and make the arms and legs flutter. Sanford was all skinny arms and legs, and nastiness. "If that happens we'll just have to make sure they won't tell anybody about it, won't we?"

His boss was unhappy at the thought. "Complicates things, but I'm afraid you're right, man. Maybe we'll be alright. Maybe we can get in and get out in the dark." He turned and looked up at the motel's second floor, waiting for the lights in 224 to go out.

A thumping noise, distant through his pillow, woke Jake. He rolled over in the bed to blink wearily at the clock that was bolted to the nighttable. It was somewhere between three and four in the morning.

The sound came again and he raised up against the headboard. It was coming from the other side of the far wall, from the young couple's room. For an instant he thought it might be something recognizable and he was momentarily embarrassed, but when the muffled scream penetrated the wall he came wide awake.

Abruptly the sounds stopped. There was a click as the door near his TV was opened from the other side. Then someone tried the door on his side of the passageway. When it failed to yield the attempt wasn't repeated. There was no pounding, no hammering against the thin barrier. That would come soon enough, Jake knew.

Scrambling out of the bed he fumbled into his clothes in the near blackness, not daring to turn on a light for fear of alerting those who surely must be watching the entire motel. Medicine, wallet, he had everything. He spared a frantic minute to make up the bed. Maybe if whoever checked the room saw no signs of occupancy they might not bother to inspect it closely. He started toward the front door. Memories of another motel recently abandoned in haste halted him.

There was a window through to the back. The fact that he was on the second floor didn't slow him. He had no choice but to take whatever escape was offered.

Sliding the glass aside, he pushed hard on the screen. It fell out, bounced off something, then went sailing like a black kite out into the night to land in the dirt behind the building. Looking out and down he saw what the screen had bounced off of; a concrete ledge perhaps a foot wide. It carried a rain gutter the length of the motel.

I could live without this, he thought as he stepped carefully out onto the ledge. He closed the window, hoping anyone who

‚entered his room wouldn't remark on the missing screen.

Stay calm, think it through, he told himself as he stood there on the narrow ledge. He tried not to think of what had taken place in the room next to his, though his imagination was working overtime.

Someone had spotted him and had notified the people who were chasing him. They'd traced him to the motel where some-one else had seen him enter the young couple's room. Since he hadn't come out of that room they'd naturally assume he was sharing it with them. He wondered that they'd located him again so quickly. That wouldn't surprise Amanda. He wished he could talk to her now.

That young fellow Huddy must want him very badly.

Keeping his stomach pressed against the wall and trying not to look down, he made his way along the ledge until he bumped up against something cold and unyielding. The fire ladder was bolted firmly to the wall.

After a moment's thought he stepped out onto the rungs and started up instead of down. The roof was flat and covered with loose tarpaper and composition shingles. As he ap-proached the far side he dropped to his knees and then his belly. Too much belly for this kind of thing, he mused as he made his way slowly toward the edge. Soon he'd reached the rim and could just peer out and down into the parking lot.

Several men stood next to a large car parked in the middle of the lot. All of them except one wore western hats. Jake couldn't see a tie in the bunch, though it was a long ways off and still dark out.

Footsteps sounded on one of the metal stairways. Half a dozen men appeared to the right, running towards those waiting by the car. Both groups entered into a noisy discussion punctuated by much wild hand-waving. Jake wished he could make out what they were saying, but they were too far away and his hearing a little too used up.

The two groups split into several smaller ones and piled into four or five cars and trucks, which went screeching out onto the main street. Cold but alert, Jake lay on the roof until he was sure everyone who'd been gathered in the parking lot had left. Something banged against a ventilator pipe and he nearly jumped over the edge, but it was only a pair of disturbed pigeons rearranging themselves in their nest.

Half an hour passed before he felt secure enough to retrace his path down the fire ladder, along the ledge, and back into his empty room.

At first he couldn't tell if anyone had come looking for him there. The front door was still locked, the safety chain still in place. The door leading to room 224, however, stood slightly ajar. A quick glance revealed a broken lock. They *had* thought to check the adjoining room, then. Carefully he pulled the door aside and stepped through.

It was dark and there was a peculiar smell he didn't recognize. He turned on the bathroom light, hoping it wouldn't be visible from the parking lot.

The first thing he saw clearly was the face of the young woman who'd offered him the ride. She was lying half on, half off the bed. Her head brushed the floor and she was staring at something unseen. One leg showed bare atop the bed and one arm lay limply on the floor like a pale snake. A steady drip, drip came from somewhere Jake was glad he couldn't see. The blood ran down her arm and pooled on the carpet, explaining both sound and smell.

Her husband lay on the floor nearby, nude and intertwined with the fully clad body of a man Jake didn't recognize. The stranger's head lolled at an unnatural angle. The young husband was bleeding from the back. Jake could see the knife wounds: straight, clean, ugly where the flesh was cleaved. He stood there with his mouth trembling and tried to make some sense of what he saw. After everything that had happened this past week, after all the attempts that had been made to capture him, he finally began to realize the extent to which Huddy and his people would go to get him back.

And that made less sense than anything else.

No witnesses. They didn't want any witnesses, he thought numbly. Either that or when they hadn't found him in the room, they'd panicked. Obviously the young man had put up an unexpectedly strong resistance. Fat lot of good it had done him.

Nice folks, those two kids. He backed slowly out of the room. They'd made one bad mistake in their young lives. They'd given him a ride. My fault, he thought. This is my fault. I shouldn't have stayed close to them, shouldn't have involved anyone. I shouldn't. . . .

Something screamed in his brain. It was distant, yet near. Far off, yet proximate.

Amanda!

She wasn't talking at him as she usually did. She was broadcasting her distress blindly. Someone, there was someone in her room, not her mother, not her father. Someone who'd entered through the window that overlooked the bay, a window that Jake knew well even though he hadn't seen it in years.

He stumbled backward and fell into the dressing table. A lamp went flying, crashed to splinters against a wall. He spun around in the darkness holding his head, which throbbed and pulsed like an overheated engine.

Amanda, Amanda! She couldn't reply. He had the feeling she was trying to scream aloud. That first shout had been a silent one, an instinctive reaction to whatever menaced her. Now she was trying to alarm her parents, to wake them, to summon help . . . and she couldn't. She couldn't because she was being gagged. Something was shutting off her breath and she couldn't make any noise. Not in her room, but she could still howl with her mind. Only one human being could hear those screams, and he was hundreds of miles from aiding her.

He could feel the gag filling her mouth, could see dark forms moving around her. Then even that was taken from him as something was pressed and bound over her eyes. She was being lifted and carried, trying to fight with her arms, unable to resist with her useless legs. The wheelchair was left behind, then the bedroom itself.

Jake slumped to the carpet, fell back against the bed, then found himself prone on the floor. Slowly he brought his trembling fingers away from his head. The throbbing was fading, receding.

Amanda was gone.

Just . . . gone. It was not at all like when she ended their private conversations, nothing like that. At such times she left him gently, smoothly. This time her mental self had been terminated with brutal suddenness.

He lay there with his legs bent, staring at nothing. He

couldn't tell if Amanda was asleep or drugged or dead. Only that she was unconscious.

Someone had grown impatient. Someone had decided it was time to stop toying with their quarry. Time to employ real leverage, time to get serious. So they'd taken Amanda away.

He fumbled at his shirt pocket. Shakily he pulled out the little bottle and threw three of the pills down his throat. It was bad when he had to use three. Not desperately bad, but bad enough to frighten him. The pounding beneath his ribs slowed; the fire fled from his chest.

Get out of this town, a voice inside his head ordered him. You can't stay here. They're bound to come back and check again. And if they don't, there are two corpses in the room next to yours. If the police pick you up, Huddy will find some way of taking you off their hands. You know that.

No Amanda to help him anymore. No brilliant grandniece to add intelligence to his common sense. He was on his own.

He used the back window again even though the parking lot showed no sign of activity. The ladder led him to the ground.

Mandy, he thought, what have they done with you, Mandy? He was almost crying. He hadn't cried in a long time, in spite of the fact that old men are commonly prone to such displays. But not Jake Pickett. Not until now. Fear and worry combined to push him close to the emotional edge.

At the far end of the motel he hesitated as he checked out the pavement. Early morning/late night traffic was sparse but present. Surely with cars zipping back and forth no one would try to kidnap him off the curb. In any case, he didn't know what else to do. He was confused and panicky, for Amanda more than himself.

The bus stations would be full of Huddy's minions now. They'd never let him on another cross-country bus. He started out across the asphalt, trying to cling to the shadows as much as possible. Then he was standing on the curb beneath a streetlight, thumb extended, holding the collar of his jacket tightly against his neck.

There was an all-night gas station nearby and he started walking toward it. The light was better there and a curious attendant noticed him immediately. It felt good to have someone watching him as he stood there by the curb, hoping desperately for a ride.

"That's him." The woman turned to her companion and handed over the binoculars. The man pushed back his hat and leaned on the hood of the car as he stared down the street, swearing with unnecessary violence at any cars which passed between him and the object of his attention.

"Yeah, it's him alright." He reached through the open door of the car and pulled out the business end of the CB. "Masterson, this is checkpoint two, repeat, checkpoint two. Come back, Masterson."

A voice crackled back at him. "What've you got, Stroud?"

"The old man's standing in front of a Whiting Bros. station, trying to hitch a ride. I don't know where he was hid out, but it's him for sure. You want us to move in and pick him up?"

"You don't just pick this old man up," said the voice. "Where is he? Out on First Street?"

"Yeah. Hell, there's not enough traffic to make it risky. We can take him."

"It only takes one bystander who wants to play hero to mess things up, Stroud. Like those jerks in the motel. Besides, we handle this guy real easy, remember?"

"Shee-it, Masterson, somebody else going to get the glory for our work?"

"Alicia, you there?"

The woman took the CB unit from her companion, glared at him. He made a face, turned to look back through the binoculars.

"Masterson, Alicia here. We'll do what you say, but I for one don't buy any of the crap Houston handed us about this old boy. He's standing out there freezing his ass off just like anybody else."

"Just follow your orders, Alicia. Keep him in sight. I'm sending a pick-up team back after him right now. They'll be there in five minutes. They'll pull into the station, make like they're buying gas, and then they'll take him. You'll get your money, don't worry."

"I wasn't." She stuck the CB back inside the car, leaned close to her husband. "You shouldn't hassle somebody like Masterson, honey. We'll get our due, don't worry."

"Damn asshole thinks he knows everything," the man muttered, his eyes glued to the binocs.

North of the central city a blue and white van sat parked in the shopping center lot. Inside, the man named Masterson put down a CB speaker and dialed a number on the van telephone. The phone rang a long time but he didn't hang up. It was early in the morning.

Finally there was an acknowledging click at the other end.

"Benjamin Huddy?"

"Yeah. That you again, Masterson?"

"It's me. We've found him again."

"So soon? Well, that's something. I thought when you'd blown it at the motel we'd have to start scouring bus stations again."

Masteron ignored the criticism. "He's standing outside, trying to get a lift. I don't know where he was hiding when we searched the motel, but that doesn't matter now. Point is we've got him under surveillance." He glanced at his watch. "My people are moving in right now. We'll have him in ten minutes." He hesitated. "I don't think I told you about the trouble we had at the motel. You ought to know, I guess."

"All you told me earlier was that you'd busted into his room and he wasn't there. What kind of trouble?"

"A couple of my people got overanxious. They didn't use good judgment. They were nervous anyway, you know. All the stories about this guy that have been making the rounds. Anyway, we've got a couple of dead bystanders on our hands and—"

"Dead!" Huddy's exasperation exceeded his anger. "What do you mean, dead? Christ, you damn Texans!"

"Take it easy, Mr. Huddy. What do you want from my people, anyway? You're such a smart guy, how come you didn't pick this old codger up days ago?"

"We had our own problems. Alright, skip it. What are you doing about it?"

"I've handled this sort of thing before. There won't be any complications, Mr. Huddy. The cops won't show up until the maids start cleaning those rooms. Maybe not until this afternoon. My people lifted the valuables; you know, rings, wallets, stuff like that.''

"I'm sure that was a lot of trouble for them,'' Huddy said sarcastically.

"It'll look just like a bungled robbery to the cops,'' Masterson assured him. "There'll be no reason to connect it to anything else, least of all the Company, so quit worrying about it, okay?''

"Sure. All I'm worrying about right now is the old man. How do you plan to pick him up?''

"I have two of my best people moving in. They have the tranquilizer rifle assigned to my group. They're going to stop for gas at the station where he's standing and plug him from the car. Maybe one witness, my people tell me. We can handle that.''

"I hope so.''

Masterson hesitated. "Look, I've heard the stories, Mr. Huddy. The whole thing sounds crazy to me. Are you sure all this is necessary? The tranquilizer rifle and all, I mean? Why don't I just have a couple of guys sneak up behind him and bop him one? He's just an old man.''

"That old man,'' Huddy explained dryly, "is probably the most dangerous individual in the country, all the more so because he doesn't know it himself. You do the pick-up the way you were instructed.''

"If you insist, Mr. Huddy. But I still think we're doing this the hard way.''

"Humor me.'' Huddy hung up.

Masterson put the phone back in its cradle and shook his head slowly. Craziest business he'd ever been in on. All this effort expended to apprehend one tired old man. People covering the whole city. Hell, the whole state. Still, his was not to reason why. Only to collect.

The CB buzzed and he lifted the speaker.

"Stroud here. Come back, Masterson.''

"What's doing, Stroud?'' A check of his watch showed the time: four in the morning. The men with the t-gun should be driving into the station any minute now.

"Trouble. Looks like the old boy's got a lift.'' Stroud

balanced himself on the car hood, holding the binoculars in one hand and the CB unit in the other. "Yeah, they're driving off. Seventy-four Ford pickup, maybe seventy-five. License number six six seven DRF. Bright blue with red, black and yellow stripes. Four spots on the cab."

"Damn," Masterson muttered. Well, they'd just have to adjust. He spoke louder. "Red, black and yellow stripes on a blue Ford pickup, check. That'll be hard to miss." He thought of the unlucky couple who'd shared the old man's room. He didn't want any more trouble like that. Messy. "Who's with him?"

"Looks like a kid," Stroud reported. "Junior college age. Naw, come to think of it he didn't look like the type. Almost out of my range now. Still on First, heading east." His wife was waiting behind the wheel of their car, fingers on the ignition key. "Want us to follow 'em?"

"Yeah. Stay close but don't press them," Masterson ordered. "Keep them in sight. Masterson out."

Stroud piled into the car. His wife nodded, said brusquely, "I heard," and started the engine. They pulled out onto the nearly deserted street.

Masterson sat thinking for a moment, then touched controls before addressing himself once again to the CB.

"Central here. Outlook four, six and nine, subject is now traveling eastbound on First Street in a late model Ford pickup; blue with red, black and yellow striping, multiple spotlights on the cab. License number six six seven DRF. Young man driving. Set up your position on First in advance of the interstate on-ramp. The kid's probably heading home after a fast night in town. Maybe we'll be lucky and he's too bombed to see much. Unit six, you've got plenty of time to set up on the bridge. Put the kid out too if you have a clean shot. I'll be there in a few minutes myself."

He replaced the pickup in its holder and hurried forward. The van engine turned over with a satisfying roar and he gunned it, laying rubber as he headed southeast. He might get there in time to witness the actual pick-up and he might not. A lot depended on how fast the kid was traveling. He still had to pass through the traffic circle. There was usually a cop sitting there, watching for people to run the stop signs on their way out of town. That should slow him down a little.

Just outside Abilene's eastern flank lay a large industrial area spotted with treed empty lots. It would be a good place to pick up the old man, Masterson knew. Not much traffic of any kind out there this time of morning. It would be neat and quick. He'd be glad to be done with it. Other business was going unmonitored while he was forced to fool around with this old man.

As he sped down the feeder road he wondered what all the fuss was about in the first place.

XIV

"I still don't understand, mister." The kid let both hands hang loosely from the top of the wheel. "What're you doin' out here the middle of the night? You don't look like no wino. If you had, I wouldn't have picked you up."

"I don't drink much, son."

Jake relaxed a little, only occasionally glancing at the side mirror mounted outside his window. There were no signs of pursuit. Only city lights fading into the distance. Outside it was rapidly becoming darker. Warehouses and factory buildings loomed large against the night. The widely spaced street lights they encountered were islands of light on the dark road.

"Down on your luck then," said the driver. Jake studied him. Couldn't be much more than seventeen, if he was that. He wondered what the youngster was doing out so late, then decided that it was none of his business. The kid still had acne mixed with his freckles. Combined with a deep West Texas tan it gave his face the look of a Landsat false-color photograph. The western hat he wore was a little too big for his head and he had to keep nudging it back off his forehead. Some unfortunate rattlesnake had given its all for that hatband.

The truck was as comfortable as its driver was awkward.

Jake began to consider the possibility of going back to sleep.

"Shoot, everybody has money troubles," the kid was saying. His words were supported by beer fumes, but he kept the truck slow and steady as it swung around the traffic circle.

"Had an enjoyable night?" Jake murmured conversationally.

"Sure as hell did," the kid said proudly.

"Your family know where you are?"

He laughed. "Shit, half the time they don't know where I am and the other half they don't much care. I'm my own man. Didn't have no luck with the ladies last night, but it weren't for lack of tryin'." He laughed again, looking more than ever like an adenoidal Huck Finn. "If you don't mind my askin', what put you down on your luck?"

Jake thought a moment, then said, "I made trouble for some people with bad tempers."

"Cops? You runnin' from the law, mister?" The boy sounded excited instead of frightened. Different from my day, Jake thought dourly.

"No." The driver looked disappointed. "I'm not completely sure who I'm running from, son. But they're not good people." He thought again of the murdered couple lying back in the motel, whose only crime had been helping him. It made him angry. His heart started to hurt slightly. Anger and tension weren't good for him, but at the moment he didn't much care. Somebody ought to be made to pay for what happened at the motel, he knew. It wasn't right that something like that should go unpunished.

The boy leaned forward until his chin was practically resting on the wheel. "Now that's funny." They were approaching the old steel bridge which spanned the Clear Fork of the Brazos east of town. "Looks like some kind of a roadblock up ahead."

Jake squinted through the windshield. His eyes were old, but he could still make out the two cars parked hood to hood that blocked both lanes at the far end of the bridge. At the same time a sudden roar announced the appearance of two more cars. They materialized from a parking lot concealed by trees and accelerated until they were tight close behind the pickup. Figures were moving around the two cars parked ahead.

"Wonder what's goin' on?" the boy muttered. "Sure a lot of excitement for so early in the mornin'." He glanced sharply at his passenger. "Hey, you sure you didn't cross no cops, mister?"

Jake didn't hear him. The intent was clear. They were going to trap him on the bridge. There'd be no escape this time, no friendly back window to slip through, no familiar old car to speed to safety in. The boy was starting to slow down.

"I'd better see what they want." His youthful bravado was fading fast and he sounded frightened and uncertain. Beer makes a lousy crutch.

"Damn them," Jake whispered to himself, haunted by the image of the slain couple who'd helped him. "Damn them all to hell." His heart was hammering away and the angina stole his breath. The fear of the moment, his anger, an overwhelming feeling of helplessness in the face of relentless pressure, the fact that this time there was no way out, all combined inside him. Maybe it was all those things and maybe it was nothing more than forced repetition, but for the very first time in his life Jake suddenly knew *how* he made things slipt.

Funny, after all these years, a distant part of him thought. How strange, all those bottles of soda opened for the neighborhood kids, all those erasers mysteriously falling loose from their pencils back in grade school. All the card tricks he'd deftly performed without having to read the instructions. Bottle caps and erasers and wheels and rags.

He suddenly didn't care much what happened anymore. Twenty years he'd spent nursing a bad heart and now it didn't seem to matter. He could go at any time anyway, whether he took care of himself or not.

But he wasn't going to go at the hands of these people, and he wasn't going to give them what they wanted from him, and he was going to find out what they'd done to his beloved Amanda.

"Pull over," someone was shouting. The voice came from one of the cars that had pulled out behind them. It was in the wrong lane now, paralleling the truck. "Come on, kid, pull it over. Right *now*." The speaker gestured with a pistol of indeterminate caliber.

Its size didn't matter to the now-pale youngster. "Yes sir. Geez," he muttered, "you wouldn't think sneakin' a few crummy drinks would cause so much trouble." His right foot started to shift from the accelerator to the brake pedal. The pickup started to slow. Jake roused himself from his stupor and jabbed out with his left foot. The accelerator went toward the floor.

"Jesus, mister," the kid yelled, "cut it out!" He put his own foot over Jake's, but that only increased the pressure on the accelerator. He tried to kick Jake's leg aside, but the oldster resolutely leaned over with his weight and held the pedal down.

The pickup responded with admirable speed. It leapt forward, leaving the paralleling car in its wake and allowing its driver only enough leeway to steer. Jake put a hand to his forehead as something happened.

Behind the pickup the paralleling car started to speed up in pursuit when the rear half of the steel bridge groaned and began to collapse. No one saw the bolts holding the key beams together turn to powder. The men in the car screamed as they went over the edge.

Behind them, the second car which had emerged from the hidden parking lot squealed as the driver frantically crushed his brakes. The back of the car went sideways and it came to a halt at the lip of the abyss. Echoes from the folding steel beams and massive chunks of falling concrete continued to reverberate through the night as they filled in the riverbed. Of the first car there was no sign.

"Oh Lord," the boy was moaning as he fought to concentrate on his steering, "we're gonna die, we're gonna die. Please, mister, you're gonna kill both of us, please!"

Jake said nothing, kept his foot on the accelerator and his eyes on the roadblock they were approaching. The men who'd emerged from the cars and started down the bridge had stopped when the rear section of the span had started to collapse. Now they scattered as the pickup exploded toward them.

"Get out of the way!" Jake found himself yelling to them.

"I don't want to hurt anyone. Get out of the way!" Behind the pickup one of the huge support beams toppled sideways, pulling the middle section of the bridge down with it. Like a falling redwood, the mass of steel fell into the side of the power substation which occupied the lower river bank. The beam and bridge section tore through the chain link fence and smashed transformers like popcorn. The air was filled with ozone and a rippling, crackling sound like frying bacon. Blue sparks and thin fireballs lit the night.

"I don't want to hurt anyone!" Jake shouted above the thunder that pursued them. His foot was still jammed against the pedal, his leg locked in position so stiffly that no two men could have moved it. He was crying as he shouted useless warnings.

One of the cars blocking their path went *WHOOM* and scattered itself all over the road. The other car did likewise a split second later, blowing itself backward into the trees. Something had slipt inside their fuel tanks. The disintegration didn't halt there. Engines and seats and even headlights explosively disassembled in the air, sending metal and glass shrapnel rocketing in every direction.

Several of the stunned occupants of the two cars, who'd expected nothing more difficult than restraining an old man, had the presence of mind to dive for cover. Those sluggish of foot and thought were shredded by the flying debris. That same debris flew lethally toward the pickup but for some reason only dust struck it, particles too tiny even to pit the windshield.

The truck rumbled through the gap where the blockade had been seconds ago. Men lay on the road and in the grass, moaning and bleeding. One lay crumpled in one place, his arm in another.

Two of those who'd been hiding in the bushes dove into the river, heedless of its depth or the presence of rocks. Others melted into the foliage. One had the presence of mind, or perhaps it was instinct, to pull a pistol and start shooting at the fleeing pickup. Jake saw him standing by the side of the road and aiming with both hands. Several shots were fired, but they never reached the truck. Then the gun blew up in the man's hands, turning them red and ugly. What was left of the tran-

quilizer rifle and its unique contents burned furiously inside
one of the destroyed cars.

The pickup raced unimpeded down the road toward the on-
ramp leading onto the interstate, carrying to safety a badly
frightened young man and a sobbing, cursing older one who
more than anything else didn't want to hurt anybody. . . .

Somerset had never heard Huddy sound so tired. It wasn't
just lack of sleep that plagued her lover. There were under-
tones of defeat in his voice that were utterly alien to him.

"Pull yourself together, Benjamin," she said into the
phone.

"You weren't there, Ruth," he said weakly over the line.
"You didn't see what happened."

"Neither did you, Benjamin."

"No, but I saw the results, and I talked to the men who did
see it, and that's as close as I ever want to get. How's the
grandniece?"

"Unhurt and sedated," she told him. "My people got her
out of the house without any trouble."

"That's a switch," Huddy muttered.

"She didn't have a chance to get to her phone, didn't even
have time to yell for her parents." She could almost see him
nodding appreciatively at the other end of the line.

"Should've done it that way in the first place," Huddy
mumbled. "But who knew? Who knew?"

"I had an idea that we were being too delicate about the
whole business when you called and told me they'd missed him
at the motel in Abilene," she said firmly. "That's when I decided to go ahead with my own ideas."

"I'm glad you did, Ruth. I'm at my wit's end."

"Come on, Benjy," she chided him, trying to raise his
spirits, "I know we've had another setback, but it's only temporary. Now that we've taken the grandniece we can back off
Pickett and he'll do just what we want him to. I know it's an
extreme move, but he forced us into it."

"Setback? Ruth, this is getting out of hand. I never expected it to go this far. I never expected Pickett to . . . " He
hesitated, stopped, started again. "Ruth, there are dead
people all over the place, others scattered around area hos-

pitals working with rotten explanations that the police are bound to see through sooner or later. Now another kidnapping, an innocent crippled girl, I just don't—"

"Don't go soft on me now, Benjamin," she said tightly, trying to keep the anger and disgust out of her voice. "This is no time to think of backing out."

"I wasn't saying that," he replied defensively. "It's too late for anyone to back out even if he wanted to. I've authorized too much, taken the responsibility for too much. We *have* to see this through to its conclusion." He was trying to sound confident and only partly succeeding.

"Those of our people who survived were told that a power station blew up. It did, but it was no accident. There are no accidents around Pickett. But it makes sense, and so far the local authorities are buying it. Why shouldn't they? There aren't any other explanations. But I don't know how much longer I can keep the lid on this. Some of these guys saw things out there no power station failure can explain. Eventually they're going to start wondering, and talking."

"Do any of them suspect the old man directly?"

"I don't think so. Materson, maybe. He was in charge of the operation. Local. But he wasn't there when Pickett broke through so he didn't see anything. I can keep him quiet. It's only a question of money. I should've been there myself, Ruth."

"You didn't have time, Benjamin," she said soothingly. "Neither of us could have made it up there in time. Now listen to me. We've made some mistakes along the way. We've had some problems. We can't shoulder all the blame because we had no idea that the old man had this kind of potential. Frankly, I don't think he knew it himself.

"When he finds out that his grandniece is missing he'll turn docile and cooperative, you'll see. I know I've taken an extreme step, but we're reduced to taking extreme steps. He won't be surprising us with any more unexpected . . . what do you call it . . . disassembling? I think he's going to be real nice from now on. You ought to be pleased. I'm finally convinced your suspicions about him were right."

"That's something," he admitted. "You're right, Ruth. There's nothing to worry about anymore." He was sounding like his old arrogantly confident self again. "Sorry if I sounded reluctant. It's just that I never expected things to go this far."

"How could you? Oh, you're safe as far as this Abilene business is concerned, aren't you?"

"You mean the confrontation with Pickett, or the unfortunate business at his motel?"

"Both."

"I think so. I was nowhere around when they happened." He didn't add that he was innocent as far as the grandniece's kidnapping was concerned, too.

"You know," she added, "what we've done is nothing compared to the damage Pickett's caused."

"Not that that's any use to us." He let out a hollow, bitter laugh. "Can you imagine trying to prove in court that he's responsible for all those deaths and injuries? 'Your honor, this man, the one sitting over there with the heart condition, is responsible for killing and injuring twenty younger, healthier, armed men.' " He switched to mimicking a judge's stentorian tones.

" 'And how did the defendant accomplish this orgy of destruction, Mr. Huddy?'

" 'Well, your Honor, he looked at them.' " Again the humorless laugh, then, "Where've you stashed the grandniece?"

"Up at CCM's Matagorda complex," she told him. "The plant manager's a fat toady named Barker, five years from retirement. The only thing he's worried about anymore is his pension. He doesn't like it one bit, but I assured him he'll be kept out of it. Of course, we can involve him if we have to, but he doesn't know that. The only threats I made were indirect, but he got the message. He won't give us any trouble."

"What about the lower-downs?"

"Everyone there's busy with his or her own job. I've got one of my own people handling outside traffic and you already know who's taking care of things inside. None of the employees saw the girl being brought in. She's in the apartment in Administration that the plant maintains for visiting VIPs. Relax, Benjy. Everything's under control."

"That's my girl," he said admiringly. "I need to let you

take some of this kind of heavy stuff off my shoulders more often."

"That's exactly what you should do." Privately she was still worried about Huddy. He sounded normal now, but the longer this Pickett business dragged on, the more he seemed to be coming apart. Damned shame if that happened. She'd hate to lose him, both as lover and coconspirator within the corporate ranks. He was important to her future. But she'd have to watch him from now on. She had no intention of going down with his ship.

"One thing worries me," he was saying. "I wonder if Pickett will believe us when we go to tell him that we're the people who have his grandniece."

"Oh, I think he will, Benjy. He's already seen that we're not afraid of going to extremes. If necessary we can let him talk to her on the phone. Relax. The two of you will be on an L.A. bound plane within a couple of days."

"I hope so. Okay, everything's set, then. You sit tight. I'll be there in a few hours, as soon as I can charter a plane out of here. Then all we have to do is wait for Pickett to show at his niece's place, learn about the abduction, and us get in touch with him."

"Right." Her tone softened. "I've missed you, Benjamin."

"I've missed you too, sweet thing. Are all the taps still in place at the niece's house?"

"No sweat. The cops down here wouldn't recognize a tap if it crawled up and bit them on the ear. Bye."

The phone clicked. She held onto the receiver, thinking, and finally decided to call Matagorda. It wouldn't hurt to make doubly certain everything was going smoothly up there. Not that she anticipated any trouble with the girl. Even if she awoke, she could hardly up and run away.

She dialed the private number. She didn't like assigning Drew the task of keeping watch over the grandniece, but he'd been in on this Pickett business almost from the start. It was safer than using a local, and Benjamin had always shown a great deal of confidence in him. At least she didn't have to deal with him much in person. She didn't like the way he looked at her. He intimidated Barker, though, and it was always useful to have that kind of man around. Sometimes a warning grunt could be the best answer to an awkward question.

The crocheted placemat which usually adorned the center of the coffee table was coming to pieces in Wendy Ramirez's hands as she twisted and pulled it absently. She needed something to hold onto, something solid. Something of her daughter's. The centerpiece that Amanda had crocheted for a school project wasn't much.

Her husband paced the floor nearby. His big, scarred hands, which had caught too many fishhooks, flexed dangerously. His normal cheery demeanor had vanished completely. Events had stunned him into a furious, futile silence.

Sheriff Benbrook looked tired. Considerably more tired than the day he'd driven out to talk to them about the vandalism of their van. Benbrook liked working in Port Lavaca. You got to know everyone and they got to know you, a situation which made solving crimes a fairly simple matter of just asking around.

Now a different kind of crime had come to Port Lavaca, and he wasn't happy about it.

The man who sat in the chair across from Wendy wore a business suit, glasses and a thin, out-of-style tie. He was much smaller than either the sheriff or Arriaga Ramirez. He was also more imposing.

It had taken quite a lot of yelling and complaining on the part of the Ramirezes, supported by Sheriff Benbrook, before the FBI became convinced that a kidnapping *might* have taken place in the sleepy coastal town. They'd finally sent a representative, an agent Roeland, all the way down from the Houston office to take their statement.

Despite the reluctance of his Bureau, Roeland himself seemed genuinely sympathetic and anxious to be of help. That made Wendy feel a little better. Much better than she'd felt during her last conversation with his office, when she'd had to explain that no, her daughter couldn't have simply wandered off because she was incapable of wandering anyplace.

Now she sat and watched while Arriaga, in response to the agent's request, disappeared into their bedroom and returned with the picture of Amanda that the man required. Nor was the photo enough. He recorded every imaginable detail about Amanda, from the make and color of the nightgown she'd been wearing when she'd disappeared to the color of eye shadow she normally used. When they'd finished he flipped his little notebook closed. It was the only sound in the living room.

Roeland put his pen back in his breast pocket, carefully sliding the metal clip over the flap so it would stay in place.

"I'm terribly sorry about the trouble you had with the home office, Mrs. Ramirez," he said. "The woman who answered didn't mean to appear flippant. But you have to understand that we receive hundreds of crank calls every month. Very, very few actually deal with real abductions." He smiled in what he hoped was a reassuring manner. "I know this isn't a crank call, but maybe it's not an abduction either."

"What else could have happened to her?" Wendy was having a difficult time staying coherent. There was a lump in her throat and tears ever ready to fall. They made talking hard. "What could have happened to her? Her friends wouldn't play a practical joke like this on her, or on us."

"I just want to find whoever's responsible," rumbled Arriaga, pausing in his pacing. He glared first at the sheriff, then the agent. "I'd just like to have five minutes alone with them, that's all."

"Believe me, the Bureau shares your anxiety, Mr. Ramirez. Truly." The agent turned back to Wendy. "I know that right now it seems inconceivable to you that there could be another explanation for what's happened to your daughter, Mrs. Ramirez, but we often run into surprising solutions to seemingly straightforward cases. For example, you must have noticed that there's been no ransom note."

Arriaga let out a short, leaden laugh. Wendy said hollowly, "We don't have any money. There are other . . . reasons for kidnapping someone. Particularly a young girl."

"But not usually from her own bedroom, Mrs. Ramirez. I think you can rest easy on that score. We've also established that nothing was missing from her room, so robbery of some kind wasn't the motive.

"After considering all the information there is only one other reason for an abduction that I can think of. At least, only one that makes any sense. This is only a preliminary hypothesis on my part, you understand.''

Ramirez stopped as if shot and turned to take up a stance behind the couch, his hands resting on his wife's shoulders. Wendy stared anxiously at the agent while the Sheriff waited curiously. Benbrook was ever willing to learn.

"The sheriff here mentioned that you were involved in an incident in front of your house several days ago, Mr. Ramirez, during which you surprised some would-be car strippers at work on your van?"

Arriaga nodded slowly. Wendy looked up at him, took one of his hands in hers and squeezed hard.

The agent continued. "It's possible that those you surprised might have been so upset that they decided to come back and take a modicum of revenge. Sheriff Benbrook informs me that he's pretty sure they were from out of town. Urban professionals would be much more inclined to risk a return to the scene of the crime to try something along that line. Especially since the sheriff tells me you apparently hurt one of them pretty badly."

"I think I broke his goddamn face," Arriaga muttered. "I should've put the pipe all the way through his head."

Roeland nodded understandingly. He looks like he agrees with me, Arriaga thought. He'd never thought that the agent might turn out to be sympathetic. Hard, professional, cool and calculating, yes, but not sympathetic. But then, maybe this guy had a wife and daughter at home, too. Everybody reacted pretty much alike where violent crime was involved, he was discovering.

The agent rose to leave. Wendy stopped him. "What do you think, Mr. Roeland? I mean, when do you think you might know something?" She would not let herself consider the ultimate ramifications of the agent's theory. If someone had taken poor Amanda for purposes of revenge, then they might not find her . . . might not find her. . . .

She couldn't hold back the tears anymore. Arriaga was there instantly, enveloping her in his arms, comforting her.

The agent waited respectfully until the sobbing slowed. "I've no way of knowing, Mrs. Ramirez. I wish I could be more informative, but you must understand that I've only just been assigned to this case and have only now arrived here. I haven't even begun my work, really.

"The first thing I'll do is inform Houston that in my opinion we have a real kidnapping on our hands here. Your daughter's description will go out nationwide, though our efforts will naturally be concentrated in this area. We work closely with all local law enforcement agencies, as Sheriff Benbrook can tell you. Hopefully we'll have something soon. As soon as we know anything at all you'll be informed." He glanced at Arriaga, then took Wendy's right hand in his own, patted it gently.

"Keep in mind that we don't know exactly who abducted your daughter or why, or even if that's what happened. My suppositions are no more than that. So there is no reason for you to be conjuring up gruesome scenarios until we know something for certain. If she was kidnapped the people who did it might have been drunk rather than coldly calculating. They may have sobered up, realized what they were getting themselves into, and dumped her quickly and unharmed. It's . . . difficult for your daughter to get around. If she was dumped in a rural area it might take her a long time to attract attention or make her way to the side of a busy road. She might be sitting in a gas station right now trying to borrow a dime to make a phone call with. Or she might be on her way to a hospital to be treated for nothing worse than exposure." He pointed at the telephone.

"The best thing you can do for her now is to stay here and wait for some word from her or from my people. If the kidnappers get in touch with you, stay calm, tell them you'll do whatever they want, and then get back to me. I'll handle things from there.

"Keep in mind that I've been in on cases like this one before, Mrs. Ramirez. The Bureau's rate of success in kidnappings is very high, much better than you'd be led to believe by the media. You can reach me through the sheriff's office."

Arriaga nodded and escorted them to the door. Wendy trailed behind, still turning the crochet-work over and over in her hands. They stood in the portal and watched as Benbrook and the agent climbed into the sheriff's car and pulled away from the curb.

XV

Jake waited until the last moment before stepping off the bus. None of his fears were realized, however. There were no anxious men standing outside the Dairy Queen waiting for him.

Port Lavaca was a small town population-wise, but spread out. After orienting himself he had to hitch two separate rides before he felt close enough to his niece's house to go the rest of the way on foot. So long as he watched himself and maintained a slow pace, his heart gave him no trouble.

Though he hadn't been to that house in years, locating it was not as difficult as it would have seemed to an outsider. All you had to do was reach the bayside area and walk down the road paralleling the water. One advantage to getting old, he mused as he strode down the street beneath the live oaks and willows, was that you got rides quicker.

He should have been excited at the prospect of seeing his niece again. Instead he was sick with worry because he hadn't heard from Amanda in several days. That was utterly unlike her, the more so under the present circumstances. Either she was unable to reach out to him for reasons he couldn't fathom, or else she was. . . .

He refused to consider the possibility that his grandniece might be dead.

The sight of the sheriff's car pulling away from his niece's house as he rounded a curve in the road did nothing to reassure him. Wendy was about to go back inside when something made her hesitate, look down the street. A tall figure was striding toward them like a walking stick on a dead log. She squinted into the afternoon sun. Then the figure waved at her and her eyes got wide.

"Arri?" she murmured uncertainly.

"Hmmm?" He was halfway back inside, his mind still full of the FBI man's words.

She took a step off the porch. "Arri." Her fear was being replaced by something like excitement, "I think that man down the street . . . I think it's Uncle Jake!"

Ramirez came back out onto the porch and looked up the street. He'd met his wife's Uncle Jake only twice before, though they'd talked many times on the phone. The figure which had aroused Wendy's interest was closer now. It certainly looked like him. Thinner across the shoulders, maybe, and wider across the belly, but the same man he remembered from his last visit.

Wendy was already down the steps and running up the street. Arriaga waited, watching as niece and uncle embraced affectionately. The fisherman was confused and upset, uncertain whether to regard Pickett's arrival as welcome or an intrusion.

No, that's not fair, he told himself. The old man doesn't know what's happened. It was ironic, though. He couldn't have picked a sadder time to surprise them with a visit.

On the other hand, his unexpected appearance seemed to have lifted Wendy's spirits, if only temporarily. Arriaga was grateful for that. They could help support one another.

Soon both were standing with him on the porch and he found himself shaking the old man's hand. He looks tired, Arriaga thought. Only natural, considering his age and the length of the journey. Arriaga was a little surprised at the absence of any luggage, but then, old people often traveled light.

"Hello, Jake. Been a while."

"Como 'sta, Arri? Qué pasa?"

Arriaga forced himself to smile. "Quite a lot, I'm sorry to say." The smile didn't last long. "Come inside. I'm afraid we have some bad news to share with you."

It was on Jake's lips to say, "It's about Amanda, I know," but he kept silent. He and his grandniece had spent too much time preserving their little secret for him to give it away now. So despite his anxiety he waited for them to explain. They wouldn't have believed him anyhow.

Once inside, Wendy sat him down on the couch in the living room and busied herself in the kitchen, fussing with lemonade and plans for dinner. It was left to Arriaga to break the bad news to her uncle. The fisherman sat in the chair opposite the couch, his hands working nervously against each other.

" . . . so we can't be sure yet, but the police think Amanda may have been kidnapped," he concluded. Arriaga waited for the old man's reaction, was surprised when none was forthcoming.

You had to hand it to the old boy, he thought when he'd finished. He was taking it well. It was a difficult thing to accept, but old folks can be good at keeping their emotions hidden. According to Wendy's stories, Pickett was a tough old bird. Would've made a good fisherman.

He said lamely into the silence that followed his disclosure, "What about you, Jake? How are you doing these days?"

"Doesn't seem to matter much now, does it? I had a feeling something was wrong."

"You did?"

"Yes. I could see it in Wendy's face when she ran up to greet me. Amanda kidnapped?" He shook his head slowly, sadly. "It doesn't make sense. And the police have no idea who did it or why?" Jake pretty well knew the answers to his own question, but he was curious to see what the authorities were making of the situation.

"Nobody really knows anything." Unable to sit still, Arriaga rose and resumed his pacing. "Nobody saw anything, nobody heard anything. We went into her room in the morning and she just wasn't there anymore. She'd vanished straight from her bed." He went on to explain the FBI agent's theory and relate the incident involving the vandalism of their van.

Jake listened with half an ear, remembering a couple of re-

cent nights when he'd nearly vanished from his own bed. But
why would the people who wanted him resort to kidnapping
his grandniece? Surely they couldn't have discovered her own
ability. He thought of all the television detective shows he'd
seen. It was a crude education in criminology, but one at least
partly valid. It didn't take him long to figure out that they'd
kidnapped her in order to get to him.

"No one's contacted you about a ransom or anything like
that?"

"No," said Arriaga. "That's almost funny, someone sending us a ransom note. If that man from Houston is right and
they're the same bastards who tried to rip off our van and they
took Amanda for revenge, there shouldn't be any ransom
note. So far he's been right."

"No one's contacted you at all about her, then?" Arriaga
shook his head once, angrily. Jake could feel the man's rage,
could share his pain, and like him felt utterly helpless. No, he
wasn't completely helpless. His mind lit up with memories of
exploding cars and fleeing gunmen. The remembrance was
unreal, another TV show unspooling in his brain. Something
else had caused those cars to explode, something else had induced the old bridge to collapse. Not him, it hadn't been him.
Not poor old, tired Jake Pickett. At least in his mind he tried
to run away from the truth, but the truth kept catching up
with him.

The memories wouldn't go away. There was the terrified
face on the boy steering the pickup down the road, Jake's foot
jammed against the accelerator. There was the roadblock
ahead, transformed into flaming metal boxes. There was himself in the middle of it all, the pain at the back of his head as
things all around him slipt.

What good did that do him now? If only his precious, dear
Amanda could get in touch with him. Never mind keeping
their secret anymore. Nothing else mattered to him. Just tell
me where they've taken you, Mandy, he thought furiously.
Give me a hint that you're still alive, a clue to your location,
and I'll come for you and I won't let anyone hurt you; your
Uncle Jake won't let anyone hurt you.

And despite his silent entreaties there was nothing, only the
same maddening, taunting silence inside his head, a silence he

felt far more strongly than Arriaga or Wendy ever could. He studied the face of Wendy's father, and the expression only multiplied his own sorrow. These people were all the family he had. Though Amanda was by far the most important to him, he also loved Wendy and this soft-spoken bull of a husband of hers.

He could hear his niece in the kitchen, trying to hold back the flow of tears and failing, could see the brawny Arriaga fighting to keep from falling to the floor to bawl like a child. Only he, alone among those in the little house, felt no need to cry, perhaps because he'd stopped feeling that deeply when his sister Catherine had died.

Or maybe it was something else. Maybe he was too angry to feel real sorrow, because unlike Amanda's parents he knew where the blame for this agony lay and had a good idea who was behind it. Arriaga had nothing, only empty fears and his own imagination and the suppositions of the FBI agent, which were insufficient to focus on.

"Don't worry, Arri," he told the father consolingly. "She'll be alright. She has to be. She'll turn up, you'll see."

"I wish I had your confidence," the fisherman told him. "Everyone's trying to be so positive about it; you, the sheriff, the agent. Everybody's so positive, but nobody knows a damn thing." He punched an unseen opponent, the fist ending up in his other palm. Beneath the anger and the fear lay the beginnings of hysteria, only just held under control.

Jake meant what he'd said. They *would* find Amanda. But the police had no inkling of what had really happened to her. Only he knew that. So it was up to him to locate her. And when he found her, he decided, justice would be done. Never before in his life had he thought of doing harm to another human being, not even during the second world war when the enemy was known and real. His draft-exempt job in the ship-yards had spared him the necessity of finding out if he could have done such a thing.

All he'd ever wanted was to be left alone to live out his life in the house on the ridge, and to make other people feel good. Like the neighborhood kids he did tricks for. Now, near the end of his life, all that was changing. It was a change he hated, a change that was being forced on him by others.

There was no reason for such evil, no reason to put nice folks like Arriaga and Wendy through this kind of hell. There was no reason for the things those people had been trying to do to him during his hurried flight across the Southwest.

Now they'd gone so far as to kidnap a sweet, totally innocent young girl. Yes, Jake was discovering that it was possible for him to feel real anger. The anger was still small, still contained. Nothing like Arriaga's barely repressed fury, but anger nevertheless. As he sat there and wondered what to do next and watched the anguish fill Arriaga's face, the anger continued to grow within him.

Somerset turned off the tape recorder. The gown she was wearing was yellow with orange trim. It plunged in front at a sharp angle, creating what Huddy liked to refer to as "the view from Toroweep Point, Grand Canyon." It was open to a point not far below her navel. Only a thin orange ribbon held it together at waist level.

Huddy lay on the bed in his underwear, considering both the contents of the tape and the nightgown.

"That's the latest," she told him.

"We should have picked him up in Abilene," Huddy murmured. "Or in Benson. Or outside Phoenix. Everything's getting so complicated. It all seemed so simple, so easy at first. Just pick him up and deliver him to Navis for testing." He laughed hollowly.

She sat down on the bed next to him. "You're making a career out of worrying, Benjy. Everything's under control. You heard. The cops don't have the slightest idea what's happened to her."

"Yeah, but now FBI. . . ."

"Cops in suits and ties," she said soothingly, caressing him. "Let Mama Somerset handle things." She was a little miffed at his preoccupation with Pickett, especially since they hadn't seen each other in days.

"What if they find the bugs we've put in the Ramirez house?"

"Now why on earth should they start looking for telephone taps?" she said irritably. "You heard what the agent's theory was. They're all looking for out-of-town car thieves."

"Pickett must have some idea that we're behind it all."

"Maybe, maybe not. You told me yourself the old man's not too bright. Not that it matters." She put her arms around his neck. "Tomorrow morning we'll find some way to isolate Pickett from the rest of the girl's family. Then we'll get in touch with him. All you have to do is mention the grandniece and he'll do whatever we want him to. Don't you see, it's over? Finished. I admit it's been more trouble than we anticipated, but none of that matters in the end so long as we're successful. And we have been successful.

"You'll pick him up and escort him to Hobby Airport, fly him back to L.A. and turn him over to your pet mad scientist, and that will be the beginning of things for us, not the end. As to the grandniece, we'll just let her go. She's so doped up she'll never be able to tell anyone who snatched her or why. And since she hasn't been harmed," Somerset shrugged, "I'm sure that her family will want to forget about the whole business as quickly as possible.

"As far as the FBI and the local cops are concerned, that'll be the end of the case. There's no injured party, there are no leads, the parents will be satisfied just to have their daughter back, and everything will be filed and forgotten. Then, if Navis can learn how the old man does it, we'll be heading for heights that'll make the presidency of CCM look like a consolation prize for the losers at a Phi Delta sorority party."

"No, 'if' about it," Huddy said. Already he felt better. Somerset never failed to make him feel better. "We'll get what we need out of him. I'm taking all restrictions off Navis." He turned to face her, finally relaxed enough to think about something besides Jake Pickett.

"I always did like that gown."

"What part do you like the most?" She sat back on her haunches and smiled at him.

"The parts that aren't there." He reached for the orange ribbon.

Endless, the dream seemed. On and on it went, liquid and black, with her as the nexus afloat in a sea of nothingness. A dark ocean buoyed her from beneath. Stars pressed close, sometimes too close. It was warm and soft and somehow still not very relaxing.

Occasionally the stars shifted, and once the dream was gently shattered by the intrusion of huge, distorted planetary bodies that assumed the form of human faces. These globular shapes seemed capable of conversing with one another in some profound planetary tone. Their words were unintelligible.

Fortunately they didn't stay long, letting her slip back into the depths of the fuzzy, uneasy dreaming, to drift alone on the supportive back of the emptiness.

Unexpectedly the stars started to fade from the dream sky, the black ocean to evaporate. Dark waves no longer moved gently beneath her, though her support remained soft and comforting. The waves went away altogether and she grew afraid the empty sky might swallow her up. Then it too began to move, falling away from her eyes, retreating into focus. The sky lightened, became a ceiling, and she knew that the stars had lived only on the backside of her retinas.

She turned over very slowly, moving almost as ponderously as the deep voices which had pontificated above her. The bed she was lying on was not her bed, the ceiling overhead not the ceiling of her bedroom. Where the window that looked out over Lavaca Bay belonged gleamed instead the great ignorant eye of a television set.

She tried to prop herself up on her elbows. That turned out to be far more difficult than rolling over, so she contented herself with lifting her head for a moment to inspect the rest of her surroundings. That made the sky start to swim again, but eventually it resumed its identity as a ceiling. She tried to orient herself. It wasn't easy because she felt that at any moment the room around her might melt and flow together, returning her to that falsely secure homogenous dream world she'd only just escaped.

The bed she lay on seemed enormous. Partly that was the result of her drugged condition and distorted perceptions, but it was surely at least a king-size. Near its footboard stood an expensive-looking dressing table, a couple of ornate chairs, and above them a light fixture weeping crystal. The only window in the room looked out onto the sky. She could see the stars through it, but they weren't the same stars she'd been watching in her dream. These were distant and real.

The light in the room came from a single nightlight set into one wall socket. Everything was dim and ghostly. The only bright light came from a crack under the door next to the dressing table. Memories came racing back to her.

The people in her bedroom, her real bedroom: no dream, that, but all too real. A cloth over her nose and mouth, a sack over her head. Something pricking her arm and then . . . the beginnings of the dream, creeping over her, stealing reality. Herself on someone's shoulder, moving rapidly. Then moving faster still, but far more smoothly. How? In a plane, in a boat, a car?

Where was she, and why?

Mom and dad, they must be worried sick about her. Taps on the telephone, bugs in the lamp, and suddenly she knew, she knew. These people who'd been after her poor Uncle Jake, they'd finally decided to stop playing around, like a fencer who'd traded in his foil in favor of a broadsword. No more finesse now. Brute strength.

She seemed to be in a fancy hotel room. Certainly there was nothing so elaborate in Port Lavaca. Houston, perhaps? It was hard to tell because she had no idea how long she'd been dreaming.

Now she could sit up, could see a little more clearly. There was another door to the right of the bed, leading to . . . where? Rolling over, she dropped her hands to the floor and pushed against the base of the bed. Her body oozed snakelike out from beneath the sheets and her legs made little noise as they fell against the thick carpet. A faint murmuring came from beneath the door, entering the dark room along with the light. Voices, freezing her there on the floor for a desperate moment. They faded, coming no closer, and she breathed again.

The effort of escaping the bed had exhausted her. She waited until the room stopped swimming, then started for the door next to the bed. Using her arms she pulled and pushed herself across the carpet until she was facing the opening. Bathroom; an extremely large curved tub, a separate shower stall farther off, dressing table, john and bidet. A very fancy hotel, she decided.

A telephone beckoned from the nightstand close to the bed. She'd ignored it because she doubted her captors would be so foolish as to leave her an open line to the outside world. It was harder to push herself across the tiled floor of the bathroom, but she managed, heading for the bathtub. Above it was a low window, and through it she could see the moon.

The side of the tub presented only a temporary problem. It was slippery, but her arms were considerably more powerful than those of the average sixteen-year-old. She put both hands on the side of the tub and pushed down, raising her whole body and turning at the last instant so that her hips swung sideways. The ceramic was cold through her thin nightgown as she sat and caught her breath. As she rested she stared out the window.

Plants rose like thin shadows from a planter on the far side of the tub, but they didn't block all of the view. She was able to see open sky, and the moon. The same moon that shone through the window of her bedroom, how far away she couldn't guess.

Using her hands she swung her dead legs into the tub. Using the handholds provided for older guests, she managed to edge her way around to the far side of the tub. A push and she was sitting on the planter, ignoring the plants crushed beneath her. Her face was flat against the window and she could look down as well as out.

She saw a second moon, an echo of the first, rippling on unknown waters. Lavaca Bay? The same Lavaca Bay she saw from her window at home? Or had she been moved much farther up the coast, or down toward Corpus Christi? There were no landmarks beyond a distant narrow, sandy spit of land running north and south. That could be the Matagorda Peninsula, she thought, or Matagorda Island, or Padre Island, or any of several other gulf barrier formations. But at least she was still on the coast. She was sure she hadn't been unconscious long enough to travel cross-country.

The moon in the sky gleamed off scrub cypress, live oak and mesquite. To the left of her prison she could make out two long docks extending out into the water. A small cargo vessel was tied up at one of them. Pressing tight against the glass, she tried to see straight down and was rewarded with visions of huge pipes and conduits, pavement and a rats nest of smaller pipes and cables. They filled her field of view and sent out metal tentacles toward the docks and into the water.

Beyond a paved walkway lay a narrow beach barely a couple of yards wide. To her right was a single thin, small dock, a stick alongside its larger commerical brothers. Several pleasure boats nuzzled up against it.

As she stared, a long barge led its mothering tug from south to north. She watched until it vanished. A glance at the clear late summer sky showed familiar stars in their expected positions.

Barge traffic implied a protected channel. She was looking out at a portion of the Texas intercoastal waterway, the same liquid highway that ran through Lavaca Bay. It only confirmed her suspicions as to her location. With her family she'd traveled up and down this coast several times. The building she was in was a good three or four stories tall. Only in Galveston or Corpus Christi were there hotels this high on the waterfront.

Unless her first guess was wrong and her prison wasn't a hotel. What other structures were likely to boast a fancy room like this several stories above the water's edge? From Galveston to the Mexican border there were only isolated, large industrial plants. Corpus Christi lay on a curving bay, and she couldn't see anything to north or south. Galveston's shorefront would be full of night-time strollers, and there were none of these. It seemed likely she'd been brought to a far more isolated location.

It didn't matter. There was one person who would be able to find her anyway. She hesitated, considered carefully before contacting him. He was an old, tired man with a bad heart. But she didn't know what else to do. She was scared, and it wasn't like he was helpless. Not anymore.

She closed her eyes and did as she'd done for all of her conscious life, reached out with as much strength as she could muster.

"UNCLE JAKE!"

The half scream, half cry brought Pickett awake as if he'd been shocked. Instinctively he started to scramble clear of the bed, then calmed himself and set his mind to listen.

"Is that you, Mandy?"

"It's me, Uncle Jake. Are you alright? Where are you?"

"I'm fine, Mandy. I'm at your mom and dad's. Everyone thinks you've been kidnapped by a bunch of angry would-be car thieves. They think you've been taken for revenge by the people your dad beat up."

"I've been kidnapped, but not by them. By—"

"I know who," he said wordlessly, interrupting the thought. "I knew right away. Are you sure you're okay? You sound funny."

"They drugged me, Uncle Jake. Took me away and drugged me. I've only just come out of it and I don't know how long I'll have before they come in and drug me again." She was watching the bathroom doorway now, not the view out the window. "I don't even know how long I've been sleeping."

"They took you last night, princess. I just got here today myself."

"So I've only been out one day. Then I'm *sure* I'm not far from home!"

"Where are you, Mandy? Just tell me where you are and I'll come and get you. I'll bring every policeman I can find between here and wherever you are."

"No, Uncle Jake. I'm . . . I'm afraid what might happen if these people think they've lost their last chance to manipulate you. If they see a bunch of police cars driving up, they might move me or . . . they might do something else. You have to come get me by yourself, Uncle Jake. You have to try. I think you can do it. I don't know what else to do."

"If that's what you think's best, Mandy, then that's what I'll do. Now tell me how to get to you."

"I can't tell you for sure, Uncle Jake. I'm on the coast somewhere, in a bathroom three or four stories off the ground. My room faces the intercoastal waterway; you know, the ship canal? It's a fancy room, but I don't think it's a hotel. I can see the water and the moon and ships moving around. There are lots of big pipes and things all over the place, and big docks with one cargo ship. It's got to be a plant of some kind. You don't feel very far away, Uncle Jake."

"Neither do you, princess. Don't worry. I'll get you out of there. Then we'll send the police in for these evil people, after you're safe and away from them."

"Be very careful, Uncle Jake."

"I will, Mandy. They won't be expecting me. I'll bet they plan on contacting me in the morning, to tell me they have you and to warn me I'd better cooperate. I have to come get you now, before they find out I'm not here anymore. I'm sure they know I'm here." He was dressing silently, pulling on worn socks, tying his shoes.

"That's right, I almost forgot. They have the house bugged, Uncle Jake, so I'm sure they have somebody watching it, too."

"I'll go out the back window," he told her. "I know that window well. You've helped me look out through it a lot over the past ten years." He smiled, wondering if she was able to perceive his feelings if not his actual expression. "I've gotten real good at going out windows lately."

"If you can get away from the house without anyone seeing you, you should be okay, Uncle Jake. Then you come and get me and we'll sneak out of here and go to the police. "We'll . . . we'll have to tell them everything, Uncle Jake. About you and me, I mean, or they'll never believe us."

"I know, princess. I didn't think we could keep our secret forever."

"How are mom and dad?" Little girl thoughts and feelings now, the fear beginning to overwhelm the rational, brilliant teenager.

"Scared for you, like you'd expect," he thought back at her. "They don't know what's happened to you or why, and I can hardly wake them up and tell them, can I?"

"No. Come and get me out of here, Uncle Jake, and we'll go to the police and everything will be alright again. Even if we do have to give away our secret."

"I can get out of the house without them seeing me," he said as he buttoned his shirt, "but how am I going to get to you? Until they have me they're going to be watching the bus station and the highway. I can't take your parent's car because they'd see me right away. And if they're watching the roads I can't hitch a ride. Princess, I can . . . I can *feel* where you are, but it's much too far for me to walk.''

"I know, Uncle Jake. I'm right on the waterway. Go out behind the house and turn north. A couple of blocks up the seawall there's a small floating dock where everybody in the neighborhood keeps their private boats. Most everybody we know has a rowboat or something to fish from. Except dad. He doesn't like to go fishing for fun. Maybe you can find one you can start. You have to, Uncle Jake.''

"Don't worry, little girl," he thought. "I'll find something. Been a lot of years since I jumped an ignition.''

"Maybe you won't have to do that, Uncle Jake. This isn't Los Angeles. People don't lock things up around here the way they do in big cities.''

"I hope you're right, princess. I'm ready now.'' He stood there in the dark room, digesting her thoughts, orienting himself to something inexplicable yet terribly real. It wasn't that difficult. He'd been orienting his mind to hers for years. She was . . . that way.

He stepped toward the window, the window he'd looked out of so many times while lying on his bed back in Riverside. It opened easily and he cautiously surveyed the narrow back yard and the seawall beyond. There was no one in sight. Of course, if there was someone out there who did this for a living and he didn't want to be seen, it was unlikely Jake would be able to spot him.

Hope for the best rather than the worst, he told himself. A light breeze drifted in off the bay, cooling him. From down the hall came the light sleeping sounds of Wendy and Arriaga. He put a leg over the sill, then the other, and pushed off.

No one confronted him as he crept toward the seawall, using bushes and trees for cover. If I'd been in the army instead of the shipyards, I'd know how to do this, he thought. But there was no reason for them to bother watching the back of the house, no reason for them to expect Jake to slip out in the middle of the night.

He reached the seawall, had a last look at the house, then dropped gratefully over the rocks. So far his heart wasn't giving him any trouble. Right now he had too much to think about to get dangerously tense. As long as he didn't have to do any hundred-yard sprints, he should be okay. If not, his medicine rested in his breast pocket, ready to work its chemical magic on his damaged chest.

Using the seawall for cover he started northward along the yard-wide strip of sand and gravel. It hid him completely from any landward observers. Ten minutes later he reached the floating dock Amanda had described, a flat square built of old timbers and planks. Old automobile tires lined its sides and pleasure craft bobbed against it like piglets nursing a sow. The slap-slap of water against boat hulls was a relaxing sound in the night.

The first two boats he boarded were secured as tightly as any low rider you might find parked on an East Los Angeles street, but the third had keys lying on the floor in front of the pilot's chair. He'd never driven a boat before. A careful inspection of the controls and instruments revealed nothing incomprehensible, however, and he was sure he could manage it.

Actually, he had a harder time figuring out how to untie the lines holding it to the dock than how to start the engine. He just hoped that the big house nearby wasn't the home of the boat's owner.

The engine rumbled to life when he turned the key in the ignition. It wasn't much different from driving a car, though he bumped up against the dock twice before figuring out how to put the inboard into reverse. A moment more and he was crawling out into the bay. The waters were calm and the new sensation was a pleasant one. No hint of seasickness. Not yet, anyway. Experimentation with the controls and switches activated the running lights and a single bright forward-facing searchlight.

"That's it, Uncle Jake." Amanda had never left him completely. She'd simply thought silly nonsense thoughts while he'd worked his way to the boat. "I can feel where you are. It's a lot easier than it was when you were in California."

"I'm a lot closer, princess."

"Start . . . start in a big circle. Head north and make a curve back southward."

"Whatever you say, Mandy." He turned the wheel, his con-

fidence intensifying the longer he handled the boat. If the circumstances surrounding this nocturnal excursion weren't so
desperate, this could be fun.

"No, wait, that doesn't feel right," she whispered at him.
"Turn north again." Obediently he swung the inboard
around, enjoying its responsiveness as it pivoted in the water.
"That's better, that's better. You're coming toward me, Uncle
Jake. I know you are. I'll be . . . I'll be on your port . . . your
left side."

"I know which way port is," he thought back at her.
"Maybe I've never driven a boat before, but I sure built
enough of them."

She went back to the nonsense talk again, the rhymes, the
monotonous reciting that served not to communicate but to
guide him. Drugged, he thought. No wonder she hadn't been
able to get in touch with him these past days. The more he
knew of the people who wanted to make a guinea pig out of
him, the less compassion he could muster for them.

How strange to feel some genuine hate for a change! Maybe
he'd been too nice all his life. He sighed. A little late to go
back and change seventy years of decision-making. Now he
wanted only one thing: to be rid of these people once and for
all and to make sure they never bothered his grandniece or her
family ever again.

He didn't care that much about himself. If someone else
wanted to run some tests on him, like the government, maybe
he'd let them. But not these people, no, not after what they'd
done to him and those he loved.

But he was sorry for Mandy. If they revealed their secret to
the authorities, she was the one who would be subjected to a
lifetime of testing. But like she'd said, there didn't seem to be
any other way.

He wanted to see some seagulls. Amanda had shown them
to him many times. Sensible birds, they were fast asleep in unseen nests. Only an occasional crane flew between the bay and
the moon, crying to the night. Excepting such isolated appari-
tions, it was quiet save for the engine's steady hum and the
splash of water against the boat's flanks.

Once he had to steer to starboard to avoid a small cargo ship
coming down the waterway toward him, but there was plenty

of room for him to pass. He was thankful for the clear night and the brilliant moon. Steering the boat through darkness and fog would have been impossible even with Amanda's aid.

The fuel gauge read full, so he wasn't going to worry about running out of gas. Hopefully Amanda was right and she wasn't too far away. There was no reason for her kidnappers to extend themselves that way because they'd have control of him as soon as they told him they had his grandniece. Evil, vicious people. His gnarled fingers tightened on the wheel.

"Don't you worry, princess," he thought into the night as he gazed over the bow. "Your Uncle Jake's going to take you away to where you'll be safe, and none of these people will ever bother you again. You just wait." Off to his left, the lights of isolated farms imitated frozen fireflies.

"I'm waiting, Uncle Jake," she thought back at him. "I know you're coming for me, I know you're coming closer all the time. I'm sorry for all the trouble."

"Why should you be sorry? I'm the one who's responsible. If it wasn't for me you'd be home in your own bed now, warm and comfortable. Don't worry though, princess. You'll be sleeping there tomorrow night." He concentrated grimly on her steady mental callings, tried to resonate in time with her own thoughts even as he scanned the western shore for the kind of building she'd described to him.

XVI

"Remember now," Huddy was saying as he opened the door and started to slide out of the driver's seat, "all we want to do is get him outside. He may be a little reluctant at first, especially if he recognizes me. I'll get the parents to one side and you whisper to him that we have the grandniece. He should know about her by now. They've had all night to break the news to him. Once he hears that I'm sure he'll come along quietly."

"Don't worry about me." Somerset exited opposite him. This is the way it should have been handled from the start, she mused. We should have picked up the grandniece as soon as the old man left California. She could sympathize with Huddy's reluctance to go to such extremes, though. The end justifies the means, however, and Pickett's now fully revealed abilities certainly justified the abduction of one small-town girl.

He'd been wrong about some things, Benjamin had, but he'd sure been right about Pickett. He'd been right about something else, too: as far as this project was concerned, the sky wasn't the limit. There were no limits. There was no telling how far Pickett might take them.

The morning came with clouds and humidity; not hurricane weather, but typical of the summer thunderstorms which haunted the South Texas coast. Fat, heavy drops spattered on the windshield of the rented car as it turned up the tree-lined street.

Huddy was first up the steps onto the porch. A stocky, muscular latino answered the door, gazing curiously at his visitors. Huddy was a little surprised. It was his first view of Arriaga Ramirez. From the report of the men who'd bungled the disabling of the van he'd expected a much bigger man. Looking down always made him feel superior.

"Hello," said Ramirez politely. "What can I do for you?"

"We're from the Bureau," Huddy told him. If Ramirez pressed him for further identification they'd be forced to show their bogus FBI ID cards.

Ramirez did not press them and Huddy breathed a little easier. They were still guilty of a number of transgressions, but so far imitating an FBI officer wasn't one of them. The world was full of bureaus.

The fisherman frowned as he stepped aside to admit them, looking past both toward the car parked at the curb. "Where's Roeland? The agent who was here yesterday?"

"He'll be along later," said Huddy reassuringly. "We're from a different section."

That satisfied Ramirez. If these people were not from the Bureau (and where else could they be from?), then how could they know the name of the agent who'd taken the deposition the other day?

"Have you found out anything about my daughter yet?"

"Not yet, sir," said Somerset. "We're working on it as hard as we can." She complimented him on the house as they went into the living room. Pitiful little shack, she thought.

Wendy Ramirez emerged from the kitchen. She wore an apron which wasn't properly tied. Her eyes were red and swollen from crying.

"I'm sorry," Somerset started to tell her. "We just told your husband. . . ."

"They don't have anything new," Arriaga said softly to his

wife. He walked past them to turn off the television.

"Actually, we're here to ask a few more questions," Huddy explained.

"I don't know what we can tell you that we didn't tell your *compadre* Roeland the other day," Arriaga replied.

"We don't want to ask you the questions," Somerset told him. "We've been informed that a relative of yours, a Jake Pickett, is visiting from California. It's him we want to talk to."

"Uncle Jake?" Wendy looked from one visitor to the other. "He's terribly fond of Amanda, but I don't see how he can be of any help to you. He only arrived here yesterday."

"We know that." Huddy smiled. "That's why we'd like to question him. You never know what he might have seen or heard on his way into town."

"If he heard or saw anything he sure didn't say anything about it to us," Arriaga observed.

"Sometimes important details go unremarked upon until you pull them out of a witness," said Huddy. "We want to be as thorough as possible. It'll just take a minute."

"I'm sure Uncle Jake will help in any way he can." Wendy glanced at her husband, who shrugged indifferently. "I don't see any harm in it. Try not to get him excited, though. He has a bad heart. I'll go and fetch him."

An uncomfortable silence ensued. Arriaga finally broke it, speaking while staring at the floor. "I still don't understand why anyone would do something like this. Amanda, she's never done anything bad to anybody in her whole life. Life's been mean to her, not the other way around. If these people wanted revenge, let them come to me. Why pick on an innocent, handicapped little girl? Sometimes . . . sometimes I think maybe the world's going loco."

"Mr. Ramirez, we understand what you're going through," Somerset said soothingly. "In fact, I can say that we have reason to believe your daughter will be returned to you very soon, none the worse for this experience." Huddy shot her a warning look but she ignored him.

Ramirez glanced up sharply, suddenly alert. "You do? But the other agent said—"

"We have access to certain other sources of information. Don't be surprised if your daughter isn't returned as early as tomorrow."

"Can you promise that?"

"We can't promise anything," Somerset warned him. "There are still a number of variables which could complicate matters. But I can say truthfully that things are looking up. Try not to worry quite so much."

"It's good to hear you talk like that," said Arriaga, "because we—"

He broke off at the look his wife threw him as she re-entered the living room. "Arri, did Jake go for a walk this morning? You know he likes to walk. I thought maybe he went out without telling me."

Arriaga shook his head. "I haven't seen him since last night."

Ruth Somerset didn't stop to ponder propriety. She rushed uninvited past Wendy Ramirez. There was no one in the spare bedroom, the bathroom, or the girl's bedroom, nor anywhere else in the back of the house. She was back in the living room in a minute.

"He's gone," she snapped at Huddy, then turned her no-longer solicitous attention on Wendy. "You're positive you didn't see your uncle go outside and you don't know where he might be, Mrs. Ramirez?"

"Why, no. I'm sure he's probably just taking one of his morning constitutionals. He'll be back soon. If you'd like to wait for him I'll make us some coffee."

"Another time, thanks." Huddy was already halfway to the front door, leaving a deeply confused couple in his wake.

He barely beat Somerset to the car. "Where do you think the old bastard's got to?"

"Why ask me?" Somerset growled back at him. "Nobody saw him go out. There's nothing on last night's tapes, as you well know, so he couldn't possibly have been in touch with the girl even if she'd somehow managed to get to a phone."

Huddy gunned the engine and the car squealed as it shot off down the street. Behind them, Arriaga and Wendy Ramirez stood on the porch and watched as it squealed a second time rounding the far corner.

"This is crazy," Arriaga was muttering. "Crazy. That woman, she was so confident a moment ago. Now all of a sudden they panic because your Uncle Jake's gone for a walk. I don't understand."

Wendy Ramirez leaned against her husband's shoulder and said nothing. The brief, bizarre visit had pushed her emotions to the breaking point. She held tightly to the only stable part of her life and tried to still her trembling.

Somerset and Huddy didn't even bother to return to the motel room. Huddy roared into the parking lot of a U-Totem and viciously stabbed the break pedal. Somerset had the door open before the car came to a stop. With the number committed to her remarkable memory, it took only seconds to dial the private number of the VIP suite at the refinery. The young clerk inside the store peered curiously out at the idling car and the elegant woman using the pay phone.

Drew picked up the receiver, wondering who would be calling the suite this early. He wore only slacks, a white shirt open at the collar, and a .45 in a shoulder holster. He waited for the phone to ring three times before picking it up, holding the magazine he'd been reading in his free hand.

"Drew here," he said quietly into the phone. Drew was always quiet. It was almost impossible to upset him, which was one of the reasons his services were valued so highly. In his line of work, inconspicuousness was a virtue.

"Drew, this is Somerset. I'm on my way to the plant." When no reply was forthcoming she added, "Ruth Somerset, Benjamin Huddy's partner."

"I know the name, lady. Where is Mr. Huddy?"

"In our car. He's coming up with me."

"Why the call? I thought everything was going to be wrapped up today."

"So did we. We went to the parents' house. The old man isn't there and they don't know where's he gone to."

"Well he sure as hell ain't shown up here," Drew informed her. "Only one's been on this floor is the regular receptionist and the meal boy from the kitchen. Nobody else. I've been here all the time."

"What about the girl? Is she still where she belongs?"

"Unless she's learned how to fly while sleeping," said Drew

sardonically. He was a little surprised when Ruth Somerset replied in deadly earnest.

"Go check on her and make sure she's still there. I'll hold at this end."

"Whatever you say, ma'am." Shaking his head in disgust he pressed *hold* on the phone console and put the receiver down on its cradle. Typical, he thought. Likes to give orders just to see them obeyed. Snooty bitch. Well, it was all part of the job. He unlocked the door barring the bedroom from the sitting room and stepped inside.

He got a nasty shock when he saw the empty bed, but Drew wasn't the kind to panic when confronted with the unexpected. He'd handled too many awkward situations in which he'd come out on top to panic now. So the girl wasn't in bed. She'd awakened from her stupor and gone exploring. That was improper, but hardly threatening.

Sure enough, there she was in the bathroom, sitting on the inside rim of the bathtub and staring out the window.

"Enjoying the view?"

She jumped slightly at the sound of his voice, turned to glare at him. He'd been standing there for a long minute before she noticed him, which meant she was still feeling the effects of the drugs. There wasn't anything outside the window to concentrate on except sunlight and water and unattainable freedom.

"You could've called me if you had to go that bad," he told her, grinning unpleasantly. "I would've been glad to carry you."

"Just get out," she said, her voice thick from the sedation. "Get out and leave me alone."

"Why, sure. Why not?" And he turned and strode out of the bathroom. Back in the sitting room he picked up the phone, pressed the *hold* button to release it.

"Somerset?"

"Yes?"

"She's still here. Crawled into the john. The effects of that stuff you sent me must have worn off. I'll redose her and get her back in bed as soon as we stop gabbing." He waited patiently, could hear her talking to someone else. Huddy, probably.

Then she was speaking into the pickup again. "We don't know where the old man is. He *can't* know where the girl is, of course. She hasn't had access to a phone or anything?"

"What're you, nuts? You know there's no line in the bedroom and I've been sitting on this one ever since she was brought in. Besides, she's been in dreamland until just now. You think she crawled out a window and got to a phone in another room?"

"No. No, of course not," said Somerset, feeling a little better about the situation. Probably Pickett *was* just out for a morning stroll. They'd return to his niece's house later in the afternoon to pick him up. She was a little mad at herself for reacting so anxiously.

Drew was another problem, however. She'd felt an instinctive antipathy toward him ever since Huddy had brought him into this business. His efficiency and discretion were not to be denied, however, so she supposed she'd have to tolerate his insolence a while longer.

"There's still an outside chance the old man might have discovered where the girl's being held."

"I don't see how," Drew said blithely, "unless someone slipped up at *your* end."

Somerset bristled at the implication but held her temper. By tomorrow they'd have no further need of the man's services.

"We'll assign blame later, if there's any to assign. Right now we have to get our people out looking for Pickett. I'm sure he'll return to the niece's house sooner or later. He's got no place else to go. Maybe he's sitting somewhere and meditating, who knows? We'll probably locate him in town."

"Sure, he's probably having a cup of coffee somewhere," Drew agreed. "No reason to get upset, ma'm."

"I'm not upset," Somerset replied unconvincingly. Damn, but she despised this arrogant thug! "You just keep your eye on the girl. If by some chance the old man *should* show up there, you put a gun on her and hold him until we arrive. Understand? Don't hurt him, don't try to take him yourself. Just pin him down until we can get there. Keep in mind that he's dangerous."

"So everyone keeps telling me," sighed Drew, sounding bored.

"You should have been in Abilene."

"Yeah, I heard about that. Everyone blew their cool and let him get away . . . again. If he pops up here, I'll have him all packaged and ready for you, ma'm."

"Just remember, you'll control him best by posing a threat to the girl."

"Whatever you say, Miss Somerset," said Drew, always willing to please.

"We'll be there soon. You do your job." She hung up.

Drew felt like spitting into the phone, but wasn't much for futile gestures. So he contented himself with thinking what he'd do to that high and mighty bitch if given half the chance. He put down the phone and considered what to do next.

The girl shouldn't be in the bathroom. She was supposed to be under constant sedation. Drew didn't imagine any harm had been done. It saved him from changing the bedsheets. That was another part of his job. Not that he minded. He was paid plenty, and there were much dirtier tasks than changing linen.

But he had to put her down again. People trapped in her situation were sometimes inclined to go a little crackers and do something crazy, like pushing themselves out a window. Or through one. If the girl turned herself into a bloody mess on the pavement outside it wouldn't go down well with his employers, wouldn't do his considerable reputation any good at all.

Easier just to put her back to sleep. Easier on him, easier on her, too. Not that he cared anything about the latter. He re-entered the bedroom and locked the door behind him. She was still sitting on the side of the tub, staring out the window down at the bay.

"Alright, little lady. You've had your exercise for the day. Time to go beddy-by again."

"Stay away from me."

Her protest was so pitiful he couldn't even laugh, just moved forward and scooped her up in his massive arms. She beat vainly at him with her fists, but he simply turned his head away and ignored them. The journey from bathroom to bedroom, though brief, was not unenjoyable. His hands moved over her casually, freely, as though he were exploring a piece of furniture. He was actually reluctant to set her back down on the big bed.

Leaving her there, he returned to the sitting room and pulled a small black vinyl case from a desk drawer. It contained several gleaming hypodermic needles, two glass syringes and several little bottles with thin membranous lids. He put a clean needle on one syringe, then stuck it through the membrane of a bottle and slowly topped off the hypo. He closed the case and returned it to its drawer, then headed back into the bedroom.

When Amanda saw the needle she stopped yelling and cursing at him. She just lay back against the bed and whimpered. Drew was enjoying himself thoroughly. He pointed the needle upward, squirted a little of the clear fluid into the air.

"You've been a bad girl, Amanda. That's what they told me your name was: Amanda. You're supposed to be resting."

"No, please." She dragged herself to the far end of the bed. "You don't have to sedate me again. I'll go to sleep if that's what you want. I'll stay on the bed."

"Will you now?" It was pleasant to toy with her. Any divertissement was welcome in what had become an especially boring job. His hands still tingled from the warm feel of her as he'd carried her back to the bed.

But his instructions were explicit. The girl was not to be harmed. Drew had always prided himself on following his instructions, no matter how onerous, to the letter. As he stood there studying her, however, he considered that there were any number of ways of defining harm. He could always put it down to misinterpretation. Yes, it was the sort of thing he could rationalize. Physical harm, now; as long as the girl didn't suffer any obvious damage. . . .

Oh, Somerset and Huddy would make noise about it if they found him out, but he could handle mere noise. It wasn't as if he'd bluntly disregarded his orders. He'd simply misinterpreted a portion of them. And if the girl was heavily sedated afterwards, Somerset and Huddy would like as not never find out.

Besides, he was damn sick and tired of squatting in that tiny sitting room, turning away the occasional employee who might appear on the floor and juggling questions from the refinery manager. Barker was an officious, unhappy little man who took out his frustration on Drew. Drew listened to him instead of breaking his neck because it was incumbent on him to do so. Yes, he was entitled to a little non-financial recompense.

As his mind debated the ramifications of his intentions, his eyes remained hypnotized by the limp body of the girl on the bed. Her lower legs were thin to the point of emaciation from non-use, but from the thighs up she was downright voluptuous. No, he wouldn't injure her. Not physically, not visibly. Carefully he put the hypo aside.

"You know what I think, little girl? I think the middle of that bed's just the right place for you. Since you're being good about staying there, I guess I won't sedate you right now."

This was going to be fun, he thought. A lot of fun. Not only was the VIP suite off-limits and soundproofed, but for once he'd have someone to play with who couldn't kick back.

He started toward the bed. Amanda watched him approach. Grudgingly, he admired the courage of her silence as he neared her. Surely his intentions were obvious. He gave a mental shrug. She'd be screaming soon enough.

What he didn't realize was that she was already screaming violently, frantically, at the only person in the world who could hear her anyway.

Jake tried to make himself move faster as he steered the inboard into the small-boat dock below the refinery. He saw the words Consolidated Chemical and Mining on the warehouse by the big dock where the cargo ship was berthed. There was no feeling of surprise at the sight of the name. He expected it. He wondered what they refined at the complex. It was a lot bigger than he'd expected.

Since he'd never docked a boat before he had to settle for cutting the engine and letting it run up on the narrow sand and gravel beach. Stepping out into shallow water he took the rope from the bottom of the boat and wrapped it sloppily but securely around one of the cleats bolted to the end of the dock.

As he worked, Amanda's desperate screams reverberated inside his brain: primal, wordless screams. They were akin to the screams he sometimes overheard when a violent nightmare would awaken her. She would apologize from her bed in far-off Texas and both uncle and grandniece would go back to sleep.

But she wasn't far away now, and she was living the nightmare with an urgency that terrified him.

Mounting a series of concrete steps, he found himself on a paved walkway leading into a maze of pipes and buildings. Sensing his bafflement and uncertainty, Amanda quelled her panic just enough to guide him onward. While she struggled to direct her uncle with her mind, she used her voice to try and delay the guard.

He was sitting on the side of the bed now. His calloused right hand was running back and forth, back and forth along her right thigh. With each loveless caress his fingers explored a little higher. The worst part of it was that she couldn't feel them. When she could begin to feel them, there would be additional reason for screaming.

He was grinning at her, a thin, antarctic grin.

"Please," she whispered, "if you're going to do this, why don't you go ahead and sedate me now?"

"Now why would I want to do that?" Drew said softly. "I think I'll enjoy it more if you're conscious."

"I'll scream as loud as I can."

"Go ahead and scream. We've above and beyond the working section of the plant. This room is soundproofed anyway. The soundproofing's to keep the noise of the refinery from disturbing important guests, but it'll serve just as well to keep your screams from disturbing anyone else." The grin widened. "They won't bother me.

"But why be nasty about it? I'd rather be nice to you. Doesn't that sound like a better idea?"

She forced herself to smile back at him. It was one of the hardest things she'd ever had to do. "Maybe . . . but you have to slow down, sir. You're . . . you're doing all this too fast for me. If you'll slow down I'll . . . I'll try and be nice to you."

"No you won't," he said matter-of-factly. "You're not the type. From what I've been told you're a real smart-ass, a real know-it-all. Too many brains for such a pretty face. I don't think you have any more intention of being nice to me than I do to you."

"But you just said—"

"I was lying. I wanted to see how you'd react. Besides, why should I bother sedating you? Half of you is permanently sedated anyway." He burst into unexpected laughter, convulsed by his own wit.

A hand came down on Jake's shoulder. He spun around, found himself staring into the face of an earnest young man in a hard hat.

"Hey, old timer, how'd you get in here? This is a Secured Area. No visitors allowed. You could get yourself hurt."

Jake tried to make his brain work. Slow, so damn slow! He envied Amanda's quickness. "I'm just going to visit a friend. Over there." He pointed to the distant Administration Building.

The young man considered a moment. "You sure wandered off the path from the parking lot. Okay. Let me see your pass."

Jake went through the motions of searching his shirt and pants' pockets. He looked blankly at his interrogator. "Must have dropped it somewhere. I walk around with my hands in my pockets a lot. Probably pulled it out accidentally."

"Uh-huh. Tell you what, old timer. You tell me who you've come to see and I'll get you another pass. How's that?" His hand still rested on Jake's shoulder.

"Oh, that's okay." Jake tried to back away, failed. The younger man's grip was firm. "I can find my way."

"No, I think we'd better go get you another pass. Your friend won't mind waiting a couple of minutes." His tone turned apologetic. "See, it'd be my neck if I let you into Administration without one and somebody found out about it. For all I know you could be from Supervision, sent down to check us out on procedure and reaction. Company's real security-conscious. They run surprise tests like that all the time." He started pulling Jake away from the Administration Building.

Uncertain how to proceed, Jake went with him. The Administration Building began to recede behind him, swallowed up by the jungle of white pipes.

"Hey, Stan?" The young man called out to another worker. The older colleague joined them, eyeing Jake curiously. "This old timer says he's here to visit somebody in Adminstration, but that he's lost his pass. What do you think? Should I let him go on in?''

The older worker's hard hat was red instead of orange. "Who're you supposed to see?" he asked Jake.

Everything was happening too fast for Jake. His heart began to thump warningly against his ribs. "Just a friend," he replied weakly.

The man opposite didn't smile. "Just a friend, huh? Your friend doesn't have a name?"

"Sure he does. It's just that . . . " Jake was looking around desperately. Behind the two men a gigantic steel globe soared several stories skyward. Pipes and lines ran from it like threads peeling off a ball of white yarn. He started concentrating on it, thinking about its interior. This being a refinery, the globe doubtlessly held some kind of liquid, some kind of petroleum derivative. It was hard making something slipt that you couldn't see, he thought painfully. Hard, but not impossible.

An alarm suddenly went off on the catwalk running through the air above them. Just as rapidly the attention of both men confronting Jake shifted to the metal globe.

"Holy shit," said the older man in surprise, "what the hell is overheating?"

Somebody yelled down at them from a third-story catwalk. "Number Three! Three's up to two hundred!"

"Christ," muttered the senior worker. "I've told them again and again they're overfilling." He started running for a nearby ladder.

"Hey, wait a minute, Stan," yelled the younger man. "What do I do with him?" He gestured at Jake.

"Run him up to Security, Bob." He was already halfway up the ladder on his way to the uppermost catwalk. Around them men and women were arriving from different areas of the plant. Alarms continued to shrill in the shattered air of morning.

"You heard what Stan said, old timer." The younger worker was no longer friendly. "Come on, let's go." He yanked on Jake's shirt.

The bucket that struck the worker wasn't large, but it was

half full of fire sand and fell from a sufficient height to make
him let go of Jake. One hand went to his head as he staggered
dazedly backward. He gaped at Jake a moment longer, then
fell over backwards. His hard hat had protected his skull, but
not his consciousness.

On the wall overhead, bordering the second catwalk, a hook
had come loose. The hook had held the bucket, which had
fallen to the catwalk, the center section of which had disintegrated, letting the bucket fall through and onto the young
man's head.

Jake didn't pause to wonder at this latest manifestation of
his long dormant ability. He'd progressed infinitely beyond
the loosening of bottle caps.

He started running toward the Administration Building as
fast as he could. His mind urged him to hurry, his heart de-
manded that he slow down. This time the mind won out.

Men moved quickly past him, ignoring him as they ran
toward the source of the still clamoring alarm. No one else
stopped to question him. No one challenged him as he strode
rapidly across the floor of the Administration Building lobby
and stepped into one of the elevators. There were four buttons
on the control panel; floors one through three and above the
last, one marked PH. He stabbed it with a thumb.

The doors opened onto a hallway decorated like the entrance to a fine restaurant. A woman was seated to the right,
behind a desk. Close, Amanda was very close now, he knew.
He could sense it. He started past the desk.

"Excuse me, sir," the neatly dressed young woman said,
"but you can't go past this point without special authorization."

"I have to," Jake said hurriedly. "My grandniece is down
there and something terrible's going to happen to her if I don't
go to her."

"I don't know what you're talking about, sir." The
woman's pleasant, professional smile abruptly disappeared.
"But I do know one thing. You can't go past this point."

Jake started down the hall. The woman reached into a desk
drawer and pulled out an impressively large handgun, pointing
it at Jake's chest. "Really, sir, I'm afraid I have to insist that
you stop right there." Her free hand moved toward an office

phone. "If you'll just wait a moment, please."

Jake stared down the hall, hardly hearing her. She seemed a nice enough young woman. Possibly she was quite innocent of what was going on only a few yards from her desk. He didn't want to hurt her.

So the gun in her hand stayed intact but her clothes did what the rag in the Benson motel had done. The receptionist gaped at the pile of colored threads which had suddenly appeared at her feet and forgot all about the old man nearby. She made a funny little noise in her throat, tried vainly to cover herself, and bolted past the elevators toward the ladies' room. She was still carrying the gun, now rendered harmless because the person wielding it had developed an overriding interest in other matters.

Jake hurried down the hall, passed one door, a second, finally halting before the one at the end of the passageway. The knob didn't resist when he turned it because the internal lock had suddenly become a pile of gray dust.

The door admitted him to a small living room-like area, elegantly decorated with couch and chairs, table and TV and other fake French furniture. A well-stocked bar buttressed the far wall. Pushing through the room, he shoved against an inner door and stepped into the chamber beyond.

XVII

Startled, Drew looked up from the bed. He sat in the center of it, towering over Amanda. Both hands were fumbling with the buckle of his belt as he straddled her, a knee on either side of her hips.

Now he let loose of the buckle and turned slowly, moving away from the girl until he was sitting on the side of the bed. Intruder and abuser studied each other.

So this is the old man, he thought calmly. I wonder how he got this far. He recalled the warnings repeated by Huddy and Somerset. Now that he was actually face to face with their inspiration, it was hard to take any of them seriously. Drew could not recall seeing a less menacing individual. The old man was panting hard, his face was flushed, and every so often he winced in obvious pain. He didn't appear to be a danger to anyone except himself.

Still . . . that part of Drew's mind which had rescued him from situations which had been the death of less cautious men caused him to consider what was known instead of what was merely visible. He disliked Somerset and Huddy intensely, but he also respected them. They were not idiots. Therefore it was just barely possible that this man was more dangerous than he looked. Drew hadn't forgotten Benson.

So he stayed close to the girl, reached over, and put one hand gently but possessively on her throat. She inhaled sharply but didn't resist. Good girl, he thought.

"I wouldn't come any closer, old man," he said quietly. "I'm still not sure what it is you can or can't do, but all I have to do is push real hard with my fingers here, and they'll go right through this little lady's throat. You don't want that, and neither do I. So don't do anything to make me nervous, okay?"

Uncertain how to proceed, Jake just stood there. Amanda stared imploringly at him, motionless.

"Don't make him panic, Uncle Jake," she thought at him. "Don't rush him into anything. We'll work something out, but don't push this man. He really will kill me."

His heart was trip-hammering on his ribs, but now wasn't the time for measuring out medication. Besides, there was the real possibility that a reach for a shirt pocket would be dangerously misinterpreted by the man on the bed.

So they stared at each other, Jake unable to decide what to do next, Drew considering how best to inform others of his situation. As it developed he didn't have to, because a breathless Huddy burst into the room followed by an equally anxious Somerset.

A strange calm came over Jake Pickett as he locked eyes with the young executive. "Mr. Huddy. I haven't seen you in a long time, but I sure have felt your presence around me. You really want me to take those tests of yours, don't you?"

"Take it easy, Jake," said Huddy. They had him, he thought with relief! They finally had him. The most important thing now was to get him to relax. "Don't get yourself upset. There's no reason for it. Remember your heart."

"Funny, but I don't care much about that anymore," Jake murmured softly. "It's hurting bad right now, but somehow it doesn't bother me." He found that he could almost smile.

"Jake," said Huddy, smiling himself, that wide, practiced, phony smile, "we can work this out. I know it's looked bad this past week or so, but that was the result of overeager people who exceeded their authority in direct contravention of my orders. I've already seen to it that they'll be suitably pun-ished. You and I, we don't have anything to do with that, do we?'' He extended his right hand and took a step forward.

"Don't you take another step, Mr. Huddy," said Jake coldly. "You hear me? Don't you take another step."

Huddy froze. He was acutely conscious of the ceiling overhead, the floor beneath his feet. They had a better idea now of what Pickett was capable of. If he could dissasemble guns and cars and bridge supports, there was no doubt in the executive's mind that he could do the same thing to floors and ceilings. So he retraced his single step, slowly and carefully, the vapid grin still locked on his face.

"You tell him, that man," Jake continued, pointing a shaky finger at Drew, "to get away from Amanda."

"I can't do that, Jake," said Huddy sadly, "until you and I come to some kind of agreement about this testing business."

"I'm not going to do what you want," Jake said firmly.

"Then I can't very well ask my friend Drew to take his hand away from your grandniece's throat, can I?"

"You better," said Pickett.

"Mr. Pickett," Somerset began, stepping forward, "you don't know me. We've never met. But I personally don't want to see you or your grandniece hurt. I don't want to see anyone hurt."

"Neither do I," Jake confessed, "but you two want some-thing, and you don't much care what you do to get it. That's the trouble with people like you. All you ever do is want."

"Now what the hell does this sideshow portend?" said a new and unexpected voice. Everyone turned to face the door-way.

The man who strode into the room had thin white hair and stood taller than Huddy and Drew. His suit and tie were silk, his shoes of some fine and unidentifiable leather. He was nearly as old as Jake Pickett. The two men who flanked him were considerably younger. They did not bother to try and conceal the presence of the guns in their fists.

Huddy's lower jaw dropped. "Mr. Rutherford?"

"Who's this guy?" asked Drew, unimpressed.

The tall figure glanced at him. "Ah, the redoubtable Mr.

Drew. They've told me you do good work. So it would appear." Drew made no response; he waited to see what would happen next.

The newcomer moved into the bedroom, careful to stay well away from Jake. His younger companions matched him stride for stride.

"Allow me to introduce myself, Mr . . . Pickett, is it?" Jake nodded once, warily eyeing this new problem and the two gunmen who accompanied him. "I am Charelton Rutherford, Chairman of the Board of Consolidated Chemicals and Mining." He executed a little half-bow, as it seemed to him that he would not be permitted the familiarity of a handshake.

"These two impetuous and not-too-bright young people" —and he gestured casually toward Huddy and Somerset— "are employees of mine. Low-grade employees. I'm sorry you've had to deal with them this past week, but I felt it best if I remained out of the picture. However, when I was informed that events seemed to be coming to a head down here and that these two appeared incapable of resolving them in a satisfactory manner, I felt compelled to fly out from New York to oversee things myself. I'm glad I managed to arrive in time." He smiled thinly at Huddy.

"Really, son. Kidnapping of an innocent second party. Foolish and unnecessary. It's one thing to try picking up an elderly gentleman like this Mr. Pickett in a motel room, quite another to bring the FBI into the business. And to use CCM property to hold the kidnapped party. . . . " He was shaking his head slowly, regretfully. "Inexcusably stupid."

"Mr. Rutherford," Somerset began lamely, "we had no idea that we would have to—"

"To what? To go this far? To make this choice? People of limited capacity rarely see all the choices. Now you've forced me to become personally involved." He saw their stunned expressions and nearly laughed.

"Oh, come now, you can't still be wondering what I'm doing here? Did you really think the two of you could play your little games in private while utilizing corporate facilities? Don't you think that I'm aware of what goes on within my own company? That I don't have people watching my own people? Don't you think that CCM takes precautions to guard against internal as well as external industrial sabotage and espionage?'' He turned away from them.

"I confess that at first I was very doubtful about the stories my people were referring to New York, but you, Mr. Pickett, you have provided more than enough proof for those tales. For that and that alone''—he glanced contemptuously at Huddy—''I give you credit, young man. The fact that you have thoroughly botched everything you've attempted subsequent to your initial discovery more than cancels out any credit you might have accrued.''

"Mr. Rutherford, I'm sorry if we—''

"Shut up,'' the Chairman said brusquely. "I've been following your inept attempts to convince Mr. Pickett to undergo parapsychological testing for the benfit of the company ever since you started putting in unauthorized requests for personnel all over the Southwest. You blazed quite a trail, Huddy.

"And you, Somerset. Extensive and unjustifiable use of computer time and facilities. Illegal manipulation of a police officer.'' She went blank for a moment and he added, "Your erstwhile friend Lieutenant Puteney was *very* angry when you didn't give him a date.'' He clucked his tongue. "The two of you have a lot to answer for.''

"But it will all pan out, Mr. Rutherford, sir,'' said Somerset. "I know we've made some mistakes, but it's all been worthwhile.'' She gestured at Pickett, who stood quietly off to one side, watching and listening. "*He'll* make it all worthwhile.''

"Perhaps,'' admitted Rutherford. "Perhaps in this case the ends might justify the means. We will see. You had better pray, the two of you, that they do.'' He looked across to the old man who was the subject of their discussion.

"I'm truly sorry, Mr. Pickett, that you've been treated so badly these past several days. This business with your grandniece''—he gestured toward the bed—''regrettable. Not the way I would have handled things if I'd been in on this from the beginning. But I'm a very busy man and many people and events make great demands on my time. I'm sure you understand that I cannot get involved in every piece of company business unless it's clear that my personal attention is absolutely necessary, not to mention justified.'' He smiled warmly. "Now that I am here, however, there will be no more uncouthness directed at you or your relatives, and we can work this out like two intelligent, mature men."

From the bed a sudden, anxious thought: Uncle Jake, don't trust him!

"Sure, we can talk," Jake said quietly. "First get him away from Amanda." He gestured at the bed.

"Ah. Now that presents a small problem," said Rutherford thoughtfully. "Mr. Drew is, after all, only doing his job." Drew grinned at the Chairman, then over at Pickett. His hand hadn't stirred from Amanda's throat.

"Now if I were to tell Mr. Drew to move away from your grandniece, I'm certain that because he is a good employee he would do just that. However, if he were to do so then we would no longer retain any leverage over your actions, Jake. From what I've been told about you, it's necessary that we retain that control for a short time yet. Once we have left this room and signed some papers and you have consented to be placed under sedation for the forthcoming journey, I promise you that your grandniece will be returned safely to her home."

"I'm just an old bachelor," Jake told him. "I don't want to hurt anybody. I never wanted to hurt anybody. But Amanda says I shouldn't go with you, and everyone keeps pushing at me, and I don't know what to *do*." His desperation was palpable.

Rutherford glanced sharply at Huddy, frowned. "I thought you told me there'd been no contact between him and the girl?"

"There hasn't been," said Huddy slowly. The meaning behind Pickett's unintentionally revealing comment still hadn't sunk in.

"No one's going to push you, Jake," said Rutherford, adopting as kindly a mien as possible. "You're going to be treated with care, the best of care. I promise you."

"You want me to go back with him, don't you?" Pickett stammered, pointing toward Huddy. "You want me to go back with him to Los Angeles so you can have a bunch of so-called doctors poke around inside me to see how I make things slipt."

"Whatever you call it, Jake. Yes, that's the general idea. You're a grown man. You can make your own decisions. Surely you don't need to turn to a sixteen-year-old child to tell you what's best for your future, not to mention your present. No one else will know about it. As to going back with Mr. Huddy, that won't be necessary. I know you don't care much for his company, and I can understand why. So no, you won't have to return with him. I'll escort you myself, if you like."

Huddy digested the words and started edging toward the door. He reached it and broke into a sprint. One of Rutherford's bodyguards walked to the doorway and fired with an air of boredom.

There was a violent explosion, muffled somewhat by the suite's soundproofing. Huddy's hand clutched convulsively at the handle of the hallway door. He twisted around and his back slammed against the wall. He stood there, still holding the doorknob, staring out into space with a puzzled look on his face. This wasn't the way it was supposed to turn out, wasn't the way it was supposed to turn out at all. He started to slide jerkily down the wall. By the time his rump reached the floor the last of Benjamin Huddy's grandiose plans had become meaningless.

The bodyguard turned back into the room, blocking the doorway and any further futile gestures.

"Please." Rutherford heard the voice and turned to look at Ruth Somerset. She was crouched in the corner opposite Pickett, all hint of bravado gone now. "Please don't kill me," she whispered fearfully. "It was his plan from the start. He dragged me into it. I didn't want to join him but he threatened me. I didn't have any choice. He told me that if I didn't help him he'd—"

"Be quiet, woman," Rutherford said disgustedly. "No one has any intention of killing you if you'll just stay put and behave in a sensible manner." He gestured back toward the sitting room. "If he hadn't panicked he'd still be here. You're not going to panic, are you?" Somerset shook her head quickly. "I thought not. That's a good little junior executive." He returned his attention to Pickett.

"That was unfortunate and I'm sorry you had to see it. I

dislike losing potentially valuable personnel, but one who panics instead of using his head automatically obviates his usefulness in any case.

"Hopefully there will be no more unnecessarily dramatic interruptions while we decide what to do with you, Mr. Pickett. You must see why I cannot let your grandniece go until I have secured your cooperation. I realize that you can also threaten me. I've seen the reports and I have some idea of what this peculiar talent of yours is capable of doing, but I sincerely doubt that you can handle all of us simultaneously."

As if on signal, the other bodyguard now directed his gun at Jake. Drew also pulled his, his other hand never straying from Amanda's neck. Three handguns were now pointed at the old man.

"You might 'disassemble,' as I believe the late Mr. Huddy referred to it, one or two of these weapons and some of the bullets, Jake, but I don't think you can handle all of them at the same time. You have to concentrate on one at a time, don't you?" Jake Pickett didn't reply.

"What I'm going to ask is that you just relax and do nothing. There is a sedative kit in the next room that Mr. Drew has been utilizing to keep your grandniece cooperative. If you will allow one of my assistants here to inject you with a modest dose, I promise that your grandniece will be on her way home as soon as the drug takes effect. Your grandniece is evidence that the drug is no more than a powerful sleep-inducer.

"Once this has been accomplished, we can proceed without intemperate words and weapons to a sane conclusion. How about it, Jake? You've run these dogs a pretty good race up 'til now, but it's time for the thoroughbreds to take over the track. There are no more motels to run to, no new places to hide. It's time children were in bed and adults made the decisions.

"From what I've been able to ascertain, Jake, you're an under-educated but rational man. So please, cooperate. If you don't, then much as I'd regret the lost opportunities for study, we'll be forced to kill you. That means the girl would have to die also. We can hardly allow either of you to go to the police to recite your recent history."

Jake stood there and listened to this completely confident, self-possessed stranger. Someone was using a heavy fist on his chest. He saw the three guns aimed at him, saw Drew's ugly hand on his grandniece's delicate neck. All he wanted just then was for it to be over. Let it be over, no matter what Amanda thought. The important thing was to get her home, back to her mother and father, home safe and away from these horrible people. For himself, he no longer cared.

Maybe Amanda saw the change overcoming her uncle. Maybe she saw it in the way his expression twisted, or maybe it was his mind that was twisting. Regardless, perhaps for some other unknown reason, she suddenly raised up in the bed, pushing back Drew's hand.

"Don't do it, Uncle Jake! Don't go with them. They'll never let me go because I can tell the police what—!"

Drew's hand moved from her neck just long enough to crash across her face. Her head slammed back against the pillow, bounced once. Blood began streaming from her nose. Jake took an instinctive step toward the bed, his uncertainty swallowed up by sudden blind, mindless fury.

"Drew, Pickett; hold it!" Jake froze, glaring at Drew, who simply grinned back at the old man. Yeah, sure he's dangerous, Drew thought. Those guys who went into the motel after him were useless. Abilene, that must've been some kind of fluke. The old guy's not dangerous enough to sneeze about. His hand pressed tighter on the girl's neck. He wasn't worried anymore. In fact, the whole tableau was becoming rather amusing.

"That will be quite enough, Mr. Drew," said Rutherford warningly. Drew shrugged indifferently.

"Please, Jake, you saw what happened to Mr. Huddy when he panicked. I know you have better sense than that." He nodded to the bodyguard on his right. The man vanished into the sitting room, reappeared a moment later holding his gun in one hand and a loaded syringe in the other.

"I know how tired you must be, Jake," said Rutherford sympathetically. "All that running for a man your age, with a cardiac condition. I have a few problems myself. You see, I understand, I can commiserate with you." The man with the hypo started cautiously toward Jake. "It's time for you to relax. You've earned a rest. I know all you want is to lie down and forget about all this."

Abruptly Jake was completely relaxed. It was almost as if the Chairman's words had provided the surcease he so desperately wished for. He knew now what he was going to do. He didn't want to do it, but as before these people seemed disinclined to give him any kind of a choice. The lump returned to his throat. If only they'd give him a choice, but they never did. They kept pushing him, forcing him to do things he'd never dreamed of doing, never wanted to do.

His heart was bothering him quite a lot now. It might worsen at any moment. These people would welcome a blackout on his part. It would save them the trouble of having to use the hypodermic. If he blacked out or had a mild stroke they'd gain everything they were after. They wouldn't even have to return Amanda.

But Amanda was sure they had no intention of doing that whether he was alive or dead, cooperative or otherwise.

He was almost as frightened as he was angry. His head was starting to hurt like it had several times in the past week, though because of the extreme angina he was experiencing he hardly noticed the other. He was afraid that what the dignified visitor said about him handling all the guns and bullets simultaneously might be true. So he didn't think about the guns, and he didn't think about the bullets.

A strange gurgling came from the man holding the syringe. His expression went sort of blank. Then it was gone altogether, along with his face. So was the face of his counterpart, and the sadistic face of Mr. Drew waiting tensely on the bed. They were all gone.

From their faces it spread to encompass their skulls, and then traveled down their whole bodies. They came apart in comparative silence. There were no ripping, tearing noises, no violent eruptions of blood and flesh. The three of them just melted from the top down. Most of the human body, after all, is water, and if you make the watery combinations inside the body slipt as Jake Pickett instinctively, fearfully did, there isn't much left and what is left isn't very solid. So everyone in the room stood paralyzed as three skeletons collapsed in on themselves atop a reddened, jelly-like mass. Unsupported clothing came folding down on top of former bodies until, under the tremendous surge of disassembling energy from Pickett, even they began to come apart.

Now Amanda was screaming on the bed. The Chairman of the Board stood alone by the doorway, a lifetime of assurance dissolving as rapidly as his henchmen. At last there were only two piles of sticky, maroon-colored sludge spreading out across the floor, mixed with some powdered bone and loose rags. The third mass of slime extended from Amanda Ramirez's throat down to her legs.

"Stop it, Uncle Jake! That's enough, stop it!"

Jake Pickett heard her only faintly. The pain in his chest threatened to double him over any second now. It was worse than any pain he could remember. Still he didn't reach for his pills. There weren't safe yet, weren't free. The agony in his chest had progressed to the point where the pills might not have done him much good anyway.

He didn't care. It didn't matter anymore. Nothing mattered except making certain that Amanda would be alright. If he heard her pleas for him to stop, he didn't react to them.

Rutherford was trying to back out the doorway while keeping the old man in sight. Pickett seemed to be in considerable pain. The Chairman's foot slid on something; a damp, viscous blob of jelly. He looked down at what had once been half of his personal bodyguard. A partially disintegrated skull grinned whitely up at him. There was only a jellied smear where the right eye had been. The left one hadn't slipt, had just fallen out of the socket. Now it dangled loosely by an organic thread, hanging against half a cheekbone. Rutherford found he was shaking badly.

"I'm sorry. . . . We can work it out. I'm going, see? I'll leave you alone. Nobody will bother you anymore, I swear it. Just stop. . . ." He reached out a hand, trying to protect himself from something unseen. "Please don't. . . ."

He never finished the sentence. It dissolved in his throat, along with everything else.

Rutherford didn't scream as he slipt. None of them had screamed. Maybe that meant it wasn't painful. That made Jake feel a little better. No, the Chairman of CCM didn't appear to be in any pain as his face slowly melted off his skull, as the hands that reached out became skeleton hands, as the flesh melted and ran down the white bone.

Slowly Rutherford slipt, sliding into his clothes, his body running like pudding out through the legs of his expensive pants. Something moved behind him and Jake half-turned his head. Powder stung his cheeks and he blinked as a few grains caught his eyes. The powdered bullet didn't have enough force to break the skin, however.

In the far doorway the receptionist-guard who'd first encountered Jake outside the elevators stared in terror as the gun slipt in her hands. It wasn't like the other times, not like in Benson or Abilene when cylinders had fallen away from their mounts and triggers and barrels had come apart. This time the handgun simply turned to dust along with the bullets, sifting through the woman's clutching fingers. Jake had spotted her just in time.

Then she noticed the mounds of ooze on the floor which had once been human beings, living creatures. Her hand went to her mouth and she disappeared down the hall. Soon the paralyzing hysteria would give way to screaming.

Jake wasn't sure why he didn't make her slipt. A lifetime of being courteous to the opposite sex, perhaps. Speaking of which. . . . He turned to regard the last of his tormentors.

Ruth Somerset was sitting on the floor on the far side of the room, her back against the wall. She was alternately laughing and crying. Then she noticed Jake staring at her. She didn't scream, didn't beg or plead, but there was a naked, helpless terror in her eyes which made Jake cringe. He was responsible for that, he knew, and he didn't want to be. All he wanted was to get along. That's all he'd ever wanted out of life.

He took a step toward her, planning to reassure her. It had an entirely different effect. Those widened eyes rolled up and she fell over sideways in a dead faint.

Alarms began to sound, hooting loudly through the building, penetrating the soundproofing via the gaping hallway door. It sounded as if they were blaring all over the plant.

The receptionist-guard was responsible for that, Jake knew. Maybe he should have made her slipt anyway. Too late for that now. The important thing was to get Amanda to safety.

He turned to the bed, and bent over as something ripped through his chest.

"Uncle Jake?" Amanda was sitting on the side of the bed, still cleaning herself. He fought to regain control of his body.

"It's okay, princess. It's okay. Come on. I'm taking you out of here."

She put her hands around his neck as he reached under her, one hand across the small of her back, the other beneath her thighs. He gritted his teeth and lifted. She came up easily, lighter than she looked because of the thinness of her legs. She wasn't a big girl to begin with, but that didn't matter. Suddenly he had a surge of real energy, felt some strength return to his arms and legs. This was Amanda he was carrying, and he'd die before he dropped her.

No one confronted them as they emerged into the hall. There was no sign of the receptionist. Her desk was deserted and so was the opposite hallway. The elevator responded to Jake's call and when the car arrived it was empty.

On the ground floor, however, a couple of security guards espied them as they exited the elevator. The sight of an old man carrying a nearly naked young woman piqued their interest immediately.

"Hey, who are you?" one of them said sharply. They both started forward.

Jake hesitated before reacting, remembering the goo that covered the bedroom floor upstairs. The memory of it made him queasy. His stomach was no stronger than anyone else's. So instead of disassembling the two guards he turned his attention to the ceiling, a part of which turned into a shower of wood and plaster. The two men were laid out on the floor, still wearing their bodies.

What am I going to do? he thought worriedly as he tried to hurry toward the entrance. Amanda clung tightly to him, her strong arms locked around his neck. I've killed so many people. Self-defense, sure, but those deaths were still on his hands, and literally on his mind. How was he going to be able to live with that?

Outside the Administration Building now, running back down a half-familiar path with his delicate burden. Alarms echoing in his ears. Out through the last gate, onto the paved walk which bordered the bright waters of the Gulf. Another spasm of pain burst behind his sternum. He found himself running while leaning to his left.

The little inboard was waiting for him. He set Amanda inside, wrestled with the rope binding the boat to the dock. A shout sounded behind him and he turned to look landward.

Ruth Somerset was standing by the plant exit, her expression wild with hate and fear. Sophistication had deserted her. It was more than that. The events she'd witnessed during the past half hour had rendered her slightly deranged. Armed security personnel clustered around her.

"Thre he is!" she screamed, pointing toward the dock. "There he is! Kill him. For God's sake, kill him!"

Jake climbed into the boat and sat down in the pilot's seat. The engine turned over immediately, but it took several precious seconds for the boat to pull free of the sand and back out into the bay. As he swung around and gunned it he looked back over his shoulder.

Somerset was still standing by the gate above the beach walk, but the men accompanying her were running down the path and piling into the two other small boats which had been tied up to the dock. A few were firing at the retreating inboard, which was just out of range.

They'd chase him all the way back to Port Lavaca, he thought exhaustedly, maybe all the way to Wendy and Arriaga's house. Maybe into the house. They might not even make it that far. He didn't know how fast their boats might be, and there was always the chance of a stray shot hitting him or Amanda. They'd chase him until they both died.

Tired. He was so tired.

So he reached out with the ability he didn't understand, would never have a chance to understand. Reached out for one of the last times with something he'd wanted to use only to amuse little kids, something which people he despised had forced him to develop to a frightening degree. It was less disciplined, less controlled than anything he'd ever done; the desperate strike of a man in the last stages of hopeless exhaustion. If he'd had more practice, more time, he might have managed it better. Certainly he didn't mean to produce such a violent sliptage.

Inside the vast storage tanks bordering the refinery, inside the cracking facilities of the refinery itself, certain molecular bonds were snapped. Perhaps a dozen new compounds were formed as a result. The subsequent creation brought forth destruction, for several of those new compounds were volatile and unstable. Within the airless confines of a few huge tanks, the result was explosive.

The big globe which squatted near the Administration Building, the one beneath which Jake had encountered the troublesome worker, was the first to go. Painted steel, catwalks and piping erupted skyward, propelled by expanding gases and accompanied by black-orange flame. Jake tried to stop it when he realized what he'd done, tried to reverse it. Even if he'd had the training and experience in the use of his ability, he couldn't have prevented what had already been set in motion.

Pipes began to disintegrate, spewing unfamiliar corrosive compounds across pavement and other structures. Cracks appeared not only in the walkways but in the earth beneath the plant. Jake had touched much more than a few liquids.

"Uncle Jake!" Someone was shaking him. "Uncle Jake, that's enough!" He blinked, looked to his right. Amanda was yelling and shaking him with both hands, pleading with him. "That's enough, Uncle Jake!"

Dazedly he turned to look back at the refinery. It was disappearing, coming apart as explosion after explosion ripped through it. The concussions were felt as far north as Galveston. As he stared, one particularly violent eruption temporarily deafened man and grandniece. A gigantic red-orange fireball rose from the center of the petrochemical complex as fragments of metal and plastic and people were blown a mile from the middle of the plant. None of them struck the fleeing boat, though plenty struck all around it. A fine powder sifted down to the water in the inboard's wake.

A serious, no-nonsense invisible fire struck his heart. He went forward, then backward in the seat, both arms wrapped around his chest. Somehow Amanda shoved him aside, gaining enough of an edge to sit on as she fought to regain control of the momentarily gyrating boat. She was crying steadily, cold with only the thin nightgown to cover her. She brought their speed down to a crawl and pointed the boat southward as she bent to her uncle.

His mouth gaped wide and a rasping, sodden sound came from his throat. She put an ear against his chest, heard his heart going mad. It would pause for an instant, then resume beating wildly.

Finally it steadied. Jake squinted at her until his vision cleared. He'd been asleep, or something. Distant, faint explosions continued to shake the shoreline behind the boat and interspersed among them, the first weak cries of approaching sirens. Lots of sirens.

Jake saw his grandniece gazing into his eyes, saw the tears straggling down her cheeks. Weakly, he began fumbling at his shirt for the bottles. Then he knew something had broken inside him. He shook his head at nothing. It was growing dark out, evening advancing in midday, the ominous evening he'd dreaded and been expecting for a long time.

"Too late," he whispered at her. She had to lean closer to understand him. "Too late for nitro now. Too late for anything. I didn't mean, didn't mean to do all that." His neck muscles didn't seem to be working, so he had to indicate what he meant by gesturing backward with his eyes.

"No one will bother you anymore, Mandy." He smiled. That only increased the flow of tears, which was not his intention. "No one will ever bother you again."

"It doesn't matter, Uncle Jake. What matters now is you. You're going to get better, get well. You have to." The bodice of her gown was dark with tears and sweat. "If you don't, I won't have anybody to talk to. I'll be all empty inside."

"Oh no you won't, Mandy. There's no void where there are people who love you, like your mom and dad and brother. I'm sorry I didn't get to see Marty. He's a good boy, your brother. And before you know it there'll be somebody else to fill any voids, somebody who'll love you forever. You'll see. There always is."

"There wasn't for you, Uncle Jake."

He tried to shrug, discovered that he couldn't. "So I'm a disreputable, cantankerous old bachelor. That was just something I never got around to, Mandy. Never met the right woman, I expect. But there's something else I have to get around to. One more thing to do.'' He went silent.

He'd never tried to make anything like this slipt before. He wasn't sure if he could manage it. After everything that had happened he still didn't really know quite *how* he made things slipt. It was funny, he mused, downright hysterical. He was going to go without ever knowing what had pushed him into it.

Maybe on the other side, he thought. Maybe on the farther shore someone could tell him how it worked. That was a nice thought. He was looking forward to seeing Catherine again.

It occurred to him that he could have tried the same thing on himself. Too late now. The time for that would've been years ago, before everything inside him got too broke down. Typical, though. Maybe if he'd thought of himself first everything would have worked out better long ago. Too late for that now, though. Too late to do anything, except consider his grandniece and strain to make something inside her slipt.

Amanda jerked back, let out a little ''Oh!'' of pain and surprise. Her hands drew away from her uncle and went to her legs.

''Uncle Jake, it's hurting me! It's hurting!''

Suddenly the import of that pain struck home, and then it didn't hurt so much anymore. Then there was only shock, and wonder.

She leaned back and put a hand on the passenger's seat for support. She pushed down hard with both hands and did something she hadn't done in eleven years. She stood up.

Only for a few seconds, because the muscles weren't there to support her body weight. She slumped back against him. The muscles would come back. All that would require was a little therapy, a little hard work. But her legs would come back. Her spine throbbed just above her hips, a throbbing that was slowly beginning to fade. She stared at her Uncle Jake. He was smiling back at her, unable to nod but able to perceive his success.

''I thought maybe I could do something like that,'' he said softly. ''It's just like the bottle caps, only more complicated. You just have to make things feel *right*. You never did feel right, Mandy. I remembered what the doctors said, all those years ago. I thought I could do something like that.''

"Uncle Jake . . . " she started to say.

"It'll take you awhile. You'll have to learn how to walk all over again. But I think that thing that was wrong in your back will be okay now." He sighed and his chest rattled like a tin drum. "I think everything will be okay now."

Suddenly his back arched forward; once, twice. Then he settled back easily into the padded seat. The air hissed out of him and was not renewed.

"No," Amanda whispered. "Please, no."

The sirens across the water were very loud now, all clustered behind the billowing black smoke and the flames. Amanda pushed and beat on her uncle's chest and breathed into his mouth the way the books said you should, but it didn't do any good. It didn't do any good because Jake wasn't there anymore. She knew that in a way no doctor could know it, because Jake's mind, always so receptive and open, had become a dark, empty place.

She sat there and sobbed while the boat chugged southward at a few miles an hour. Eventually she wiped at her face and retook the wheel. That was how he'd expect her to react, she thought. This is what he'd expect me to do. The boat accelerated, parting the water as it sped toward the open expanse of Lavaca Bay. Occasionally Amanda used her legs on the controls, the legs her Uncle Jake had returned to her.

No one to talk to anymore. No familiar, warm thoughts to cuddle up to at night in bed. But she was a smart girl. Everyone talked about how smart she was. She'd study hard, and she'd learn, and she'd try to find out what the bad people had wanted so desperately to know about her Uncle Jake.

She thought about his last words. Maybe she would meet some boys now. Maybe her brother could introduce her to some. Surely they'd be different in college, more serious, more grown-up. She'd finally have a real life, all the more real because of her Uncle Jake's final act. She'd get married, yes, and raise a family. If she had a boy she knew what she'd call him. She'd have a couple of boys, and a girl, too. No, make that a couple of girls and a boy.

She'd be able to tell them all about her wonderful, sad, gifted Uncle Jake. That made her feel better, helped to keep back the tears, as she steered down the center of the inter-coastal waterway.

And as she steered the boat toward the tree-choked shore later that afternoon, toward the oh-so-familiar yard and house, it did not occur to her to wonder if just maybe whatever she held inside her genes, whatever Jake Pickett had possessed inside his, might be waiting patiently within her own body, a tiny insignificant twist in a strand of DNA waiting to be passed on to a child not yet conceived.

Maybe a new twist.